PRINCE ALBERT

Evoking the colour, scent and light of the Kentish countryside...

It was in the Kentish Isle of Sheppey that the young Burbages, soon after they were married, bought their farm, 'Doggetts'. After the negative frenzy of war, the healing joy of the country and the arrival of a baby daughter, Madeleine, made up for the endless labour of the prospering farm. They took on an extra hand, Tom Small, who quickly grew devoted to the baby, but his birthday gift of a pony, 'Prince Albert', unwittingly almost brought disaster to the Burbages' idyllic life. The real value of loyalty and honesty is confirmed as the family is re-established.

PRINCE ALBERT

Prince Albert

by

Richard Church

Magna Large Print Books
Long Preston, North Yorkshire,
BD23 4ND, England.

British Library Cataloguing in Publication Data.

Church, Richard
   Prince Albert.

      A catalogue record of this book is
      available from the British Library

      ISBN   0-7505-1683-6

Published in Large Print 2001 by arrangement with
The Estate of Richard Church, care of Laurence Pollinger Ltd.

Magna Large Print is an imprint of Library Magna Books Ltd.

Printed and bound in Great Britain by
T.J. (International) Ltd., Cornwall, PL28 8RW

To

CEDRIC AND HELEN WATKINS

FOR

ANABEL (1943–1962)

'I am afraid of things which can be hurt.'

(from *The Clown*, by Elizabeth Jennings)

ONE

1

Matthew Burbage was wounded during the intensified attack on German towns in 1945, before the Allied armies crossed the Rhine, to bring the war to an end. He flew a Mosquito, laden with radar-baffling devices, a heavy equipment which forbade the carrying of arms. For a safe return, he had to depend upon height and skill in evasion.

That last journey began with ill luck. His briefing instructed him to precede an attack on Pilsen, to obscure the arrival of the bombers, and then to return solo. But when he left the ground, and was still circling the airfield, he saw that his altimeter was not working. He radioed down and was ordered to try to land.

To think over this order and how to accomplish it safely, he circled twice, and saw the ambulance and the fire-engine crawling out of their kennels below. He realized that the delay would hold up the whole operation, browning-off the crews and generally lowering morale. He signalled that he would first do the job, and attempt the landing afterwards.

This he did, but the preoccupation of mind caused by his efforts to recall the visual aspects of a normal landing slowed down his responses to what was happening in the alien sky over Pilsen. Though his machine was painted black, the German searchlights caught it and, before he could realize that he had been circling too low over the area, a stream of anti-aircraft fire came rocketing round him. As he darted upward, a bullet cut through the fuselage and lodged in the calf of his right leg.

With one half of his anatomy numb, and the rest of it raging with pain, he made for home, trying meanwhile to concentrate on recalling the behaviour of the landscape during a landing. He pictured buildings, trees, roads and every landmark with their angles of approach, by which roughly to judge their distances and his own height from the ground.

He made a perfect landing, then fainted in his seat, from loss of blood through the improvised tourniquet.

This exploit was rewarded by a reprimand for disobeying orders, and with a D.F.C. It also put an end to further adventures in the air. By the time he was out of hospital, the war with Germany was over.

Just before the period of three months spent in similar operations on this dangerous mission, he met a young woman in the W.A.A.F. on the station where he was training for the job. They hob-nobbed in the canteen, and more privately on one or two official journeys when she had to drive him. To his surprise, she was his first visitor in hospital after the bullet had been dug out of his leg and the broken bone re-set. Her name was Anna Waltham and she was twenty, a quiet, matter-of-fact girl, reticent about herself, but warm and willingly interested in him, his talk, his plans.

For he had plans, even then. During her visits to the hospital, he told her about them. He came from the Durham coalfields, where his father, and grandfather, were deep-set in the mining community. But his mother's family were farmers.

He told her, with some hesitation, that his mother had died during the war, leaving his married sister to look after the widower. So there was no duty to call him back to the North.

At this point he realized what he wanted. Looking shyly and awkwardly at the girl, he knew that life would be worth while if he could spend it with her.

She must have read his thoughts – and feelings. Even the thick uniform could not disguise the warmth, the womanly kindliness, of her figure, her face, her hair and strong hands. She was a healthy creature, with hair that could be attractive when fussed up somewhat. Her gaze was level and steady. Her blue eyes reflected the glare of the naked bulb over Burbage's bed. The setting for his proposal could not have been more unromantic. He took one chapped hand in his, and thus began his confidence.

'The fact is, I've fallen in love with the South here – with Kent. I want to farm. It's peace I want. To stay put; to grow things, not destroy them. We've got to make up for what we've done, Anna. Don't you realize that? And what it's done to us?'

She said nothing. She looked at him, and her hand turned in his and closed firmly round his fingers. That was enough.

'That's not the only thing I'm in love with, Anna.'

Then he told a permissible lie, for he half believed it himself:

'I wanted to speak while I was training for that job. But the risks were too high. I wasn't justified until I knew I was safely back. I want to marry you, Anna.'

She leaned forward for a moment, breathing a little less serenely: but she did not relax the pressure of her hand round his.

'I wish you had spoken then, Matthew. It might have helped you. It would certainly have helped me.'

'You mean that, Anna?'

'I mean it, Matthew. I love you too.'

14

They decided to marry in uniform, to save expense. They needed every penny they could muster to further their plan, which was to buy a small farm in Kent, immediately, while prices were still petrified.

Kent was shabby and littered with debris after five years beneath the major defensive air-battles. Her fields were pocked with dew-ponds where bombs had puddled the soil. Shell-splinters in the fields threatened the farmers' machinery. Farmhouses, cottages and barns were dilapidated, some in ruins.

The business-like young couple pooled their gratuities, and both contributed a little of their own small capital. Burbage had fifteen hundred pounds which since his mother's death in 1942 had been on deposit. So he held a thousand back, to live on during the first two years, and he put six hundred-odd pounds into the purchase money.

Anna's parents were both school-teachers in Wiltshire, but they were also of farming stock, and approved their daughter's purpose. Their profession forbade their doing much more. They could offer only a small marriage-portion from the savings put by, profits on the schoolmaster's bee-keeping, an art in which he was expert and adviser to the County Council. Anna consented to accept two hundred, on the understanding that it was an investment rather than a dowry.

The young couple bought a pre-war baby car and began to search, quartering Kent west of the Medway. The weeks of that first winter of peace, or what seemed like peace, dreamed over the stunned world. The Burbages, man and wife, found it to be paradise, with only a tiny serpent of un-ease. They decided that they must not settle too far from a market for the certified milk in which they proposed to specialize.

'We'll build up a herd of Jersey cows,' said Matthew confidently. 'We can get advice from the Ministry experts and the people at Wye Agricultural College. Everybody's help-ful nowadays, for the population's got to learn to feed itself.'

No married couple could have been more harmonious. They both wanted to do the same thing, and to do it together. They knew it would be an uphill job, but they were young and healthy. The only draw-backs were a small capital and Matthew's limp.

During one of their home-hunting ex-peditions, he apologized to Anna for this latter disability.

'It has slowed me down,' he said. 'I know that up North, in my own country, it wouldn't be amiss. I should be one in many among the miners, who all reckon to take a knock sooner or later at that job. But down here, among these Kentish farmers...'

He looked ruefully at her across the car-rug spread over a patch of frosty grass under the wide winter sky, on the Isle of Sheppey. They had stopped to picnic, on their way with an order to view yet another small property. The search had been in operation, over the turn of the year, since their wedding in November. Optimism survived, but somewhat dimmed. The young war-riors, man and wife, were finding that the warm community spirit of wartime was cooling off. People had begun to look more to their own interests again. This drop in social temperature may have added a touch of dejection to Matthew's ruefulness.

'It's not going to be easy, Anna.'

She was splitting and buttering a new bread-roll when he dropped this defeatist remark. She looked up at him, while reaching across to the packet of cheese, to complete the sandwich preparing for him. The low midday sun dazzled her, and she screwed up her face, blinking sensuously at the unexpected warmth.

'Do we want it to be?' she whispered.

'No; but I mean – the handicap. A man

will need to jump around fast if he's to hold his own with these southerners.'

'I'm a southerner, Matt. At least, a south-westerner. And I'll be with you now, all the time.'

This restored them both to gaiety. Burbage took the roll, and also the hand proffering it. The bridal pair were thus bending towards each other, and a kiss sealed the promise and blessed the meal.

It appeared also to bring them good luck, for that afternoon they found what they wanted. It was a small farmhouse, called 'Doggetts', its roof and walls hung with rose-red tiles, with warm-tinted lower courses of brick. It stood flanked by half an acre of walled garden, with a rusty iron gate under a round arch through the wall into a small orchard of old apple trees, picturesque with moss and gnarled limbs. Four meadows behind sloped gently up from the estuary, protected by a copse which had grown out of a former windbreak eastward.

The house stood at the bottom of the farmland, facing south across the narrow water to the mainland, opposite Sitting-bourne and the flats of that old Roman shore. From the front windows the young couple looked across, to watch the sun riding down to the hills beyond the flats.

'This is our place, Anna, isn't it?'

He spoke gravely, and his wife put her arm

round him, as though to protect him from his own emotions.

'Far enough round the corner of the world, eh, Anna?'

'Yes, but near to Queensborough, Matt. Not a long drive each day with the milk.'

'Oh, we shan't have to do that. Didn't you notice the raised platform along the roadside as we turned into the drive? That's to hold the churns. Somebody else collects them; wholesaler, co-operative, I don't know what, but we shall not have that chore.'

'But won't that mean selling ourselves to a middleman?'

This amused Burbage. Anna's practical turn of mind reassured him and gave him confidence in his own ability to deal with the hard facts of the post war world.

'But look at the place! Isn't it just right?'

The sun was now reddening into the line of mist above the downs: a winter scene of still-early afternoon, the hour touched with melancholy, but also with cosiness, and the promise of something to come, something generous and larger than life.

'Yes, this is for us, Matt. Let's go to the agent before somebody else finds it.'

3

Thus began a period of hard work and happiness. Everything the Burbages planned gradually took shape. For the first three months they slaved so doggedly that they had neither energy nor courage to start a family. But working alone together taught them a lot about each other. They were still lovers, when not too physically weary; but they were also man and wife, welded soul to soul by the monotony, the prosiness of daily, hourly life on the farm. The slow tempo of the byre, the meadow, the dairy steadied nerves overstrung by the abnormal conditions of wartime. At first, Matthew could not fall into the rhythm. Sometimes, while following the cows down to the dairy at milking-time, he found himself sweating with impatience, and had to prevent himself from shouting at them and whacking their obstinate haunches to urge them along.

Anna observed this nervous distress. On his twenty-fifth birthday, in their first month on the farm, she bought him a Corgi puppy.

'He'll nip their heels for you, Matt, when I'm not there to drive them in.'

In a hundred such little ways she studied him, and helped him over the difficult transition from heroic life in the air to a plodding existence on the soil. For herself, the change over from war to peace was simple. She loved the quietude, the solitariness. Camp life and the pseudo-military discipline under women officers in the

W.A.A.F. had soon palled. She was a country woman, descended from a long line of fore-mothers born and bred to isolation in cottage and farmhouse, and the company of livestock. So now she had her hens and the first cows of the Jersey herd, accepting them as a beneficent dispensation of nature. She was content to wait for greater blessings.

Her happiness and good content shone like warmth from the sun. Matthew basked in that warmth. He felt it healing his brittled bones. The ill effects of the murderous, destructive tasks of his service as airman gradually sank out of sight. He hardly recalled them. He even lost interest in the company of his wartime comrades, and gave up attending the dinners and reunions of the vanished squadron. None of that was real: that nightmare of violence, fear, distortion. Life with Anna was real. It was sane, fulfilling. It meant something coherent, constructive. He thrived in it, stretching his mind and relaxing his nerves and bones. He felt that he could stand before her and fling out his arms. It would be almost a gesture of worship, certainly one of thanksgiving.

After little more than a year of this serene duet, Madeleine was born.

She came into this home which was already fecund with living things; the ever-growing herd, the hens, the cats, Gwylliam the Corgi, and the chorus of birds which Anna encouraged in spite of her farmer ancestry. The baby was one more living soul to add to the mystery of creation around them, this husband and wife islanded in happiness.

But Anna could do less on the farm, and Matthew had to employ labour, a troublesome business in the post-war world. Here again, he was lucky. He was shopping one day in Sittingbourne and, while having a snack and a drink in a public house, got into conversation with a man who worked in the Employment Exchange. He told Matthew of a fruit-farmer who had just died, whose son was unpopular with the men. Two of them had registered at the Exchange. One of them was a fellow who had been stationed during the war on an anti-aircraft gun-station on the Tyneside coast.

'That sounds like my man,' said Matthew. 'He'll be likely to understand my North Country ways.'

He was right. Tom Small was contacted that afternoon. He was older than Matthew, and unmarried – which explained his independence over choosing his jobs. Though trained as a fruitman, he was willing to work on a dairy-farm, especially when Matthew told him about the neglected orchard behind the house-garden.

'I'll have a look at that,' he said: his manner of accepting the offer.

A week later Tom Small reported for work. Anna, meanwhile, had found a lodging for him in a coastguard's cottage, where another bachelor lived, looked after by a sailor's old widow, named Mrs Weston.

Anna approved of Tom Small because he immediately showed an interest in Madeleine which soon developed into worship. The gratified parents suspected that his proposal to 'do something' with the orchard near the house was confirmed by the fact that the baby spent most of the day sleeping in her pram under the shelter of the wall near the door into the orchard.

Some unmarried men have this curious, avuncular attraction towards young children – shy, with a shrinking sensuality about it, a kind of substitute passion. As soon as Tom Small noticed that Madeleine spent her daylight hours between meals outdoors by the gate into the orchard, he began to work on these old apple trees. He sawed out the crowded wood, sprayed them with tar distillate, lagged their trunks with sticky bands, grafted better strains onto poor stock, and worked over the ground with hoe and fertilizer.

When the bill for the chemicals and artificial manure came in, Matthew tried to take a stand.

'I didn't reckon to grow fruit, Tom,' he said. 'It's not much good putting in a lot of time in that orchard. We ought to grub the lot. We could make a nice little market-garden there – salads and soft fruit.'

Tom put on his Kentish obstinacy, and looked sheepishly evasive.

'Nothing wrong with them trees,' he said. 'I been at fruit all my life. We all have, where I come from, Tunstall way. It's the old tree that gives the flavour to an apple. Young saplings is all acid, to our way of tasting. Once I get that orchard cleaned up and in good shape, we'll make a profit on every bushel.'

Matthew had to let him go his own way, for no complaint could be made that Tom neglected his work with the herd and on the fields. It was to some purpose also that Anna found a cord of apple logs cut and stacked in the tool-house near her back door. The orchard looked no thinner for it, and indeed, when spring came, the blossom there was so thick that fairyland stood beyond the walled garden. Day after day, the pink-white glory stood beyond Madeleine while she slept, breathing the almond-flavoured air as though she were consciously inhaling its richness.

One day Ann went down to see that all was well in the pram, and she found Tom Small standing just beyond the gateway, with sun-dappled hand shading his eyes, as

24

he peered at the infant.

'Why, what's this?' she said, picking up a carved wooden image from the coverlet.

'Just an old bit of applewood,' said Tom. 'Took my fancy, the way it had grown, so I finished it off. She'll like to hold that, later on, and help her teeth on it.'

Neither he nor Anna could say more. Both took it for granted; but from that day Anna felt no anxiety about the child's sleeping out of sight from the house. Tom took a step farther in his proprietary attitude, one rivalled only by the passive devotion of the Corgi, who followed the pram, more in sorrow than in anger, wherever it might be, to act as sentinel.

It was a vintage year, and weather that is good for the vine is good for the apple. Tom's promise was fulfilled: the orchard made a profit, and Matthew was able to add substantially to his Jersey herd.

4

So the latter-day bucolic idyll developed, month by month and year by year, in the modern world of industrialism and expansion. The nearby towns of North Kent grew more populous, and every village tried to overcome its housing shortage. The demand for milk and vegetables swelled, and the Burbages' farm prospered.

So did Madeleine. Some elusive quality of lyrical peace from that apple orchard saturated the child's daytime sleep. It augmented what she inherited from her parents out of their happiness in each other. Their mutual trust was an almost tangible influence throughout the farm and the neighbourhood, and Madeleine was a codicil to it.

Tom Small shared the privilege. The Burbages accepted him wholly, and had the illusion that he must always have been a part of 'Doggetts'. Indeed the farm became a little universe, secure, permanent, and all-providing.

It made its demands: work from before dawn until after sunset, constant planning, austere economy, wholetime devotion. But how much it gave in return: tonic air sweeping in on the estuarial tides; the rich river-soil; the gesture of the skies over the creeks and the traffic of sun, moon and stars over the Kentish downs beyond; the birdlife and the procession of ships coming and going; the tang of the sea and the ever-changing seasonal perfumes of the orchards, byres, marshes and hills.

One light June evening in 1950 Matthew and Anna stood at the top of their ground, with only the copse of oak and sweet chestnut rising behind them. They were looking south over their roof and the water to the mainland, Anna picking out detail along the ridge of the downs with binoculars. Matthew stood beside her, breathless after chasing the three-year-old Madeleine, with the dubious help of Gwylliam the Corgi.

'You know, Matt,' said Anna, still with the binoculars to her eyes, 'that world out there is changing fast: new buildings everywhere. All these Dutch barns, and cold stores. Don't you feel we're losing touch. Too concerned with ourselves?'

Matthew warded off the child, who was attacking him with a thick stalk of cow-parsley, and shouting with delight, as the tiny confetti of the umbel clung in her father's hair.

'We've enough on our hands, haven't we? This young monster for one, Anna! Look at her! She'll keep us busy for years.'

'I know. That's what I mean. We're too much concerned with our own, Matt. I don't know. Sometimes I feel that it's too good to last. Don't you understand how those hills are watching us, waiting for a chance to...'

'Look, Anna, you're being morbid. We're doing well enough; but we work for it. Maybe that's what is wrong. You need a break. Things are well set for a few weeks. Let's send Tom off for a holiday now, and bring your parents down during school

27

holidays, so that we can get away for a couple of weeks.'

Anna looked at him in surprise. She still held the glasses up to her face, and their shadow hid her eyes. The western sunlight glanced up from the river and touched the rounding of her cheeks and chin. Every feature was firm and statuary, shaped in metal. Matthew turned from the child, and saw this trick of sunlight.

'You look secure enough, my dear. You might be the Rock of Ages.'

'Don't darling, don't say such things.'

'Asking for trouble, eh? Look, Anna, let's be thankful for what we've got. Don't we deserve it?'

She was still more disturbed.

'That's what I mean. We're in danger of being pleased with ourselves. It's not a matter of needing a holiday. We ought to take part in local affairs, be more friendly with people. It was like that during the war, and somehow I felt safer then than I do now, Matt.'

Nothing more was said, but the conversation marked a development in their life. Before the autumn of 1950 set in, Anna joined the Women's Institute, and Matthew began to attend the meetings of the local branch of the Farmers' Union. During the winter he was elected to the Agricultural Committee.

Madeleine did not suffer from neglect. Already she was assured of her world: Mother, Father and Tom. The last was not least. He was her Prime Minister. What she willed, he carried out, and thus she built up an assurance too strong to be shaken even by the frightening first term at a private kindergarten school. A reasonable balance was held, however, between home and school. She was not a spoilt child, though an only one.

There was that little cloud. No brother or sister came along. Matthew and Anna were puzzled. Sometimes they discussed it, and asked themselves if the pause might be due to delayed effects of the wartime strain on nerves and emotions. There was no answer. They did not care to seek advice, and the years moved on. Madeleine remained an only child.

Now the apple-orchard was a well-ordered asset of the farm. The child spent so much time in it, with Tom Small at her service, that it was named 'Madeleine's Piece', and its profits put into a separate Savings Bank account under her name.

The pedigree herd of Jersey cattle also grew. In its daily movement between the pasture and the mechanical milking-byres, it paraded a corporate personality: warm, confident, enriching. In more ways than one it symbolized the cream of life. It dominated

Matthew's character, and drove out the wartime fears, the nausea of violence and the conjurings with death. He could plan ahead now, with long-term certainty, based on his well-stocked farm, his complete and perfect marriage and fatherhood.

Thus firmly anchored, he attracted a gradually increasing attention in the farming communities of Sheppey and North Kent.

5

Tom Small was reluctant to take a holiday, and another twelve months passed before he consented. During that delay, Madeleine thrived, and day by day unconsciously strengthened her domination over Tom. On her birthday he disappeared after the morning chores in the milking-sheds. He did not return until tea-time, leading a small pony, a shaggy creature with huge, liquid, friendly eyes.

He knocked at the kitchen door while Anna was buttering the toast. Madeleine dodged in front of her father and struggled with the latch, which she could just reach. Matthew watched, amused by her wilful intensity.

'Where have you been on my birthday, Tom?' she demanded. 'I brought my new tricycle down to the orchard to show you, and you were not there.'

She stamped her foot: a bit of play-acting, a pretence of anger.

Tom grinned; but Matthew noticed that his face was pale.

'I been to Dartford to fetch my present,' he said, his voice husky with feeling. 'He's a gentle lad, you'll soon master him, to ride about the farm, and his name is Prince Albert.'

As though to justify this flattering reference, Prince Albert stepped forward under Tom's arm and into the kitchen, snuffing his way towards the pile of toast which Anna had just set on the table. He was about to lift a slice with his humorous lips, when Madeleine's arms were flung round his neck, and her head pressed against his broad, shaggy forehead. He waited patiently during this demonstration of love at first sight, then stepped forward again towards the toast, dragging the child with him. A neat twist of his upper lip, and a toss of his head, and the top slice was gone.

During the burst of laughter from the three grown-ups, Prince Albert chumbled the toast, submitting meekly to the caress and scolding from his new mistress.

'You wicked – wicked...!' she murmured, as convincingly as Titania into Bottom's hairy ear. But she could not find the word for so incredible a creature. She turned on Tom, but without daring to release Prince Albert from her grasp. 'Oh, Tom! Who told you? Who told you?' she cried, and then began to weep.

'Come now, young Madeleine, I ain't that sort of chap.'

Tom's voice was equally troubled. The parents too were sobered.

'What have you done, Tom?' whispered Anna. 'Spoiling her, that's what it is.' But she betrayed her recognition of his kindness and Matthew looked anxiously from one to the rest of the emotional trio.

'What about tea?' he said. 'We're late with the milking.'

'Nobody told me,' said Tom to Madeleine, ignoring his employer's effort. 'You always wanted a pony, didn't you?'

With this, Madeleine released Prince Albert and transferred her embrace to Tom Small, flinging her arms round his legs and butting him in the groin with her head. She released him only when her father dragged her away, to pick her up and sit her on the pony's back.

There, for a moment, the tableau stayed. Then the tension broke, and Tom was allowed to lead Prince Albert out to the yard and tether him there. As Madeleine took her place at the table, Matthew appealed to his wife.

'It's getting a bit much, Anna?'

'Oh, Matt, no! It's well meant. He's got no other outlet. How can you say such a thing?'

'What *have* I said?'

Matthew was bewildered. But he wanted to say more, to make clear to Anna something that was not clear to himself. The effort was cut short by a warning glance from Anna, which indicated in dumb-show that the child was aware of this concern on her behalf.

'It's a wonderful present, Madeleine,' said Anna loudly. Then she added, in an undertone to Matthew, 'I'd trust him with her life, Matt.'

'Nobody doubts that,' he said, 'but we've still got the milking to do, so let's get on with our tea.'

He was not prepared to feel more about the matter, but even so, he did not address himself to Tom, when that devoted fellow reappeared and took his place at table, to submit to a barrage of questions, self-answered, from Madeleine, who was now flushed with cloudless excitement.

The cake was cut, after Madeleine had blown out the birthday candles, and everybody was bidden to wish.

'I don't want any more wishes,' cried Madeleine, working up to another bout of tears as another shadow passed over her uncontrollable universe.

'Then you can come and help in the byre,' said her father, 'and cool off before bed-time.'

Anna watched them go, and turned to see Tom moving after them. She laid a hand on his arm.

'Nobody has thanked you, Tom,' she said, gently.

He nodded, shifted his feet, then looked into her face for a second, with an intensity that almost frightened her.

'I don't reckon to be thanked, Missus. That's young Madeleine. I know her ways.'

He followed the others, and she saw him moving solidly after them down the yard. Madeleine was on the pony, her father leading it by the halter of rope. The group was gilded by dusty evening sunlight.

'A lot of gipsies,' said Anna aloud, as she turned to clear the table. Her eyes were still dazzled, for she had been looking from the western window of the kitchen, which gave on to the yard and the farm-buildings, with the end of the orchard behind them. That background was now a thicket of pink and white blossom, blazing coldly in the level fire as the sun sank. For a moment, the conflagration blinded Anna, and she had to pause, blinking her eyes, before she could begin to clear the tea-table though the kitchen too was filled with the sunset, every object glorified.

6

Serenely, meekly, Prince Albert reigned over the whole community at 'Doggetts'. He conducted himself with an air of knowing a good thing when he saw it, and he had instantly decided that 'Doggetts' was an uncommonly good thing. He recognized his little mistress and submitted with docility to her tyranny. In this, he modelled his conduct on that of his donor, Tom Small. In this service, the pony had the advantage, because he carried no other obligations. Tom had to tear himself away, to his work on the farm. He now had help, for Matthew, by a stroke of luck, had been able to buy twenty acres when the adjoining farm was split up after the death of its owner. This carried Burbage's pasture further westward, towards Elmley and the south-western angle of Sheppey. The bridge connecting with the mainland, carrying the road that led to Queensborough and Sheerness, was near his new western boundary.

A bungalow was built for the new man, who brought a wife, another pair of hands that might help on the farm and in the house. The couple were elderly, and inclined to fill in time until they could claim their Old Age Pension. Meanwhile they were willing to oblige, so long as nobody interfered with their independence or expected any new-fangled ideas, or ways of doing a job. They were content to be background figures, and kept themselves to themselves. They had sons and daughters scattered about the neighbourhood, mostly working in the factories. From time to time one or other of the family visited the parents in the new bungalow. They drove up in second-hand cars, or on motor-cycles, and if they encountered their parents' employer, or his wife, they did not bother to pass the time of day. Or they might nod. But they had left that kind of nonsense behind when they left the land. They now also left their litter behind: cigarette packs, ice-cream cartons, a worn-out tyre. Every Monday Tom Small, who was a stickler for tidiness because litter might carry disease to his apple trees, went around the new acres and cleared up after the week-end visitors, burning the refuse. He did not consider it his place to speak to the farm-hand about this. That was the boss's job. But Matthew and Anna were too shy to remonstrate on a question of good and bad taste, with people old enough to be their parents.

Matthew reluctantly allowed Tom Small to extend the orchard westward by two acres, which were planted with Cox's apples. Ten acres were ploughed and sown with winter fodder and hay-seed; the remainder on lower ground was left as pasture. Matthew added five more pedigreed heifers to his herd.

This heavy outlay took place in the spring of 1951, at the time Prince Albert joined the family.

'Now we stay put for a while,' said Matthew, when the comings and goings of the whole business were settled, and the extra work mastered. 'That's about anchored us down. We're slaves of the bank, Anna.'

'Yes, but we're building up one of the finest herds in North Kent, Matt. It's something to show, after such a short time. We're taking our place in the country, and Kentish people don't accept newcomers easily. People are friendly, and we're lucky in having Tom Small.'

'Oh yes; Tom! he said drily. 'Our paragon!'

'Why d'you say that?'

'I don't know, my dear. Perhaps I'm jealous of his efficiency.'

'But he's loyal, Matt. That means everything. Compare him with that pair we've just taken on!'

'Yes. I can't get used to that. It's odd, but I hardly remember their name even. What is it; one of the local tribal...'

'That sounds snobbish, Matt. Moxon. I always call her Mrs Moxon – more in fear than affection! She holds me at arm's length too. I feel that I serve her purpose, for as long as it suits her.'

'Yes. Democracy in action. Sometimes it terrifies me: all the human warmth frozen out of it.'

'Well, Matt, I suppose the relationship between employer and employed has always been much like that. It's the exception which keeps things working smoothly. There are still people with a sense of service. For example...' She hesitated, looked swiftly at her husband, then spoke with more emphasis than was necessary. She might have been accusing him of something. 'There's Tom Small.'

She saw Matthew guard himself. She saw also that he was sincerely puzzled, and she recognized his honesty and effort to be open-minded.

'Yes; yes, you're right,' he said slowly. 'But d'you understand him, Anna?'

She did not reply, and Matthew struggled to explain.

'I mean his devotion to Madeleine. Is it – is it quite balanced?' Then he added: 'And is it going to do her any good?'

'You mean he spoils her? That's all right, as long as we don't. It balances things up for an only child, who tends to be either indulged or oppressed.'

'An only child? That's not our fault, my dear.'

38

This being a curtain dialogue, half whispered on the pillow, its conclusion led to more intimate and tender experiment, all doubts and questionings relinquished, for the night at least.

7

Everything promised well. The apple-blossom set firmly, with no attack from late frosts. The newly sown acres sprouted green overnight as the days lengthened. The yield of milk from the herd responded at once to the young growth of the warming pastures. Even the Moxons were cheerful, working almost with a will.

Maytime smothered 'Doggetts' with blossom. A great tide of foaming umbels rose along the field ends and spilled into the roads, powdering the tarmac with pollen and a shaking-out of tiny petals. The first honeysuckle appeared, hanging its little candelabra along the hawthorn hedgerows. The ground blooms, which delight children and botanists, shook out again in carpet fashion, a recurring play upon a few colours, white, yellow and blue, but as rapturous in one medium as the songs of the stormcock and blackbird in another.

The Jersey cows waded belly-deep in the pasture, their profitable udders swinging unseen in the green flood. Their breath added to the sweetness of the air, element in an unlocatable perfume blending all the sources of life itself. With some faculty above reason, the Burbages could breathe deeply of hope and confidence.

Matthew came out one morning, after taking Madeleine to school. She had been unwilling, for sunlight on a May morning plays havoc with regular human plans and disciplines. There had been tears at breakfast, and some briskly thought-up arguments about Prince Albert's disappointment if his mistress did not take him out. Only Tom's arrival appeased her. He promised to lead her on her pony round the new orchard that afternoon, while he inspected the posts and wire-nettings that protected the saplings.

Tom was in the old orchard when Matthew reappeared. He saw Tom on the tractor, dragging a spraying-machine that threw up a yellow fan of chemical over the newly-set fruit. Tree-trunks and branches, after his passage, gleamed soapily and the general flower scents were lost for a while under an astringent tang, sharp and saline.

Matthew stood watching him wind his way in and out among the avenues of trees, ducking and dodging as he approached branches that threatened his head. The spray had settled on his old mackintosh and cap, transforming them to light armour made of an alloy not of this world. He looked half-fabulous, a papery creature, cousin to the locust.

Then he drew up beside Matthew, stopped his engine, and got stiffly down, to fumble for his cigarettes. Matthew offered him one, which he took, nodding as he wiped his face with a handkerchief extracted from an inner pocket.

'Ah,' he said, groaning as he stretched, 'bad as driving a tank at Alamein! Stuck in one position. Does me no good, cramped up like that. We all had constipation out there.'

Matthew watched him pull luxuriously at the cigarette, which his fingers had already stained with the chalky fluid. He inspired confidence. No mortal could be more carefree, more wholly concerned with the immediate job in hand.

'That young Madeleine,' he said at last, 'I wouldn't blame her, on a day like this. 'Tisn't natural!'

'No, Tom. But she's got to make a start. It's an artificial world we live in; and if we don't master the technique...'

'Aye. But she's only a little 'un; it's still soon...'

'Not too soon, when you think what–'

'Think? Yes, that's it. Thinking! Look what we're coming to, with all this thinking. Likely to be the end of us, seems to me.'

41

His beaming face belied his words. Both men stood contentedly together for a while, trustful in each other and in their work together, all differences, if any, submerged.

Matthew looked up beyond the orchard, to the rising pastures below the wood.

'What's happening up there, Tom? The cows are running around. It's that pony! He's got amongst them again, the little devil. Pure mischief.'

'He likes a bit of company, that's all,' said Tom. 'He was down the yard when I came out, looking for young Madeleine to saddle him.'

Matthew hurried off across the orchard, with the Corgi at his heels. Tom followed slowly, but stopped at the farther gate, leaning over it and contemplating while Matthew went on and sorted out the cows from Prince Albert, who now stood penitently among them, after the prancing and heel-flinging which had so disturbed their grazing.

It was a peaceful picture. Matthew stood beside the pony, slapping his shaggy flank as he pretended to scold him. Tom was too far away to hear that. But he saw the little fellow listening and rubbing himself against Matthew's hip, while the cows formed round, their inquisitive heads polarized to the intruder. They floated on the pasture like wooden ships, high in the poop, and broad-beamed.

Behind them the wood was colouring up, with livening twigs, catkins, treacly buds, and some foliage already fanning out. Flashes here and there showed blue-tits at work. Stationed in the tops of the taller trees, songsters were shouting their triumphant challengings.

Tom, though not enthusiastically interested in the cows, was at once attentive when he saw his employer suddenly leave the pony and hurry to a cow that stood apart from the herd gathered round Prince Albert. She was conspicuous because the morning sun highlighted her broad flank against the shadowed background of the copse of oaks and sweet-chestnuts which crowned Burbage's land.

Tom saw him stoop, then smack down the Corgi who had leaped playfully at the creature's snout. He heard Matthew's summoning cry, and at once began to hurry up the slope, scattering the herd as he passed through them. Prince Albert turned and followed him, ignoring the Corgi who was now circling round, to drive the couple towards his master.

'Tom, d'you see anything wrong with this animal?'

'Why, she's a bit lonely like, standing up here all by herself.'

'But why is she? Look at the way she hangs

her head. Here, girl, come on now! Move yourself!'

Matthew slapped the cow on her flank, and the skin shuddered under his hand as she moved a few paces, away from the herd.

'Why, she's limping, Tom.'

'Aye, she'll have got a thorn or a stone lodged in her hoof,' said Tom. He examined her feet, one by one.

'Can see nothing there,' he said. 'Only a sore spot, kind of blister, on this one, here at the top of the hoof. That shouldn't make her limp.'

The two men looked at each other, as though both guilty of a crime. Then Matthew spoke.

'Better have the vet, Tom. We can't take a risk with an attested herd.'

Tom said nothing. They drove the cow slowly down the field and shut it off with hurdles in a corner of the home paddock. It stood there disconsolately under the spring sunshine, neither grazing nor moving. It had not moved when the vet came while the family were finishing their midday meal.

Matthew, who had said nothing to Anna, disappeared at once when he saw the car coming up the drive.

'Who's that, Tom?' asked Anna, scenting trouble.

Tom was evasive. He nodded warningly at Madeleine.

'One of the Jerseys a bit poorly,' he said. 'No need to worry.'

'Why, Tom, what is it? Matthew said nothing. No need to worry? What do you mean?'

But Tom had fled. He followed Matthew and joined him and the vet as they walked over the paddock to the temporary sick-bay.

The vet examined the sore hoof. He said nothing. Then he put on a pair of rubber gloves, and forced the disconsolate animal to lift her head. He turned down the lip, and after a tussle got the mouth open.

'See?' he said, pointing to two white water-blisters in the mouth. 'I'll have to call in the Ministry people, Mr Burbage. Sorry about that. But I must keep away now.'

He took off the gloves and dropped them into a canister.

'Is that what it is?' Matthew heard his own voice, whispering from a distance.

'Afraid so. It's already broken out near Dartford. We'd better lose no time. There might be a hope...' The lie was too obvious to bother about. 'I'll see to it. You'd better be around for the rest of the day.'

They watched him drive off, and then they returned slowly to the house.

'What do we say to young Madeleine?' asked Tom, as they saw her appear at the door with her mother. She had caught the infection of fear, for instead of running to

45

meet the two men, she clung to her mother's apron, and stared stupidly, a thumb in her mouth.

Matthew lost his temper.

'Is that what worries you?' Then he attacked the child: 'Take that thumb out of your mouth, Madeleine.'

She looked at him, as over imaginary glasses, her eyes owlish. Then she hid her face against her mother's skirt. Anna was too much concerned to be able to comfort her, and during the next few minutes of anxiety and embarrassed interchange of questions and replies, Madeleine was ignored. Nobody noticed, or cared, what she observed and registered.

Three Ministry officials, with the veterinary surgeon, arrived at sundown.

'We're late, I'm afraid,' said one of them, 'but the light's good.'

The sick cow still stood motionless. Ropes of saliva hung from her mouth. She lowed miserably from time to time. After the examination the vet nodded to his colleagues. Their leader addressed himself aggressively to Burbage, then tempered the abruptness by putting a hand on his shoulder. 'There's no doubt, Mr Burbage. It's foot-and-mouth. The rest will be showing it by now, I expect. Is that the herd up there?'

He pointed to the upper field, where the

Jerseys were gathered round the gate, bellowing impatiently, all but two of them, who remained up field.

The grim procession crossed the farm. The two separate cows were examined, and the dreaded symptoms found.

'I'm afraid we must isolate you. It's a tedious business, but you know how it is.'

Burbage left Tom to help the two Ministry men with the job of setting up notices at the gates, and preparing tubs of disinfectant to be used on the shoes of people coming to and from the farm. He led the vet and the officer to the house, introducing them to Anna, who at once knew the worst, from the bearing of the three mutes. She made a fresh pot of tea while forms were produced, filled in and signed.

Madeleine, still ignored, looked on owl-eyed. When the men got up to leave, the vet noticed the child, approached and spoke to her.

'Do you go to school, young woman?'

She shrank back, and murmured something inaudible.

'What time do you set off, eh? Quarter to nine?'

He turned to Anna, and spoke quietly, intending that the child should not hear.

'Sorry about this, Mrs Burbage. I'll arrange that we're not here before nine tomorrow morning. Just as well, don't you think, if you stay out of it too, until the job's done?'

'I suppose so,' said Anna dully. 'Though my husband may want my help.'

'Don't talk nonsense, Anna,' said Matthew, who had left the table and was offering cigarettes to the executioners. He spoke irritably, as he had snapped at Madeleine when he saw her clinging to her mother at the door.

'No, dear,' said Anna. She laid a hand on his arm. 'I know what you mean. But I want to be with you.'

He looked at her, drowningly.

'That's all right,' he said. 'But it's no job for a woman.'

'Not even an ex-W.A.A.F.?'

The vet interrupted: 'Very brave of you, Mrs Burbage, but it will be better to keep out of the way.' He indicated the child with a half-glance, which her sharp eyes did not miss. 'You could be more use with her, too. Why not take her off for the day? Keep her mind occupied, I mean.'

It was a sensible suggestion, and Anna agreed. Until the men from the Ministry had gone, and the unusually docile Madeleine was in bed, Anna controlled her distress. She prepared supper, and while at work in the kitchen heard Tom come in from the yard, before going off for the night. Matthew was still out, after seeing the visitors off.

'What does she know about it, Missus?' said Tom, as Anna turned from the stove to greet him. 'Wouldn't do to get her worried.'

'We're all worried, Tom. How can such news be kept from her? The whole air is poisoned for us. What *are* we to do? I must think it out. I can't let Matthew face it alone.'

He studied her intently.

'No call to worry about him, Missus. So long as you're his wife, he'll have a way out.'

'What *do* you mean, Tom? You make it worse – you make it sound ominous.'

'No, not I, Missus Burbage. That I don't mean. But I'm thinking of young Madeleine. I saw what she saw, while the talking was being done. She don't miss much, that little party. And I wouldn't have her set down. It gets on my mind, to think that. This is a visitation, all right. Puts us back properly. But we can see beyond it, as I know you feel. And you will tell it that way to the Boss. But young Madeleine won't see it, y'know. I'm asking what we're to do about that.'

He was so distressed that Anna left the stove and approached him. He smelled of the byre, with an over-scent of the disinfectant, and a remote survival of the spray lingering from his morning's work. The earthiness of all this reassured her. She looked into his troubled eyes almost with

49

amusement, certainly with kindness.

'I think you love her as much as we do, Tom.'

That embarrassed him. He flushed, turned away, then faced her again, with a gesture of desperation.

'She's a rare one, Missus Burbage. I don't presume that way. A bit lonely, maybe. You and the Boss, you've got each other, but she's like me, I'd say: got nobody else.'

'Oh, Tom, don't be so fatal about it. She's a happy child, surely. You wouldn't have us spoil her?'

This again embarrassed him.

'Sorry, ma'am. I think we're all worked up today. But what's coming tomorrow is an ugly business, and I saw that young Madeleine knew it.'

'Oh, nonsense, how could she? Nobody spoke a word about it.'

'But it's all around us. That's what I mean.'

'Well, I can only keep her away, Tom. But don't think I, and her father, too, don't appreciate what you feel, and all you do for her.'

'Oh – her father!'

With this exclamation, he frowned, turned, and walked out, leaving Anna ruffled, not quite sure whether she was indignant or merely bewildered. But at the back of her mind was a half recognition that Tom's unaccountable devotion to Madeleine was an assurance, and she wished Matthew would see it so.

She was pondering on this when Matthew returned. He came straight through to the kitchen and sat down, a defeated man.

Anna, a soup-ladle in one hand, stooped and kissed him.

'Don't, Matt. It'll be all right.'

'Don't what?'

His voice was lifeless too.

'Don't let it beat us. We've got each other.'

'Yes, that's fundamental by now. I can't imagine, Anna... I mean it's impossible to think of anything coming between us. It's hard even to remember what life was like before we met.'

Matthew rambled on, recalling precious moments and scenes from their first days together. Anna was both affectionately moved and alarmed. She realized that he was more vulnerable than she had believed him to be.

'Matt! Is there something else on your mind? Tell me what it is.'

He stopped talking, and looked at her hungrily, but also with some irritation.

'What d'you mean? Isn't this blow enough? Don't you realize that we're practically ruined?'

'Look, Matthew. You're exaggerating: working yourself up like this is no use. Isn't it enough that we can start again together?'

'Together?' he interrupted with a bitterness that dismayed her. She left her cooking and took him in her arms, but he would not let her kiss him. He held her off, fiercely and sadly. 'That's it, you see. I can't do without you, my dear. I've been figuring this out. It's the sort of luck that comes to most farmers, but they're not shaken by it. They don't come crying to their wives.'

'You don't know what they do, Matt!'

He ignored this.

'Maybe my nerve has gone, Anna. It's airman's malady, long delayed. Sooner or later we all show the effects of those nights on the big raids.'

He shivered, and made another effort to escape from her. But she clung to him in a paroxysm of protectiveness, kissing him and murmuring: 'Darling, you mustn't! It just is not true. No man could have done more than you since we began. Don't think I've not watched you; your work and hopes. And we've done it together, Matt. We've got Madeleine now. We're still young. We can start again, and the farm is ours: no debts, Matt. And there will be some compensation, at least. And Tom Small's orchard, too!'

'Tom Small's orchard! *My* orchard!'

Anna laughed, reassured by his indignant claim. It was a sign of self-respect.

'Yes,' she said, 'but it is Tom's province, and it may have to support us this year.'

'What, a couple of acres of apples?'

'But he's got all that soft fruit under the trees.'

'Oh, yes, and all the rest of it. Tom almost runs the whole show.'

'Don't be an idiot, Matt. You make me angry.'

'Oh, I make you angry? Well, hasn't it occurred to you that we owe this damned business to Tom Small? D'you know what the vet said to me, Anna? He asked me where that pony came from, and how long ago. When I told him it came from Dartford only a week ago, he said, "Well, that's it then. These gipsies wander about everywhere".'

'How'd you know he bought it from the gipsies?'

'How else could he afford it? Besides, look at it. He and Maddy together still haven't got that coat into shape. It's as rough as when the little brute came. And he was careering about with the herd only this morning, when I went up to see what was disturbing them.'

'Matthew, you're too anxious to blame Tom Small. It isn't fair...' Anna turned away and wept. Matthew, unrepentant, stared at her, until she recovered.

'Unfair!' he repeated several times, accusingly.

'Even if it's true,' said Anna at last, appealing to him again, 'we mustn't, Matt, we dare not let him know! Promise me that! For Madeleine's sake.'

'Oh, it's for her, is it? I thought you'd be worrying about him.'

'You know you don't believe that, Matthew. If I thought you did, it would be the end of everything, worse than losing the herd, or everything we've got. But you can't believe it, Matt. Don't you see what I'm trying to tell you; how much Tom means to Madeleine? She depends on him for most of her world. I don't understand where it all comes from, this devotion of his, but it's real enough, Matt; and it's something true, and beautiful. If we spoil it we shall never forgive ourselves.'

She wept again, but fought against her distress and conquered it.

'Promise me, then, Matt; promise you won't say a word to him. I believe he would go if you did. We should lose him. And is it fair to him? Even if he *was* responsible, he's not to blame. Think what it meant to him, this gift. Be fair to him, too, darling. Not a word to him; never! never!'

Matthew, reassured by Anna's violent repudiation of his jealousy, tried to comfort her. The caresses now came from him, and he gave the promise demanded.

'That's over, my dear. I'll say nothing. You can depend on me there.'

At this moment, Madeleine came in, a

wan little figure, shrunken and pale. Both parents at once forgot their own troubles and turned to her, alarmed by the discovery that she knew what was to happen next day. They had to work hard, supporting each other in the effort to comfort her, to make her eat her supper and go to bed. The last words Matthew heard Anna say to her as her eyelids closed over her fears were, 'Yes, darling, we'll soon have another herd of cows, and they won't be poor sick ones, will they?'

He paused at the bedroom door, over-come by love for these two. It was almost a convulsion, gripping his limbs as well as his will. Suddenly, he relived the moments of that grim night when he disobeyed the order to make a crash-landing. He had gone on then, and done the job. Without carrying the memory further, or consciously apply-ing it to present circumstances, he went downstairs. But the resolution was there, giving him courage to face tomorrow in a way which he knew was part of his own character. He was almost happy in this second demonstration of self-confidence.

8

Anna set off at eight o'clock next morning,

to take Madeleine down the estuary to Broadstairs. The day was fair, and from the cloudless sky sunlight and sea-breeze swept the Isle of Sheppey clean. Anna stopped the car after reaching the mainland. She looked back across the island, and the irony of its sweetness and brilliance made her lean for a moment or two over the steering-wheel, while bitterness gripped her throat. In a mood of self-torture she wished she could drive along the shore, to look over to 'Doggetts', not to watch the proceedings, but to appreciate more fully this dreadful indifference of the universe. The open country of the island, gently sloping up to Minster, thus greeting the sun as though responding to a caress, made her long to turn back, to share Matthew's ordeal during the slaughter of the cattle.

'Why have we stopped, Mummy?'

Anna looked down at the wistful inquirer, and for a moment saw her almost as an intruding stranger.

'I was just wondering, Maddy,' she said guiltily.

'I'd like to go back too,' said Madeleine, her voice shaken with tears.

'Oh, no! No, darling. We must go on. We'll have such a happy day on the sands. We'll build a castle together, and then...'

'Will Tom be helping them, Mummy?'

Anna stared ahead, helpless. She tried to

conquer the guilt, the sense of being shut out from her daughter's misery. But the relentless inquiry continued.

'Will they – kill Prince Albert too?'

'Of course not. You must not imagine such things, Maddy. Now let us forget all about it, and plan what we shall do when we get to Broadstairs.'

She drove on while she talked, trying to draw the child's interest away; but her own heart was cold with misery and worry, a weakness which she recognized and was struggling to overcome. Anna looked down at the little figure from time to time, to see what effect her forced chatter might be having. She saw a flushed face, brown eyes – Matthew's eyes – staring fixedly through the windscreen, shoulders hunched and hands clasped between a pair of bony knees.

Anna recognized not only Matthew's eyes, but his temperament. The inheritance was more pronounced than ever. A passion of protectiveness carried Anna clear of her own despair. She told herself that she must fight for these two people, and for the home that sheltered them both from themselves and the world. She longed to stop the car, to turn back to 'Doggetts', and to face the battle. Passing cottages and farmhouses, she felt the tug at her heart as she pictured the families at home in them.

'I must watch the road,' she said aloud,

pausing in her effort to distract Madeleine. An overtaking van had startled her. She had neglected to see it coming, and the driver glared at her as he passed. 'I mustn't talk so much, Maddy. You watch too, and tell me what is coming.'

But she knew that she must not daydream; must not blind herself with anxiety over husband, daughter, and the future of their home.

'We'll start again, Maddy,' she cried, with such vehemence that the child was at last pulled back to the present moment, and so to health.

'You don't mean to turn back, Mummy?' looking up at her mother with living curiosity in those brown eyes.

Anna laughed; both laughed.

'No! Onwards. To Broadstairs; our sand-castle! And then home again to Daddy.'

'And to Tom, Mummy.'

This was another problem. But Anna's resolution was now firm enough to face that too. It sustained her for the rest of the day. It built the sand-castle and furnished it with Madeleine's reawakened confidence. It fortified her during the hours of absence from Matthew and that ordeal at home. She believed that she could handle this crisis, and overcome it.

Dusk was falling when she turned into the drive at 'Doggetts'. A strange quietness lay over the farm. Under the lowering light the fields stood empty, except for a long mound – like a neolithic barrow – of raw earth, along the hedge at right-angles to the wood at the top. The clay still gleamed damp, reflecting the western sky. It might have been a pile of gold. Madeleine did not noticed it.

'I must feed Prince Albert,' she cried, scrambling down almost before the car stopped. Anna was relieved to get rid of her for a while. She was weary after the strain, weary but happy in the newly discovered strength brought back to 'Doggetts', to bring it to life again, to give new hope to Matthew.

But it was Tom Small who first appeared. He came into the yard as she emerged from the garage. Madeleine had already disappeared into the pony's stable.

'Well, Missus,' he said. 'She's quick enough, tonight. Not taking it too badly then?'

'Where's Matthew, Tom?'

'No need to fret about him, either. He was a bit shaken while the killing went on. Took us all morning. By that time the bulldozer came and had that trench dug before three o'clock. We got the whole lot covered up by five. I got him to go down and make tea for the chaps. Take him away, like. He must have done a bit of thinking too; for when we all went down to the house, there he was, cheerful as a cricket: a new man, I reckon. He and I watched them go, and he turned to me when we was alone, and he shook me by the hand; kind of ceremony he made of it. "We start again, Tom, as soon as the isolation is over. The Ministry isn't too bad over compensation, after all." That's what he said, Missus Burbage. And I reckon that's as much as any man could say.'

Anna heard this. It revived the resolution which had met her on the road to Broadstairs.

'I'd like to shake you by the hand, too, Tom.'

She did so, as he stood somewhat shamefaced by this second, un-bucolic display of feeling, so foreign to Kentish manners.

'And there will be the apple-harvest from your orchard, Tom.'

He nodded.

'So long as we don't get a frost in May.'

Then his interested veered back.

'I better see how young Maddy's getting on with that feed.'

'And I'll find Matthew.'

'Aye, we've been up the orchard, looking round. I left him up there. First time he's shown an interest in that crop.'

Anna laughed aloud as she parted from Tom Small, crossed the yard, entered the walled garden and made for the gate into the orchard, calling, 'Matthew! Matthew!'

They approached each other like bride and bridegroom, rather than man and wife with several years of the ups and downs of marriage behind them.

TWO

1

After that disaster the sun shone on 'Doggetts'. Nothing could be done that spring towards starting another herd, so Matthew turned to arable farming, investing some of the money paid by the Ministry as compensation for the slaughter of the cows. He found that Moxon approved, had an experienced knowledge of cereals, and was a skilful hand with the plough and all jobs connected with corn crops. Matthew raised catch crops of barley and oats that summer, and a fair tonnage of potatoes. Moxon was responsible for all this, and his pride in it made both him and his wife more amenable and friendly. They grew less suspicious of the foreigners who employed them.

Matthew and Anna had to forego the hoped-for holiday, but there was rich compensation. They had ridden their first bad storm, and the adventure brought them closer together in this next year of their marriage. Their working days that summer were a second honeymoon, undimmed by habit, nothing between them taken for granted.

In that revival Madeleine flourished too. The pale cheeks filled out, rosy with health. The brown eyes lost their load of premature thought. The more she was dominated by her devotion to Prince Albert, the more she consolidated her ascendency over Tom Small. They were the two poles of her small world, which whirled round them, bearing her parents on varying parallels, according to her moods and their behaviour. Tom and the pony were absolute, fixing her universe securely.

Her parents did not mind. They had each other in renewed certainty, and needed no other possessiveness; at least nothing so fierce. They were indeed glad to relax their hold on Madeleine, knowing they would have to do so should other children arrive. It was wise to be ready before the event: wise for themselves and for her. They did not tell themselves that; but they implied it in their contentment with each other.

One hot day at the end of June, Anna and Madeleine came up the meadows carrying a clothes-basket between them, loaded with a picnic luncheon for four. They were halfway towards the copse when Gwylliam spotted them from his post beside his master's jacket hanging on the fence which Matthew and Tom Small were repairing. The dog came racing down, invisible but leaving a green wake in the thick pasture grass sown in the fields ploughed immediately after the disaster. Ideal weather of sun and rain had drawn up a miraculous crop.

'Out! Out, Billy!' shouted Gwylliam's master. 'You'll ruin that hay.'

But Gwylliam, short-legged, was lost in the jungle. His jubilant bark turned to cries for help, as he ran in circles, making patterns of agitation in the pasture.

Matthew's voice echoed and re-echoed from the walls of the house and farm-buildings, and this confusion of carefree sounds was repeated when he shouted, 'Hi! There you are then! We're up here. Keep to the edges; and call that dog out!'

This long speech tumbled over itself, un-recognizable by the time it reached Anna and the child. It might have been a trumpet-call, but it was joyous enough to set Madeleine shouting in reply, her treble cutting the air like a knife. It guided Gwylliam, who suddenly appeared, leaving the grass none the worse for his hysterical geometry. He grinned at the basket, raising his head and sniffing.

Madeleine was about to stoop and brush a smear of buttercup pollen from his head, when there rose a whinnying from the stable down below. Prince Albert had heard his mistress's voice.

'Oh, Mummy! What have I done! I'm coming, Prince; coming!'

She was off down the fields, so excited that she left the first gate open, then the second.

'Gates!' shouted her mother. But Madeleine could hear only one demand. She disappeared, her shrill voice answering the cries of the pony.

Anna went on alone, balancing the basket on her hip. The dog trotted behind her intent on the prospect of a share in the picnic.

Matthew left Tom at work, and came down to meet her.

A spur of the wood gave them a momentary solitude.

'Why, you're breathless,' he said, tenderly. He leaned across the basket and kissed her. The warmth of their mouths, and the healthy sweat, roused both to passion. The basket between them creaked and narrowed.

'More than ever, Anna, more than ever! You're all my world now.'

He slipped his hand into her blouse and cupped her breast. It was damp yet cool. She responded, mature, obtainable.

'Not here, Matt,' she said. 'Madeleine will

be coming up. And where's Tom?'

He said nothing, but relaxed, content to wait. Both their lives were before them. He realized that, as he took the basket, and felt her bare arm along his as she clung to him.

A curious note of mockery sounded from the woodland as they approached the fence: the voice of a belated cuckoo, stuttering on, two or three weeks after its fellow gipsies were silenced. The married lovers laughed together.

They passed round the spur and came upon Tom Small, who was wiring spiles. He set down his tool on top of a standing roll of half-inch netting.

'We'll need to set that against them rabbits before tonight,' he said, taking out his tobacco-box to roll a cigarette.

But Anna and Matthew had not yet returned to the workaday world. Tom looked at them indulgently as he twirled the weed in the paper.

'She bringing up the pony?' he asked.

It was as though he had summoned Madeleine by telepathy. She appeared round the spur, riding Prince Albert, her back straight and knees only just clasping his broad flanks.

'You shut those gates?' demanded her father, his voice still lazy with postponed desire. She was too happy to reply.

By the end of that summer, Matthew was building up another herd of Jersey cows. He might have started earlier, for the Ministry had notified him weeks before that the district was free of infection. But he had already put much of the compensation money into other ventures. Moreover, he was nervous about starting again, and might not have done so that autumn if Anna had not been so eager. It was she who first approached the expert at Hothfield and invited her over to discuss the matter.

This professional, a titled woman named Lady Beverley, whose sharp, petite beauty startled even Anna to admiration, warmly approved of 'Doggetts' as the setting for a carefully selected herd. She approved also of the Burbages, and invited them to her home to discuss the problems involved in establishing pedigreed stock on limited capital. She admired their courage, and advised them to add a small insurance to the guarantee of governmental cover in the event of another outbreak of foot-and-mouth disease.

Lady Beverley had also much to offer about the technical skill needing in raising and maintaining cattle. She was as generous with advice as with friendship, though she forced neither upon the young people.

They profited by both. Her confidence in them was a tonic to their courage, much needed after the setback in May. She came to 'Doggetts' frequently during the summer, and her praise spurred on the work being done on the stricken farm. During that time, as new beasts arrived, there was often no money to pay for them. Lady Beverley smoothed out that difficulty, by standing in for deferred payment until the autumn. Even when the harvest was in and sold, the margin of profit on so small an acreage was not enough to cover the investment to which Lady Beverley had committed the Burbages. Anna was at first frightened, almost hostile.

'Why is she doing this, Matt?' she demanded one October day after an evening spent by her and Matthew on their bills, receipts and bank statements. 'She'll be owning the farm if we're not careful.'

'Don't be cold-blooded, Anna. Life isn't as tough as all that. She's taken a liking to us – to *you*, I suspect and enjoys helping us. She knows we won't let her down. After all, my dear, we're working all out, and she admires us for it. We've come through. What more have we to fear?'

Anna looked at him. Lady Beverley's trust had renewed him. He was vigorous and confident again. To his surprise, she leaned across the table, took his head between her hands, and kissed him despairingly.

'Don't boast of anything now, Matt. We've come through so much: the war, *our* war, and now this year. I'm still bruised. I don't know what to trust. It's not that I'm afraid. But everything is on the move. We'll stay together, won't we? Say I'm part of your life, Matt!'

'What's biting you?' he said, as she released him. 'You don't resent a bit of help from outside, surely? She's not giving us anything, my dear.'

'But she *is*, Matt! Her time, thought, energy. And we're not used to it. We dare not fall into debt. That's what we're heading for. I want us to save up for another child!'

Matthew was startled. He got up, stooped over his wife and buried his face in her hair.

'It's not been for that reason, sweetheart. God knows it hasn't. Things just haven't gone that way. Over four years now since Madeleine came, we've done nothing since to prevent it.'

'I don't know, Matt. I think it must have been fear.'

'Fear? What are you talking about? We've been prospering, until the last blitz. Fear? You're not ill, Anna? Nothing the matter?'

'But compare our position with that of Lady Beverley. She's got everything: security, expert knowledge; and look how beautiful she is!'

Matthew, still leaning over her, drew her back and caressed her tenderly, as he whispered, 'But she's a widow, and elderly. And you've got a man, and he worships you, my dear. Why not compare ourselves with Tom Small? He could well be jealous of us.'

'Jealous?' she said, suddenly angry. She jumped up, causing him to step back. 'Jealousy doesn't come into it, one way or the other.'

They were both puzzled, and looked at each other almost in dismay. Before Matthew could reply, the Corgi began whining and scratching at the door. Matthew opened it, and heard Madeleine calling from her room.

'She's not asleep yet!' he said, directing his dismay to something concrete.

Anna left him to get on with the paperwork alone while she went up to Madeleine. He heard their distant voices upstairs; Madeleine's treble pouring out a flood of some excited confidence, Anna's voice almost inaudible.

Matthew could not concentrate. Receipts and expenditures for the moment lost all reality. He was driven to follow Anna upstairs. He hesitated at the door of Madeleine's room, half afraid of the perplexity of emotion still storming within him. Madeleine sat up on her pillow, wide awake, her eyes bright with inquiry. Her mother was leaning over the bed, sorting out and tucking in the tumbled sheets and blankets. She had her back to Matthew. Her hair was ruffled. Madeleine had obviously been clinging to her. He could see the child's eyes shining.

'Mummy, why hasn't Tom Small got a wife?'

Anna was too busy to reply.

'He's older than Daddy, isn't he?'

'Perhaps he doesn't want to marry anyone.'

'Yes he does. He wants to marry me.'

Matthew felt the blood beating in his head. He walked round Anna and confronted the child.

'What's this nonsense? Where did you get that idea?' He shook Anna's restraining hand from his arm. 'We don't want to hear such things, Madeleine. D'you understand?'

Madeleine looked up at him, innocent and puzzled. 'It's not nonsense, Daddy. Tom Small gave me—'

'Call him *Mr* Small!'

She paused again after this correction, trying to understand it.

'Mr Small gave me Prince Albert. He gives me everything.'

'Not everything, Madeleine,' said her mother, gently hand-coaxing her to lie down and be tucked in. Matthew's mood of devotion, the force which had driven him

70

upstairs, was curdled into anger. He glared at the child, and at Anna, like a cat turned out of doors into the rain.

Matthew felt Anna's restraining hand again on his arm. It was trembling, but her voice was calm.

'Think of what Daddy gives you, gives us all, Madeleine. We shouldn't be here, should we–'

'Oh, stop that, Anna. It's over her head. She's precocious enough already, with that rot about Small. I don't like it.'

Anna nodded, warning him.

'Now to sleep, darling,' she said, touching the child's forehead with her lips. 'Enough for tonight, for it's getting late.'

'Why doesn't Daddy kiss me, then?'

Anna pulled him forward, and he leaned over; but his kiss was sulky.

Downstairs, nothing was said for a while. Both were embarrassed. They returned to their work on the accounts, but after a few moments Matthew spoke.

'What's it all mean? I've nothing against Tom Small. You seem to think I have.'

'No, Matt. Noting in the world. You imagine it. How can you expect a child of four to be fair? I don't understand either. We're all full of surprises. We've no right to suspect. He's a simple man, and he does nothing but good, everything open and above-board.'

'That's just it. If he were – well, any other way, I'd pack him off. But he's worth his weight in gold on the farm, always willing, always capable: as good as half a dozen of the modern, chip-on-the-shoulder sort.'

Anna could not resist a poke at him, now that the storm had subsided: 'Perhaps you could ask Lady Beverley's advice about it?'

He glared at her, but was instantly reassured. The lamplight fell generously over her, from the shaded globe above the table. He realized that she was a little fuller in the figure, after nearly six years of marriage and hard work at 'Doggetts'. But her vigorous looks had not fallen away. She had more poise than ever: a woman to rely on.

'Yours is good enough for me,' he said gruffly.

'My what?'

'Your advice; your partnership.'

'You idiot!'

The word was a caress. It touched him with a confidence that held his world steady again. He was suddenly conscious of what he owed her, though she might not solve this problem of Madeleine's detached manner and the oddity of his own, cross-grained delusions, a neurotic airman's legacy.

'Tom Small's all right, darling. You're right about him. Your instinct, I mean.'

3

The following winter was uneventful, except for the troubles of frost and fog, and a plague of pigeons on the green-stuff. 'Doggetts' thrived, and the growing herd, still under Lady Beverley's care and provided with a full barn of winter fodder and a long clamp of root-crops, moved contentedly between pasture and byre. Profits from the milk began to appear. Tom Small showed a healthy credit account from fruit and vegetables.

Madeleine's birthday came round again. For this anniversary her parents took her to London to buy her a pair of riding-boots. Lady Beverley, on her way to a sale of cattle, met the family by chance on the station, heard about the cause of the expedition, and suggested meeting later for tea in Town. She appeared triumphant at the rendezvous that afternoon.

'I've secured two heifers, Matthew. Shapely little ladies. They'll be good yielders after they've calved next year...'

She paused, to select a small parcel from several in a huge string-bag, and to hand it to Madeleine, who sat pensively beside her at the table in the tea-shop, tired after the day's excitement, and the concentrated uniqueness of having a birthday.

'There, my dear; another little contribution from an ageing friend.'

Even the small figure beside her could not by comparison rob her of that petite beauty which so effectively disguised the astute business-woman and expert on cattle. In her gay springtime hat and tailored suit, her expensive Italian shoes and gloves, she might have been a character from a Mayfair comedy, rather than a gentlewoman interested professionally in stock-farming.

The conversation paused while Madeleine thanked her demurely, and somewhat incredulously, during the process of opening the parcel and discovering a peaked riding-cap in deep brown velvet.

'Try it on, child,' said Lady Beverley, ignoring the curiosity of the tea-table public. Nor was Madeleine any more aware of the crowd. She put the cap on, and it blended with her hair, eyes, and winter-weathered cheeks, like the cup with the acorn. Her parents were so proud of the picture that they half expected applause from the dozens of onlookers.

'Yes, it fits you, child,' said Lady Beverley, giving Madeleine an approving pat on the shoulder. 'Another thing, Matthew, I've found a man who is likely to be useful to you. His name is' – she whiffled through her notebook after searching for it in a vast crocodile handbag – 'is Kingdom. Suitable name for a carrier. I imagine ringing him up – "Can Kingdom come?" Forgive me, Anna, in front of the child too! But isn't it perfect? He's bringing the cattle over from Sussex. And as his headquarters are in Sitting-bourne, he could be useful to you for tran-sporting produce. Remember his name, *Kingdom Come!*'

She was wafted away by her own activity, after dropping a butterfly kiss on Madel-eine's nose, and the Burbages made their way to Charing Cross Station. Tom Small met them at Sittingbourne. Madeleine fell asleep, lapsing into the curve of her mother's arm before the car was clear of the town. Tom, sitting in front beside Matthew, looked over his shoulder from time to time.

'Anything wrong?' muttered Matthew through his teeth, without glancing away from the road. The half-light of dusk, against the street-lamps and side-lights of cars, demanded close attention from the driver.

'She's had enough for one day I reckon!'

'Who, Mrs Burbage?'

'No, young Madeleine.'

Matthew snorted, but said nothing, and Tom withdrew into silence, his features growing more and more inscrutable as the last of the April daylight dwindled away over the open country. A half-moon hung in the southern sky, and after they had crossed the bridge and turned to the right off the main road, Anna saw the white replica pulsing in the waters of the river. The image was broken by a tug, pulling barges up to Queensborough.

A warmth, rich in the smell of mud, and a less definable whiff of approaching summer, came off the fields and backwater. Anna drew a deep breath.

'It's good to be alive,' she said. Madeleine stirred, fretted, then woke.

'Are we home, Mummy?'

'Nearly, Maddy.'

'Then my birthday's over,' she said, weighed down by the heavy thought.

Tom Small chuckled. 'Don't you worry, m'dear; you ain't quite home yet.'

She leaned forward and put her arms round Tom's neck.

'Tell me, Tom! Tell me!'

'No, you just wait. You've only five minutes to go.'

'Sit back, Maddy, you'll make me run us into the ditch!'

The child obeyed her father, and looked up at Anna questioningly, so tired that she was ready to be tearful under this sharp reprimand.

'Listen, Maddy!' whispered Anna. 'A nightingale! D'you hear it? More than one of them in the orchard.'

The car was slowing down along the lane beside Tom's apple trees. The song came from those shadows, those moonlit patches. It pulsed, whirred, and rose to a piercing cry, then started again, phrase after phrase of imitation grief.

But Madeleine wasn't interested. Her attention was fastened on Tom Small's hint of yet another birthday surprise.

'Daddy, hurry up. Why are you so slow?'

Matthew ignored her. He drew up, so that Anna could hear the music from the apple-boughs. He leaned on the wheel, listening too.

'Be quiet, Madeleine. You won't hear this for long.' Then he spoke more kindly. 'What's it mean, Tom? A good summer ahead? We can still do with one. Last year was kind, but we want two or three more like that, to make up.'

'Aye, that we do. But it's asking a lot,' said Tom, rolling and lighting a cigarette. The spurt of flame from the match must have startled the birds, for the singing stopped abruptly. Matthew sat up, murmured, 'All over,' and set the car moving again.

With Gwylliam leaping at them and moaning with rapture, they entered the house. Tom stood by the car for a moment, thoughtfully watching them disappear. Then he got into the car and backed it to the garage. He had just turned off the engine when he heard Madeleine.

'Tom! Tom!' She ran straight into his arms. 'Oh, Tom, I love you, I do love you!'

He stooped over her.

'That's right, little Maddy. You'll be a proper horsewoman now, eh?'

She held up a little riding-crop, with stag-horn handle and a silver band.

'It's a real one, Tom!' She pulled at his coat. 'Let me kiss you for it.'

He felt her sleepy little mouth on his cheek, clumsy as a moth in the darkness.

'That's about it, Maddy. Now you come along indoors. You've had enough for one day.'

He took her hand, then saw that Matthew had followed her and witnessed the scene. He stood still, and released the child. Matthew claimed her.

'That's a bit much for a child her age,' said Matthew. 'Makes a hole in your pocket, doesn't it?'

Tom locked the garage door before he replied. 'I don't reckon that, Boss. I've got nobody, you see. Nothing but my own needs. You wouldn't deny that, would you?'

He walked away, leaving father and daughter to return to the house. The nightingales, more distant now in the orchard had started singing again, but without an audience.

Lady Beverley's introduction of Harry Kingdom, the Sittingbourne carrier, proved to be a happy one. He was a bluff, hearty character, who brushed his way through formalities. 'Pay when you like,' was his slogan, 'and I'd sooner you made it in notes! Not much use for banks and all that bookwork, I haven't. No time for it. Not afraid of work; and I like to be on the road myself. Don't hold with too much office life; skyscrapers and briefcases, when what we want in this modern world is houses to live in, and freedom for family life. Leave a man alone, is my idea; less of these rules and regulations.'

He was an example of his creed: vigorous healthy, casual and generous, pushing his way quite comfortably in the post-war world. His only personal complaint was that, as he got on in what he called 'the bun-struggle', he found less and less time to take the road in one of his growing fleet of lorries and vans.

Lady Beverley fascinated him. Her minia-ture beauty, her quick wits and expertise on animals, especially cattle, had him spell-bound. And she was profitable as his patron; for instance, this young chap Burbage: a nice connection there, at 'Doggetts'. As the months passed, he took over all the transport work for the farm, at rates cheaper than any quoted by rivals.

He would not admit, however, to having any rivals. 'Here's my hand!' was his motto. His gusty personality became part of the setting in which this second act of the play of prosperity was staged at 'Doggetts'.

Madeleine reflected that prosperity too, though she remained without brother or sister. Prince Albert, gentle, docile and shrewd, filled the gap. Wherever it was possible for him to follow her, there he was to be found. She treated him as though he were a law of nature: permanent and ever-present.

She became an expert horsewoman, and developed no contemporary skill with scooters and bicycles, and was car-sick on all except short motor journeys. Because she could not ride Prince Albert to her kindergarten school in Queensborough, she hated school, and made a martyrdom of the drive to and fro each week-day morning.

Gwylliam, the Corgi, made no attempt to share the pony's ascendancy. He knew it was useless. Besides, he had his own preoccupation, his master. The whole neighbourhood made a legend of the two loyalties down at 'Doggetts': the child and the pony, the master and the dog. Pub-talk offered bets as to whether or not either couple ever broke apart when out of doors.

One summer day Prince Albert fell sick. His mistress found him shivering in his stall. He ignored her when she appeared, and he refused to eat.

Anna was alarmed when a distressful little figure came running into the kitchen, incoherent with the news. Father must come at once. Tom too; and Mother. An inspection followed and a decision made that while Madeleine was at school Matthew would ring up the vet.

That was not enough. Madeleine's distress broke to hysteria. She wept, became violent, refused to go to school until the vet had been to see her Prince.

'Look here, Maddy–' began her father, but he was talking into the storm. He turned away to the shelter of the telephone, leaving Anna to deal with the distraught child, who was now crying out for Tom Small. But Small had gone off to his farm-work after the pony was inspected. He knew nothing about Madeleine's rebellion.

Anna succeeded, however, but only after surrendering to Madeleine's demand to stay at home and to be present when the vet came. She had to confess this to Matthew, when he returned to the kitchen.

'He'll be along on his way out,' he said. Then he added, aside, 'How'd you manage it?'

So Anna told him.

'Well, I hope it's all right. You're making a rod for your own back, though. That child is getting out of hand, you know. Where is she now?'

'I expect she's gone after Tom. She was crying for him. But it's only natural, Matt, since he gave her the pony.'

'It's damned unnatural. She ought to turn to us in a crisis.'

'You're being the Victorian father, Matt. It won't work in the modern world. All those supports have been knocked away.'

'But blood's thicker than water. Good to be old-fashioned in some things, eh? You know what she needs, Anna: it's a counter-influence, a young brother or sister.'

Anna hesitated. Then she said quietly, 'Well, I'm not certain she may not get what you want, Matt.'

In the eager and intimate conversation which followed, Madeleine was forgotten. It might have developed further had it not been interrupted by the arrival of the vet. Man and wife, still in a paradise of their own, led him to Prince Albert's stall.

While he was examining the pony, Madeleine came running from the orchard. She was calm now, and stood with her hand in her mother's, listening to what the vet would say, though she seemed confident that all would be well.

'Tom says it's nothing,' she murmured, as though instructing the vet what to discover. He looked at her with amusement and took her by the chin with thumb and finger.

'Tom Small? Yes, I remember him. Didn't he bring the pony here from the New Forest gipsies – and the foot-and-mouth virus on that rough coat? You've cleaned the little fellow up since then, young woman. Smart as paint now! He's a credit to you, nothing dangerous about him.'

The child's face flushed, then turned white with anger. She jerked her head away from the friendly hand.

'It's not true,' she said. 'Tom wouldn't do that. Daddy, it wasn't Tom, nor Prince.' She stamped her foot. 'It's hateful! Hateful! I shall ask him.'

Matthew caught her as she tried to bolt from the stable. She struggled for a moment, then subsided into tears.

'Listen, Madeleine,' said her mother, taking her from Matthew, 'nobody blames Prince, or Tom either. You mustn't say anything to Tom. It will hurt him. Promise now – promise you won't say a word.'

Further coaxing calmed the child, to the relief of the embarrassed vet, who had vainly tried to ignore the scene. But he could not conceal his sense of guilt.

'Stupid of me,' he said. 'Forget it, young lady. Nobody's fault. And now for the sick man! Have you been spreading nitrate of soda on the pasture, Mr Burbage? That may have upset his water-works. Better watch his feed, and stick to this diet.'

He wrote out directions for the daily feed and handed the slip of paper to Madeleine.

'Now, my dear. You keep that, and follow the rules strictly. Show it to Tom Small, and your father, and see that they carry out my instructions. Meanwhile, I'll make him up a dose, and you can ride him down to fetch it. Exercise will do him good. No more worrying, m'dear!'

He was still embarrassed, but he bluffed his way out, and drove off as quickly as possible, leaving the Burbages to return for another look at the pony. Madeleine ran into the stall, as though to protect her darling from unjust accusations.

Matthew and Anna paused at the half-door, both recollecting the theme of the annunciation made by Anna before the arrival of the vet. Matthew put his arm round her, and kissed her sunburnt neck.

'Shall we tell her?'

'Not yet, Matt. There's a long time to go, and anything may happen.'

'But what *could* happen?'

'Well, it won't be due until next spring, and that's a long time for a child to wait. She's inclined to take everything a bit too seriously. She must get that from you, darling!' She kissed him in return, 'No, leave it for now. We must get over this new upset, too.'

That sobered Matthew.

'Yes, it puts me in the wrong again. I *did* fertilize with nitrate! That damn pony brings me nothing but ill luck. It's as though Tom Small had planted him on me!'

'Matt! Don't be absurd. Well, he must never know what the vet said. That's one thing we can be certain about!'

'Well, I don't know. It's his doing. Anyway, it's all over, so let's forget it. I've said nothing to him, and don't intend to.'

They did not observe that Madeleine had been listening intently to the latter part of this conversation.

5

Nothing more occurred to darken the summer holidays for Madeleine. Prince Albert quickly recovered, and his mistress's worries seemed to vanish. She behaved in what her father called 'an old-fashioned way' over the problem of the pony's diet, as revised by the vet. She almost watched the feed, mouthful by mouthful, and would allow no one but herself to prepare Prince Albert's meals. Neither Matthew nor Anna made any other comment. They were fully occupied with their own happiness and new hopes.

'Do you realize that the baby will be born only a few months before Maddy's birthday? She'll be six.'

'Too big a gap,' replied Matthew. 'She'll be like a mother to it; more precocious than ever.'

'You criticize her as though you meant it,' said Anna. 'You don't mean it, do you, Matt?'

He laughed, and said nothing. Anna, who was resting in bed after a bout of morning-sickness, watched him disappear into the bathroom. She lay back, still in the clutches of the reassuring nausea, and half-listened to the hum of Matthew's electric razor. She was also aware of the late-summer silence outside: a robin soliloquizing wistfully, hens chattering, and the occasional moan of cows waiting to be milked. She knew the lovely creatures were crowding up to the gate leading to the milking-shed, for it rattled on its hinges from time to time as an impatient cow lunged at it.

'Everything's all right now, darling,' she called.

'Good; no more sickness?'

'I don't mean that. I mean everything in general. We're lucky really, Matt. The farm going well. And Madeleine's happy, isn't she?'

'Yes, why d'you ask?'

'Well, sometimes I think we're so happy together, you and I, that we shut her out.'

Matthew looked round the door.

'Find something else to fuss about: make a change. Madeleine can look after herself. I should say she gets too much attention, what with being a ewe-lamb, and having Tom Small dancing attendance. But I don't mind.'

'Are you sure you don't?'

Matthew ignored this.

'I'm expecting Kingdom to deliver a lorry-load of fertilizers today. He said sometime on Saturday.' He looked again round the door and grinned. 'No nitrate of soda this time, mind you!'

But Anna missed the joke, for she was dozing off, relaxed in the early weariness of her second pregnancy.

In the afternoon of that same day, Madeleine and Tom Small were mucking out Prince Albert's stable. This was Tom's idea of a half-day off. Being a lodger, he had no homelife. If he had any cronies at 'The Woolpack' in Elmley, he never spoke of them, and none ever followed him out to 'Doggetts'. Anna had once asked him if he was lonely, but he hardly understood what she meant. The idea was outside his range of consciousness.

He and Madeleine made a serious pair.

87

They had little need to talk. Happiness filled them to the brim. The five-year-old might have been fifty, so solemn and deliberate were her movements with the broom as she brushed out the milky carbolic water swilled over the floor by Tom. They face each other, Tom backing out towards the door, Madeleine with her back to the manger.

She was concentrated on the job, putting far more energy into it than was necessary. Tom looked at her once or twice.

'Don't you wear out them bristles,' he said.

She disdained to reply, or even to look up.

Time stood still, at the middle of Saturday afternoon. A ship's siren from the river broke the peace from time to time. But peace settled back more surely than ever. Wood-pigeons, in the copse at the head of the farm inland, talked in their sleep, breaking off each phrase abruptly. A covey of sparrows and a robin fluttered about the workers, their chatter too monotonous to be noticed. Not a breath of wind. The air was hot, heavy with dusty sunshine and the many smells of harvest time: fruit, chaff, and a suggestion of farmyard animals; a harmony of smells, not unpleasant, but deep, familiar, very old; the smell of time, an ancient land and people; the smell of a way of life.

It was Tom's life. He need not stop to

remark on it. He breathed it and it was in his blood, his bones. The sharp smell of the disinfectant may have been an intrusion, for when the pail was empty he took up another broom and joined Madeleine at the task of brushing out the stable, taking on the milky foam which swirled before her broom.

'There, that's done,' said the child, implying that it was all her own work.

'Aye,' he said. 'Now the new hay.'

He carried the two brooms to the tool-room beyond the stable, and brought out a pitchfork.

'I'll handle this, Maddy. You don't want it in your eyes.'

'No, Tom, but remember what Mr Harrison said.'

He looked slyly at her.

'What, that old vet? I could have told him that. I knew what was wrong.'

'Then why didn't you stop me before, from giving Prince too much linseed cake?'

Tom chuckled.

'Me telling you? That doesn't seem probable, Maddy, does it? You don't take cautions kindly, I reckon.'

Madeleine was indignant.

'What *do* you mean, Tom?' She then registered distress. 'I'm not unkind to you ever: am I?'

This was so serious a matter that she had to emphasize it by touching him. He stopped work, as she clasped one of his hands in both of hers. He looked down at the perplexed little face, but could not speak. He cleared his throat, swallowed, and made an effort, but no words came.

'You know I love you, Tom.'

He shook his head sadly, still towering above her. The dimness of the stable folded about them, making them one figure in the hot shadows, close and not quite definable.

The spell was broken by the sound of a lorry rounding and stopping where the drive ended in the farmyard.

'That'll be the fertilizers. The boss said he was expecting Kingdom to bring the stuff over himself.'

Madeleine darted out before he could move. He followed her. But the driver of the lorry was not Kingdom. A young woman in brown dungarees stood where she had jumped down from the driver's seat. She was sweating, and was busy snatching a handkerchief from her hair and mopping her face and neck. With the other hand she held out the garment from her throat and breasts, and wiped as far down as she could reach.

'Ah! Observed!' she said, as Tom and Madeleine appeared. 'But it can't be helped. Stuffy in that cab. I nearly melted. You Mr Burbage?'

This outburst was accompanied by a smile

equally candid, directly solely at Tom Small, and ignoring the child.

Tom put her right, indulgently because she was not a figure with whom one could be either formal or severe.

Madeleine, however, did not appreciate being overlooked. She took one glance at the ample bust, the cloud of blonde hair that was released from the handkerchief, the strong mouth and teeth that gleamed in the sunlight. Then she ran off to the orchard, where Prince Albert had been routing about during the cleansing of his stable. He had been sniffing at the green windfalls with his velvety nose, and puffing them off disdainfully, sometimes flicking up his hind legs to show his disgust at such unlikely fodder. He now came picking his way between the apple trees to meet his mistress, prepared to tease her on so free an occasion. She responded instantly and forgot the intrusion into the farm-yard behind her.

The young woman continued to study Tom Small approvingly after he had corrected her.

'Dad couldn't come after all. He forgot he'd promised to play cricket. We're playing against Tunstall.'

'Why, that's where I come from.'

She was instantly interested.

'Don't know any Smalls there.'

'No, my folks are dead; the old ones. Got

one sister out in Canada, and a brother, he's older than me, in South Africa.'

She laughed.

'He *must* be an old one, older than you.'

'Oh, I'm not so old as all that.'

She looked him up and down, more intimately.

'No, I'll bet you're not.'

This amused them both, though Tom was not quite sure about it, as Miss Kingdom began to let down the backboard of the lorry.

'Where does it go, Mr Small? Have you got a barrow?'

Tom fetched one from the barn, and for the next quarter of an hour he worked with Miss Kingdom, unloading and carting the bags to the barn. At the end, they were both hot, and once again the young woman wiped herself down with the coloured handkerchief with which she had tied up her hair during the job.

'Just had a wash and a set this morning,' she said, noticing that Tom was admiring her blonde crown. 'It'll be ruined again after this. Never mind, it's given us a chance to meet.'

Madeleine overheard this remark as she came out from the orchard, leading Prince Albert back to his stable. She ignored both the grown-ups, and stared straight ahead, hostile and miniaturely grim.

Miss Kingdom watched the procession disappear into the stable. Then she looked at Tom with a guarded interest.

'That your youngster?'

'No. I ain't married.'

'Not married? Well, I never!'

The guardedness left her.

'Anyone would think you were father and daughter, the way she treated you.'

Tom looked sulky.

'Oh, well; I mean she was so fond. No offence.'

'That's all right. I've been here since she was born.'

'Of course,' she said, slowly. 'And not having anyone of your own, I mean–'

Both hesitated. Then Miss Kingdom held out a hand, and gave his a healthy shake. Her grasp was firm and had a coolness that belied the rest of her warm, mature person. Tom felt himself responding oddly. Then he saw Madeleine standing behind the stable door, the lower half closed and hiding her. Only a little head appeared, with two brilliant eyes, fierce and critical.

6

Summer was unending that year, and the Kentish acres responded luxuriantly to the ardour of those late August days. It did not matter that the sun's caresses were shorter. The impress of their fierceness lasted through the lengthening nights.

Anna, in her gravid heaviness, felt the heat and slept indifferently. Bedroom door and windows were left wide open. The salt air from the river was the only cool contact. It drifted about her, like half-remembered qualities from childhood.

Childhood! Her universe was filled with it, during these months of pregnancy. She grew apprehensive. She worried about Madeleine. One hot night she lay awake, fretting. Something physical disturbed her mood. A bat had flickered through the open window and was quartering the room. She put her hands up instinctively to her hair and called out to Matthew, waking him.

He groped in the moonlight, put out an arm and felt across the space between the two beds, and touched Anna's thigh.

'What's the matter?' he whispered. 'You've lost the bedclothes. Anything wrong?'

She turned on her back, towards him, and his hand was shifted to her belly.

'Get it out, Matt. I can't stand it.'

The bat's paper wings rustled, or seemed to, and could be seen as tiny shadows in the tarnished light of the moon. But for the moment Matthew was spellbound and could not obey. He had felt a movement of the child within the womb. A deep, sensual

94

delight, fearful and awe-stricken, yet triumphant, mastered him.

'Anna!' He leaned across and pressed his cheek, and then his lips, to the swollen belly. Anna's arms closed round his head.

'Yes! Yes! But get rid of that creature first.'

He stumbled up, and drove the bat before him. After a few circlings at increased speed, it was gone suddenly, either by door or window; but it left the room in peace, a deep silence.

From the orchard came the thud of an apple falling to the ground, then the pull of a rope in the stable, as Prince Albert fidgeted in his sleep. Silence again after that.

'Has it gone?' Anna spoke from beneath the sheet, which she had drawn over her head. Matthew did not reply, but withdrew the sheet again and lay beside her in the single bed. Then they were lost, united, lost again.

At last Matthew spoke: or he may have communicated without speaking. They were so close, man and wife, one flesh.

'I felt it move.'

'I know! I know,' she whispered, almost impatiently, as though he were late, or stupid. After a while, she spoke again, more removed, back in the world.

'Madeleine won't mind, will she, Matt?'

'What's fretting you now?'

'I mean she won't be jealous, will she?'

95

'Well, if she is, it's no new thing. And it won't last, if we're sensible and handle her properly.'

'How, handle her?'

'Why, let her know she's not the only pebble on the beach.'

This disturbed Anna. She tossed about for a while, then ordered Matthew back to his own bed. He settled down and was almost asleep, when Anna spoke again.

'You know, Matt, I think it's a blessing we've got Tom Small.'

He did not want to hear. He was drowsy after the recent delight. Then suddenly he realized what she had said.

'What? What's that? Tom Small again? Why drag him in? What's he got to do with it?'

'Don't be silly, Matthew,' spoken severely. 'You know what I mean. It's our happiness. Sometimes I think it keeps Madeleine out. And it will be worse when the baby comes. I know it will. She's so strange already: so old. I don't understand her; and now I'm in this condition I don't feel I've got the will-power to contend, or to sympathize with her. It frightens me; *you* must take charge, Matthew.'

He saw her sitting up. The moon had floated round and sent a shaft across, like a sword-blade between the beds. The shadow of a rose-bough at the window was carried through, and it flicked to and fro over Anna's ghostly shape. It made her vulnerable, in need of protection.

'I didn't hurt you, darling?' said Matthew.

'Listen to what I say, Matt! I'm all right. I'm talking about Madeleine.'

'Oh Madeleine...' but he was asleep, his voice trailing away after him.

Anna sat alone in the night, her arms clasped painfully round her knees. But the position caused a protest within, a violent kick that made her gasp, in surprise rather than pain. She looked cross at Matthew, and saw the sword of moonlight approaching the unsuspecting head on the pillow.

'You're as hopeless as she is,' she said, only half-aloud, speaking really to herself. Then she wept a little, to regain courage.

7

Shirley Kingdom was puzzled by Tom Small – puzzled and attracted. A few days later she brought up a second load of fertilizers, arriving soon after breakfast.

'We loaded up last night,' she said to Matthew, to both the Burbages, whom she met for the first time. She was instantly aware of Anna's condition, and gave her a friendly look.

'Then it was *your* little girl I met the other

day!' she exclaimed. 'Quaint little soul! Bit of a handful, can't she be?'

'Horrible child,' said Matthew playfully. 'Makes our life a hell!'

Anna protested, linking her arm in his and delaying the work of unloading. She, as well as Matthew, was attracted to this young woman, so like her father Kingdom, the open-handed, easy-going carrier.

'I'll bet you worship her,' said Shirley Kingdom. But she was thinking of something else, for her gaze wandered round the farm-yard, pausing at the doors: the stable, the barn, and the distant back door of the house.

Tom Small did not appear, however, until she and Matthew had shifted half the lorry-load of sacks and bags. There remained a dozen or more sacks of caster-meal, soft, cumbersome stuff, at the front of the lorry.

Anna had gone indoors.

'I'll leave you to it, Tom, if you don't mind, said Matthew. 'Good to have this meal so early. We'll get it spread before the weather breaks.'

Tom said nothing. He took off his coat, folded it and put it beside the driver's seat in the cab.

'All my belongings there,' he said to Shirley.

'They're safe with me, Tom,' she replied.

Hearing his Christian name used so easily

at a second meeting, he glanced artfully at her, surprised, perhaps suspicious. But there was nothing to suspect, as he could see. She was a comely girl: a picture of health and good will. Besides, she was not his boss, or his boss's wife: safe to be easy with her: safe in any case, so far as he was concerned. He didn't know why he thought so, but it was reassuring to a man not much used to women.

'That's all right by me,' he said to her. 'I like to know where I am.'

'Yes, I'll guess you are a caution,' she said.

They were now up in the lorry, lumping the bags back to the tail. Both seized on one sack at the same moment. Instead of grasping the sack, Tom grasped Shirley's bare forearm, so firmly that she winced.

'Here, do you want me too?' she teased him. 'Haven't you got full weight?'

It was too good to let go at once. He felt the muscles beneath the soft, round flesh: the muscles and the small bone.

She looked up at him. It was a game, a challenge. Then she brought her other hand over the top of the sack, and gave his a hearty smack.

'Hands off!' she said: but the way she said it, meant otherwise, and he knew it.

When the job was done, Anna came out and invited them both into the kitchen for a cup of tea. Tom stood behind the open door, looking out to the yard and the empty lorry. The two women sat at the table, enjoying their tea and gossiping, almost in undertones. All were conscious of the heat. Indoors and out the air was heavy, sun-soaked already: no morning freshness. The tea remained almost too hot to drink, and had to be sipped at.

Then Madeleine appeared. She came in from the fields carrying an armful of wild flowers: scabious, ragwort, honeysuckle. The scent at once freshened the air in the kitchen, overpowering the faint, domestic aroma of tea and cigarettes. The tang of old apples from the ragwort battled with the nostalgic honeysuckle perfume.

The child rushed in breathless, eager to show her treasure.

'Where's Tom, Mummy? I want to ask him their names. Look what I've got.'

Then she saw Shirley Kingdom sitting opposite her mother, looking outward, and at the untidy mass of flowers and foliage. She also saw this stranger glance beyond, amused at something. Instantly Madeleine shrank back, shy, even hostile. She turned abruptly, either to run out, or to see what the woman was smiling at. She saw Tom behind the door. He was looking at her.

'Oh, there you are!' she whispered. 'I've got something for you, Tom. Here it is!'

Deliberately, while out-staring the stranger,

she selected a sprig of honeysuckle, broke it off from the stalk, awkwardly because of the flowers still in her arms, and approached Tom Small.

'Bend down,' she commanded. 'I want to put it in your buttonhole.'

The ceremony took place, watched benevolently by Anna, with quizzical surprise by Shirley Kingdom. Tom, who had been silent, spellbound, since the child came in, was now the first to speak. He straightened up, fingered and sniffed at the flower in his buttonhole, and smiled. Then he spoke, as though breaking the spell which bound him: 'Mind that there ragwort isn't full of those stripey caterpillars, m'dear.'

'Silly!' she said, 'I shook them off. The hens had them.'

Shirley exclaimed, almost with a little cry of alarm: 'Well! That's a caution. A little girl too!'

Madeleine turned on her, the hostility settled into a frown. Before she could retort, her mother broke in: 'Madeleine! Come and say good morning properly to Miss Kingdom. You've not met before.'

'Oh yes we have.'

She still stood at a distance.

'Aye, the afternoon we mucked out the stable,' said Tom, who could not see the hostility in Madeleine's eyes. He had not moved from his post behind the door.

Shirley made a friendly gesture towards the child.

'Come and shake hands, dear,' insisted Anna, moving clumsily to her and urging her forward. 'I'll take the flowers.' She did so, while pushing Madeleine forward. She was both embarrassed and annoyed.

Shirley leaned from her seat, prepared to kiss the sullen little face, but Madeleine held back, reluctantly putting out a left hand at arm's length.

'You know better than that, dear,' hissed her mother.

'Well, she's shy. No need to be shy with me, little girl. I was young once, like you. And I'm still shy today. That's right, isn't it, Mr Small?'

Madeleine said nothing. She looked away, as from something indecent.

'Let me have my flowers please, Mummy,' she said. 'I've done what you told me.'

Shirley Kingdom laughed, and put a hand to her mouth.

'Oh, my goodness! What have I done? Won't you give me a flower too, my sweetheart?'

Madeleine took the bunch from her mother, gravely selected an umbel of ragwort on which a caterpillar still clung, and presented it to the young woman, who took it, shuddered, and indifferently dropped it onto the table.

'There now,' said Anna, 'take them through to the scullery and put them in a bowl of water while you find a vase. They're wilting already in the heat.'

As Madeleine disappeared, Shirley took up this remark.

'They say flowers wilt on a flirt. She's a proper little one. Got her eye on you, Mr Small. And when I saw you together last week I thought you were father and daughter. Fancy that!'

Anna looked sharply at her, but said nothing. She saw them both out, and was still watching them curiously while Tom helped Shirley up into the driver's cab. She noticed that the girl lingered for a moment while mounting, thus causing Tom to retain his hold on her arm.

'Ah, that's it!' said Anna, aloud to herself. She did not know whether to be relieved, or vaguely jealous: jealous, at second hand, for Madeleine, to whom she now retreated. She decided to say nothing to the child about her rudeness to the visitor.

8

Next day Tom did not appear as usual at the farmhouse after the day's work. It was his habit to come in for a cup of tea before going along to his lodgings, where Mrs

Weston prepared an early, badly-cooked meal for him and his fellow-lodger, a farm-labourer of the pre-mechanical age, who spent six evenings a week at 'The Wool-pack'.

Tom had fitted up a shed, removed from the cottage, where he could be to himself. He had a bench, an amateur's collection of tools for woodwork, others for his real work as a fruit-man. He had fitted a shelf to hold his few books, most of which were nursery-men's catalogues and growers' manuals.

He owned other books, too, and had lately begun to add to them again, spurred on by Madeleine's growing demands upon him for information: a book on wild flowers, another on birds. Since the child first went to school, and increasingly after she began to read, Tom had also resumed the habit dropped during and after the war, when youthful curiosity died down. Now he was intent again, for he had a purpose. At her kindergarten, Madeleine began prematurely to learn French. Tom must follow suit, and Hugo's *Grammar* and *Conversation,* in paper backs, now stood alongside a botany primer.

He became more ambitious, too, with his woodwork. He was now making a set of doll's-house furniture. A bedstead, two chairs and a sofa stood under a newspaper on the bench, and parts of a sideboard and dining-table were taking shape, made from cigar boxes which he picked up from a tobacconist in Sittingbourne. The suite, with the house to contain it, was to be presented to Madeleine for Christmas: a nice job for the autumn nights ahead, with the oil-stove beside him, and no interruption. The portable radio was an ally: company that also left him alone.

On this hot summer evening, however, he was neither at his bench nor his books. During that moment when Anna observed him as he lingered over helping Shirley Kingdom up to her seat in the lorry, the couple had agreed to meet and take a walk together, an old-fashioned plan which had since puzzled him. He asked himself who suggested it, and he could not be sure. But the young woman pleased his fancy because of her candid manner. She might be a bit rough, but was no fool: good company for a man who must be at least fifteen years her senior. He told himself that, and looked forward with a cool, amused curiosity to the rendezvous. He would admit no more.

Before going to his shed, he changed from his workaday clothes, and came down to the kitchen to shave. His old landlady glanced at him shrewdly, and retreated from the sink to a chair outside the back door. She was not much interested in the two men, one elderly, the other middle-aged, who lodged in her cottage. So long as they paid regularly, she was content that their habits were equally regular. She wanted no trouble. A bit of gossip, a bit of scandal, that was all right, so long as she did not have to seek it.

'Ain't yer going down to the shed?' she asked, speaking from her chair outside.

'Why?'

''Tain't like you, changing yer clothes on a weekday. Courting, or something?'

Tom did not think that Kentish pleasantry worth a reply. He finished shaving, went up to his room, put on his jacket, and left the cottage by the front door, to avoid another encounter with the old woman.

He hesitated by the gate. He would much rather have gone down the garden to his shed, to potter about there, or perhaps to work a little on the doll's furniture for Madeleine.

'Blast!' he said, and shook his head, silently accusing the landlady of being in the way, at her seat, staring down the garden.

He strolled along the lane, increasing his pace as he drew away from the cottages. He was about to turn down the footpath leading to the riverside, when an open sports car overtook and drew up alongside him.

'Who gets there first, Tom?'

He had been so absorbed thinking about her that for a second he did not see Shirley Kingdom.

'I was cutting across the allotments,' he said, pointing down the footpath.

'Jump in, and we'll go a bit farther afield.'

Again he hesitated, hardly willing to recognize her, she was so smart in a green nylon dress. That shock of fair hair was tidied up too. She looked a little older, thus groomed. The lowering daylight, with gathering shadows, subdued her more obvious qualities: the fullness of bust, the muscular limbs. Her arms, bare to the shoulder, stretched out to the steering wheel, were cool, statuesque. Tom felt flattered.

'Why not?' he said, with both conscious and unconscious intent.

Shirley drove off, down river, the sunset beginning to colour up behind them and throw stage-lights over the level fields and up the northern rise of the island towards Minster. It lit up the façades and flashed on the window-panes of buildings. Woods deepened and became mysterious, brooding over their dry foliage. Occasional glimpses of the waterway gave the illusion of strings of lanterns, a carnival in preparation. The world lost its ordinariness; time and place offered a *ballo in maschera,* a relinquishing of responsibility.

'I'm enjoying this. Are you, Tom?'

Shirley spoke, peering ahead as she switched on the sidelights.

Tom did not reply, and she glanced at him, seeing him slumped awkwardly beside her. She put a hand on his knee.

'Nothing to say?'

'Too much to say, Miss Kingdom.'

This was rather beyond her.

'What *do* you mean? And why can't you call me Shirley?'

'I'm not a quick mover, Shirley.'

'That's better. I don't think I want you to be, Tom. I'm more staid than I look, maybe. Because I drive a sports car, and like a bit of life, doesn't mean that I–'

'Why are you explaining? D'you take me for an old man? I remember you thought I was a family man. Well, I'm not. I like my freedom. But that doesn't mean–'

'Who's doing the confessing now? What's got into us, Tom? Anyone might think we were going to church.'

He ignored this.

'It's the time of day. I always reckon night-fall is solemn-like.'

They fell silent while she drove in the difficult half-light. It was already dusk when she turned down a lane to the river, through open country, mudflats leading to grassy banks of broken clay at the water's edge. Shirley switched off the engine, and silence cloaked the car and its occupants.

The lights of Sittingbourne to the right, and of Faversham to the left, began to strengthen as the sky deepened. So, too, was the moon gathering body. It began to influence the Kentish hills southward, as the last fires of sunset left them. The tide incoming lipped at the shore.

'What's it all about, Tom?'

Shirley spoke sadly, out of character, and Tom turned to her with greater interest.

'That's a funny question, when you're out with a man.'

She left the car, and he followed her. As they began to walk, he took her arm, and she did not withdraw.

'That's what I mean. You think I'm fast and easy-going. Maybe I behave that way. But I don't want it like that. I can tell you, life at home is not how I'd have it. Dad is all very well, but we never know where we are with him.'

Tom was taken aback by this confidence.

'Are there more of you then?' he asked lamely.

'Three of us girls, and Mother. I don't know. We all need something to steady us. The trouble is, I feel it in myself, Tom: easy come, easy go. I'd like to change all that; frankly I would.'

He was thoughtful. Her aims began to come within the scope of his own, and he could sympathize.

'Aye,' he said at length, 'I know what you mean.'

'I knew you would. You're a reliable chap. That's why–'

She stopped, and withdrew her arm.

'Go on; why what?'

Excitement began to stir within him: excitement, and a half-guilty recognition of it, guilty because of his surrender. He took her hand and drew her arm through his again. Its warmth made him even more reckless.

'That's right, Shirley. I'm old enough to–'

'Oh, don't say that, Tom! That's what they all say!'

He hardened.

'How many others? You like them older, eh?'

She returned, perhaps feeling defeated, to her more easy, habitual self. She laughed.

'Older or younger, it doesn't mean much.'

He felt the warmth of her arm again. It may have been part of the warmth of the belated summer night. Tom saw the tide pulsing under the rising water. The rhythm was infectious, and his blood responded.

'We're not quarrelling already, are we, Shirley?'

He spoke almost tenderly.

'You're not one to quarrel, Tom.'

With that they began to make love, relinquishing their personal problems and distinctions. They lost themselves in the indulgent mood of the night, exploring the cheat, emerging from it an hour later, strangers still, but somehow committed by the simulacrum of familiarity.

'Make me one of your cigarettes, Tom,' she said, as they walked back to the car.

He did so, settling the paper in his palm, adding the pinch of tobacco, and rolling it. He was aware of her looking on. He heard her breathing deeply. She was still excited.

He handed the open cigarette to her gently, so that the tobacco should not spill before the paper was gummed down.

'No,' she whispered. 'You lick it for me.'

He looked at her, sharply, almost sternly.

'You want it that way?'

'Yes. I want you, Tom. Stay near me.'

He licked and closed the cigarette, and handed it over. She leaned forward and kissed his cheek while he was fumbling for matches.

'I meant it, Tom. I meant it all.'

He was trembling. The match flickered in his hand, and the darkness round the tiny flame suddenly seemed cold.

'Not too fast, now, my dear.'

She could not examine what he meant, and was still too physically exultant to be able to think ahead.

Even when they drew up outside the cottage, parking on a roadwork lay-by in front of a heap of stone chips, Shirley was still reluctant to return to reality. When Tom shyly suggested that she might like to see inside his shed, she took the compliment for granted, and was not too sensitive to hold back.

He led the way round the cottage and along the path. The chair at the back door was vacant, and neither of the pair noticed Mrs Weston, who appeared for a moment to take the chair indoors.

She shaded her eyes from the moonlight, and peered after them, nodded her head complacently and vanished, richer for this titbit.

Tom, in his own setting, returned also to a formality which Shirley might have interpreted as irony. At the moment, she was more interested in the room, and Tom's efforts to make it cosy.

'You're comfortable here, then?'

He was busy filling a small kettle and lighting a Primus stove.

'Cup of tea, eh?'

She went, like a cat in a strange room, from one object to another. Her warmth added to the cosiness. Tom felt it around him, and he grew sleepy. He almost lost her as a person. But she was everywhere in the room, flooding it with animal vitality. He could scarcely recognize his own bits and pieces. Everything shrank in size, and lost its value.

'You upset me, you know,' he said,

handing her a cup of tea.

She nodded, and stared into the cup as though trying to read the future. What she saw there made her smile secretly.

'What d'you expect, Tom? You see, I took to you from the beginning. And it's worth something. I'm not a teenager. I've had some experience, and I've not kept it from you.'

'Why d'you say that?'

He stood over her, and put a hand on her bare shoulder. A moment passed before she looked up at him, and he felt her trembling.

'Because you're different, Tom. I'm a fool. I don't understand this; but I love you. That's the difference. I realized when we – when we were out there.'

She glanced through the open door. Tom moved deliberately, and shut it.

'That all right?' he asked. She put down the cup and saucer, and held out her arms.

Tom hesitated again, then he surrendered himself, and felt her clinging to him, possessing him.

'I don't know about this, Shirley. I'm not prepared for it. A bit of fun is not the same as a lifetime together. I'm a solitary chap, as you see. I like my own company, and a lot of it.'

She spoke from lips still close to his mouth: 'I could do with that, Tom. It would suit me to sit quiet, to go about my own jobs. I'm not so modern as I look, Tom. Maybe I've done my flaunting. And I know what a noisy home is like. I've had enough of that too.'

The explanations died away into love-making, and time stood still. When the couple were conscious of it again, Tom picked up the cup which Shirley had set down.

'It's stone cold,' he said, and opened the door to fling out the contents. He peered up the garden and saw the back door of the cottage still open.

'The old girl hasn't gone to bed, Shirley.'

'Why, is it all that late?'

She was exploring again, while combing her hair. He turned back as an owl hooted from the 'Doggetts' copse. It was a derisive cry, and it made Tom lose what he was about to say.

Shirley stopped at the bench.

'What have you got there, Tom?'

She lifted the newspaper, and saw the miniature chairs, sofa and bedstead. She laughed, and picked up the bedstead.

'Darling! So you've got it ready for us!'

The owl hooted again, nearer and louder. Tom scowled, and said coldly:

'Put that down, please. Put it down!'

Shirley was amazed. She stared at him, the toy still in her hand.

'Whatever–?' she began.

'Put it down, I said.'

Shirley obeyed, and clumsily covered the little furniture with the newspaper.

'What have I done, Tom?'

She was almost in tears, shocked by this sudden outburst of temper, following such tenderness as Tom had shown in his love-making.

He controlled himself as quickly as he had attacked her.

'Sorry,' he murmured. 'I'm sorry, Shirley. But that's something else. Doesn't belong to us.'

'Who, then?' She was amused now, or seemed to be so, relieved by his return to the gentle self who had courted her that evening. 'It's for that kid, isn't it? Well, what's the fuss?'

He evaded a reply. He didn't know. They were both puzzled, and let the matter drop.

The spell of summer madness was broken, however, and they said good night soberly, with no more kisses. They did not even shake hands when Tom had led her to the car.

'Don't wake them all up,' he said, as she revved up the engine.

'You're a funny one, you are!' she said; and that was her parting word.

Tom stood by the heap of granite chips, staring down the road, a statue in the moon-light.

He remained there after the car, and its noise, had vanished. The moon moved a fraction of an inch, shifting its scrutiny of the immobile figure.

At last he turned, put his hand to his head, and in doing so, caught the whiff of Shirley's scent on his fingers. Angrily, he shook the hand downwards, as though trying to cast off a dirty glove. Then he went back to the shed, rearranged the newspaper over the toys, doused the lamp, locked up, and disappeared into the cottage.

THREE

1

Next day, autumn school-term began, and the 'Doggetts' household swung back into more regular habits. The only difference in them from those of the summer term was that Matthew, instead of Anna, drove Madeleine to school.

That first morning she was reluctant.

'Why can't Mummy take me? She did last term.'

'Well, things are different now.'

Matthew drove fast, irked by the job because both Moxon and Small had failed to turn up at the usual time for the milking. The cows were muzzling and grumbling round the gate to the milking-shed as he drove past with Madeleine. He could understand Moxon's being late, for that was habitual; ten minutes to a quarter of an hour a day, as a regular thing, from Moxon's point of view, showed his independence. He was not conscious of it as a historical Kentish trait. When Matthew sometimes summoned courage to mention it, Moxon merely grunted, and said nothing. He did not even show resentment. He might have done so, had Matthew gone further and accused him of being a thief.

'Why are they different, Daddy? I don't like things to change.'

'You may not like it, Madeleine, but you'll have to get used to it. That's how things are. Nothing stands still.'

'"Doggetts" stands still.'

'Well, I mean life doesn't stand still. Now *does* it?'

She thought this over, almost defeated. Matthew glanced at her, mollified by her silence. He saw a sun-burned elf, temporarily neat with her hair-ribbon (Anna was behind the times in these matters), her dark blue tunic, her sandals and satchel. She had grown and put on a little flesh during the long summer holidays and freedom from the enormous, miniature anxieties of

117

the mornings at school. Her dark eyes, bright with perpetual inquiry, were intent this morning on what might lie ahead. Matthew felt he should say something paternal, reassuring, though he did not believe in all these infantile problems that Anna made so much fuss about.

'You go back now, able to read. That's more than you could do last term.'

'Yes,' she said, as they flashed past the cottage where Small lodged. 'It's Tom who did that. And we do French together. He helps me in everything. That's why I love him.'

'Love him? That's a bit strong, Maddy. Do you love him, as you call it, like you love Mummy and me?'

'Oh, that's different. I *have* to love you and Mummy. But I love Tom because I love him.'

'Well, don't shout about it,' said Matthew irritably. 'Better keep those ideas to yourself.' Then he added, after some moments of brooding: 'You've only got one mother and father, you know.'

Madeleine, as though searching for evidence of this statement, began to rout among the contents of the open shelf below the dashboard, disturbing maps, minor tools, paper napkins, bills and receipts, string, a biscuit-tin.

'Don't stir up all that rubbish, Maddy. You're not thinking about what I said.'

Matthew regretted this even as he said it. But that only increased the little flare of anger. He had to restrain himself from slapping down the small hand. Instead, he spoke again: 'You're making a mess of the car. Clear it up again.'

Madeleine obeyed. Her face was expressionless.

'And you and Mummy have only got me,' she said.

Matthew's anger vanished. He glanced at her, and saw her diminished, pathetic and lonely. Before he could restrain the impulse, he blurted out, 'Well, before long Mother and I are going to alter all that.'

Madeleine did not reply. She leaned over her satchel, pressing it into her stomach. Her silence irritated Matthew again, and he returned to the attack.

'Yes, you'll soon be having a small brother or sister. About time, isn't it? You're nearly six years old.'

Madeleine still repudiated the news.

'April the eighteenth,' she said, almost desperately, still hugging the satchel. 'I wonder what Tom will give me. I believe I know. I looked in the window.'

Matthew was defeated. He was also ashamed of himself. He had gone behind Anna's back. He had been a bully. But in spite of this remorse, the anger still rumbled distantly.

'What window? When?'

Madeleine stared into the future.

'It looked like furniture,' she said. 'I hope it isn't for Christmas. Everybody has Christmas, but my birthday belongs to me.' Then suddenly she changed, melted. She sat up, turned to her father, and spoke confidentially, inviting him to share her secret, a great compliment to him: 'The other afternoon. That very hot one on Sunday. You and Mummy were asleep upstairs, and I could not think what to do. So I went to find Tom. But he wasn't there. The door was locked, so I couldn't go in. I looked through the window, and I saw – I saw–'

She hesitated. Superstition pulled her back.

'But I mustn't tell. Something terrible might happen.'

The terror of this fairyland possibility put its mask over her face. She became a tiny Tragic Muse. The speed of all this, and the working of her mind, quite baffled her father. It frightened him too.

'Go steady now,' he said, drawing up outside the schoolhouse gate. 'Just keep your feet on the ground. See?'

Madeleine, who had climbed down, bent forward and studied the offending feet. Then she laughed.

'You *are* funny, Daddy. Good-bye. Don't be late fetching me, will you?'

He nodded, and watched her walking demurely up the drive to the house, her satchel dangling loosely, an object of no significance to her. She paused on the step, looked back, and waved a hand.

Matthew motioned her on, pretending to be brusque. But he drove away reluctantly, and was many yards up the road before he recollected the delays on the farm. Then he put on speed.

2

Anna came out of the milking-shed to meet him.

'Did she go off all right? Not too depressed?'

They both laughed together about their daughter's odd little ways, and challenged each other to say from where she inherited them.

'Not from my family,' said Matthew. 'We're tough matter-of-fact Northerners. You can't come from a family of miners and be a neurotic.'

Anna's blue eyes twinkled. Her good humour and serenity were formidable weapons.

'What about D.H. Lawrence? Would you call him a well-balanced realist?'

'Oh well,' Matthew shrugged it off. 'But

we must get the milking done. What's happening? Have the men come?'

'Tom's there, and I've been helping him. But he seems more gloomy than usual this morning. Can't get a word out of him.'

'Where's Moxon?'

'He hasn't come. He was complaining yesterday about his wife: said she wasn't well. Perhaps I'd better go along to the bungalow.'

'Yes. I don't like you bending about, lifting all that stuff in the sheds.'

'Don't be an idiot. I'm not a porcelain milkmaid.'

Anna took off Matthew's white coat, which she had been wearing, and held it up for him to put his arms into the sleeves.

Matthew looked at her when he turned round. There was a moment's pause in the day's proceedings. They kissed gently.

'Don't overdo it,' he said. 'And don't worry about that kid. She can always look after herself. We had an example of it just now, on the way to school.'

'What d'you mean? You've not been bullying her, Matthew?'

'Oh, I say! That's hardly fair. No; but I got a bit short when she started rooting out all the muck in the car. She complained of being lonely. Before I could stop myself I blurted out the news about the baby.'

Anna stared, frightened. Then she recovered, sighed, and turned to go, saying, 'It can't be helped, Matt. She'd have to know sooner or later. Better, perhaps, to have the news casually, than for us to make a ceremony of breaking it to her. You've done no harm, darling. You may be right; she can certainly look after herself. See how she has enlisted Tom Small. He's just her slave.'

Matthew frowned, and spoke emphatically, intent on his reaction to her last words. For a moment he did not notice that Anna had walked away, and could not hear him.

'You always bring him in when we talk about Madeleine–'

Anna called back, without looking round.

'I'll see what's wrong at the Moxons', and what can be done.'

Matthew joined Tom Small at the milking.

Anna enjoyed the stroll to the bungalow, along the lane towards the public road. She was not deeply concerned for Madeleine and the first day at school. The sun was glorious. She felt it seeking out her limbs, her cheeks and hair. It was like another lover, more remote and even more ardent than Matthew, if that were possible. She smiled as she considered that loose thought, and the impossibility of anything, or any power, coming between her and Matthew.

The little garden of the new bungalow was a sordid patch. The only cultivated part of it was upturned, where Moxon had lifted his potatoes and left the haulms in a heap. There were no flowers, except for a few self-sown marigolds among the groundsel that flourished from fence to house wall. Brambles sent out armoured shoots from the overgrown hawthorn hedge, which was bright with the bramble bloom, and streaks of bryony.

As Anna reached the gate, the Corgi came rushing after her, bidden by his master. But he stopped at the gate, sat down panting, unwilling to enter the garden. He and Moxon were not on speaking terms.

'Wait there then, Bill,' said Anna, unnecessarily.

The interior matched the outside: rural squalor begrimed the wretched furniture which had accreted, caddis-worm fashion, round the couple during their long married life. Mrs Moxon lay on an iron bedstead in the living-room. No explanation was given for this immigration from the bedroom next door. It could not be a matter of negotiating stairs. A sheet and a blanket, both sallow and greasy, covered her.

She complained immediately Anna greeted her: 'He's out the back. Says he ain't up to the mark. 'Tisn't as though he goes down to "The Woolpack". But it always takes him when I ain't the thing. And I been that way, off and on, since Tallulah, my

124

youngest, was born. They've all gone now, Mrs Burbage, all five, and doing well too. But they only come here to swank with their motor-bikes and cars, and radio sets. Never a sign of them girls when you're in trouble. You don't expect the boys to do anything much; but them girls! All alike nowadays. Smart enough in their ways; but when it comes to a helping hand! "Blood's thicker than water," I says to them. And all they answer is, "Mum's on at it again."'

Moxon came in from the kitchen.

'Mornin',' he said, sulky and suspicious.

'I came to see what's wrong, Moxon.'

'Everything's wrong, Missus. She's gone down again–' he indicated the figure on the bed, '–and I'm near crippled with this 'ere back. Nobody to do a hand's turn for us. Just trying to get cleaned up and something for a bit of dinner.'

'Good job I came then,' said Anna. She looked about for an apron, but found only a towel left on the bed-end. 'I'll tidy up, and get old Mother Weston to come over and see to the meal for you. Both her men are out all day: Tom Small eats with us, and the other lodger goes into "The Woolpack", I hear. So she can't be busy. I'd stay myself only I have four to feed, as you know, Moxon.'

He looked slyly at her.

'I expect you got all them appliances, though.'

Anna ignored this.

'Well, we were late with the milking. I left them both at it, the cows nearly crazy. Have you called the doctor in?'

Moxon was scornful.

'Call him in? That's old-fashioned talk, anyway! Now these doctors are Government, they don't study the likes of us. We have to go to them nowadays, even if we have to crawl there.'

'But Dr Wilson comes to us, and we're all on National Health. He gets no more out of it.'

'Oh, well, I dunno. Some he favours and some he don't.'

'Well, I'll ring him up and have a word when I get back. But he'll be out on his rounds by then. I'll ring at midday. Meanwhile, you'd better rest too, after I've cleaned up the room. Now, Mrs Moxon!'

Anna put in an hour, and left the old woman looking more human, but still grumbling.

'Now you'll do until the doctor comes,' she said, 'and I'll just call in on Mrs Weston; it's not far out of my way.'

Her cheerfulness did not penetrate. Its expenditure merely tired her. The glory had gone out of the morning, though the sun still shone, and fields, orchards and copses glittered and rustled, rich, like herself, with fruitfulness.

She found Mrs Weston willing, her incompetence therefore an improvement on that of the unwilling Moxons.

Anna was anxious to get home, to prepare the midday meal, but Mrs Weston wanted to talk.

'Seems to me if that young woman has her way, you'll soon be building another bungalow down the lane.'

'How's that, Mrs Weston?'

She was so old, she had to be humoured.

'Why, ain't you noticed it up there? She's fastened on my young lodger with grappling irons, as my husband would say. Only last night she came and fetched him in that flash motor she swanks all over the place in. And when she comes purring back, up they go to his shed, and makes tea like a married couple. Up there till near midnight they was, and she driving off after it, bold as you like, waking all the neighbours.'

'What, you mean Mr Small? But that's good news, Mrs Weston. He'll make a good husband: kind and hardworking. And he loves children. He's devoted to our Madeleine.'

'Aye, she's always around here looking for him. Old-fashioned as you like! What'll she say to this, ma'am? Put her little nose out of joint, won't it? Specially when the babies start coming. Mind you, I don't hold anything against the Kingdom girl, except that she's a bit too willing.'

'Well, if she settles down too, both of them will benefit.'

'Maybe you're right.' Mrs Weston had by now collected a small knitted cape, a hand-bag, and a pail with brush and rags: 'If I knows that lot, she won't have a thing to hand. Better take me tools, for that kitchen will need a clean up before I can cook in it, new as it is.'

As she left Anna, she looked at her keenly and said, 'You better sit down a bit. The morning's coming up hot and you look moithered, m'dear. Make yourself a cup o' tea. You're right welcome.'

She nodded her head at Anna's noticeable waistline. 'Another on the way, then? You want to be careful with so long between them. Nothing drastic like, and don't let yourself get excited.'

Anna, having seen her off towards the Moxons, gladly obeyed the old woman. She was surprised by her tiredness, after that unthanked labour at the bungalow. She was too shy to make a pot of tea in Mrs Weston's kitchen, but she drank a glass of water, and sat for ten minutes, bemused by the silence of the cottage, which was emphasized by the sounds of the world outside, from the sparrows gossiping on the path before the door, the wistful song of a robin near by, to the clatter of a reaping-machine at work down towards the river. She felt that she was the only idle creature in the universe. The novel sensation, something along her nerves rather than in her mind, was luxurious.

She found herself dozing. Then, as she pulled herself together, she saw, through the window over the sink, Tom Small's shed at the end of the neatly-kept garden. Lazily, she recalled Matthew's story of Madeleine looking into the shed and seeing something that she dared not talk about.

Her own curiosity was stirred, and she walked down the garden, to peer into the shed as her daughter had done. The bench stood immediately against the window. Anna saw the toy furniture, the chairs, the sofa, the table, newly painted and left un-covered to dry.

She was puzzled. Tom Small was late this morning, and the old woman's story had suggested the cause. But Anna could see that the paint was wet. Tom had done the finish-ing job this morning; so he did not oversleep.

She fell to wondering about it. Not even a full-bodied love-affair could interfere with his devotion to Madeleine. Misgiving chilled her, but she instantly repudiated it, and hurried home without more delay.

When she reached 'Doggetts', she saw, behind the house and garden, Matthew and Tom setting up the fruit-picking ladders in the orchard. It was a reassuring spectacle.

Nature was kind to farmers that autumn. Hot, windless weather lingered on, day after day, and the air was dusty with harvest.

The apple orchard at 'Doggetts" was not big enough to carry casual labour. Pickers at five shillings a bushel would have swallowed the small profit.

Next morning, when picking up the churns of milk, Kingdom, who was to carry the fruit to Maidstone, offered the service of his two eldest daughters. Later in the morning, only Shirley appeared, driving an empty lorry into the yard.

'Can't I get up into the orchard with the 'bus?' she cried, to the empty yard.

Anna appeared from the house. She opened the door of the cab and looked up at the trousered girl. She was aware of health and cleanliness, and a pair of blue eyes beneath a little knitted cap. Shirley smiled down at her, with a gleam of mischief, or of conspiracy. It was obvious she intended to make no secret of her conquest of Tom Small – if it was a conquest.

'No,' said Anna. 'Matthew looks on the fruit as a sideline, and won't do much about the orchard. It's a miracle how Tom Small got that extension out of him; such a long-term policy too!'

At the sound of Tom's name, Shirley's smile suddenly clouded, then beamed out again. Anna saw, but said nothing.

'Then we'll have to wheel the boxes down,' said Shirley. 'Whew! That'll be hot work!'

'But I thought two of you were coming? Your father said so.'

'Father said so! He doesn't know what's going on. He meant Mary, for she was the only one at home with me. But she's gone ladylike: taken up shorthand and typing, and has found an office job in Sheerness. Rides in on her Vespa every day.'

'I'm afraid I can't help this year,' said Anna.

Shirley leaned down and touched her shoulder. 'Why, Mrs Burbage? Do you mean it? Oh, I envy you. Lucky you!'

She was standing beside Anna now, and put an arm round her.

'I wish–' she began.

'I know,' said Anna. 'It may not be so far off, I hear?'

'Why, what do you know? There's nothing yet. Only last night – nothing decided!'

'News travels faster than fact in the country, Shirley. Tom's a good man.'

'Of course he is. I liked him at first sight. And I don't mind telling you I've had a good look round. I wasn't born yesterday.'

Anna laughed.

'Well, you won't take him away from "Doggetts". We can't lose him after all these years.'

'No need to worry, Mrs Burbage. Tom's tied here so long as your little girl's around.'

They looked at each other, sharing something they could not understand, and dared not approach. After the pause, Anna retreated.

'Matthew will be back any moment. He's taking Madeleine to school this term. I found it a bit much, with no help in the house.'

'Why, Mrs Burbage, I could lend a hand there, for a couple of hours a day. Dad's talking of taking on another driver, and that will release me, except for the odd job when there's a rush on. He's doing so well that he's buying another lorry.'

'What, even though the farmers are complaining?'

Shirley laughed uneasily.

'He doesn't depend only on the farmers.'

Anna paid no attention, for Matthew drove in and greeted the two women.

'Not your sister, Shirley?' he said.

She explained again.

'Oh well, we can manage. That'll be three of us, though I'm expecting Lady Beverley during the day. You remember, Anna? She wanted to look round, and talk about a few more heifers.'

'Yes, but don't be persuaded to take on too much. You're working hard enough, Matt.'

He grinned.

'I've got a big family to keep, eh, Shirley?'

But Shirley did not reply. Tom Small had come out of Prince Albert's stable, leading the pony, who minced along self-consciously beside him, like a virtuoso being led on to the platform by a respectful conductor.

Shirley approached him, and he stopped. Prince Albert rolled his eyes, questioning the delay.

'Do we start straight away, Tom?'

'Start what?'

He avoided her warm approach. He would not look at her.

'Picking I mean. What'd you think I meant?'

'Why, I haven't heard of it.'

Matthew broke in: 'No, I've not had a chance. Moxon still being off. He should be back next week, the doctor said. But we need help in the orchard, Tom. Kingdom said this morning that two of his girls were free. But only Shirley can come. That's all right, eh? You know each other.'

'Yes, we know each other, don't we, Tom?'

Small turned abruptly, still leading the pony, and made for the orchard.

'Good Lord, what's biting him now?' said

133

Matthew, looking from Anna to Shirley. They both hesitated, and for a moment the only sound was that of Tom retreating, out of sight through the gate in the walled garden.

'Shall I say?' whispered Anna.

Shirley answered for herself.

'Tom and I are talking of getting married, Mr Burbage.'

Matthew stared, then solemnly shook her hand.

'But that shouldn't make him look so surly. Just like Tom, though. No knowing him – though I suppose you do, as you've got so far. Not that I'm being critical. Tom's reliable, sound as a rock.'

He turned to his wife.

'How long have you known about this, Anna? Things going on under my nose.'

'Only five minutes, dear; and I've already made sure we shall not lose him.'

Matthew laughed.

'No, you've got a little rival here, Shirley. Our Madeleine. They're inseparable.'

'Include Prince Albert, Matt.'

Anna said this because she had seen that quick shadow of doubt in Shirley's clear eyes. It was the second time.

'Well, it's into the orchard then. You and Tom can call it the Garden of Eden if you like. Take care not to let the Serpent in.'

He followed his wife into the house.

Shirley paused in the walled garden. Here in this private place she tried to shake off the misgiving, the uncertainty, which had teased her since that unloverlike parting from Tom.

Gwylliam, the Corgi, had deserted his master, and now came trotting smartly after Shirley.

'Why, boy?' she said, and he showed his approval of her by collapsing and rolling on his back at her feet. She stooped and fondled his silky ears. 'What d'you want then? Want to be friends? That's a comfort, I'd say. More straightforward than some!'

She lingered with the dog for some minutes. He sat panting while she talked. He looked up at her from time to time, sadly rolling his eyes, as though sharing her perplexity.

'This won't do, old boy,' she said at last. The dog followed her into the orchard, and waited at her feet while she stopped beyond the gate in the wall, to look round for Tom Small.

He was already picking, at the near corner where the mature trees joined the new saplings, and where the old wall turned away at right angles. Shirley could not see him. But she located him by the agitation of the foliage above one of the ladders.

'Where do I start, Tom?'

She peered up at him from the spread base of the ladder. He answered without looking down. She saw the soles and heels of his boots, and the man above them fore-shortened, his head hidden in the greenery, his back by a loose canvas bag slung from his shoulders.

'Want me to get these Bramleys off tonight. You'd better start next door here. I'll shift the ladder when you're ready. It's a tricky business and you might bruise the boughs if you haven't got the knack.'

Still he didn't look down. Shirley waited. She wanted him to say something personal. But he went on picking, his body leaning against the ladder, both arms moving rapidly, his hands pausing as they groped for the bag, to drop the plucked apples there behind him without damaging their ripe skins and flesh.

A twig fell and struck Shirley across the forehead. She blinked, and her eyes watered.

'Can't you get started, then?' said Tom, sharply.

'If that's all you can say, I might as well.'

As she answered, Shirley saw his face. He stopped picking and frowned at her, moving his head aside to dodge a spray of apples still swinging on the bough.

'Now, look, Shirley. We've got a job to do. We're short-handed as it is, with this lady coming to keep the boss talking about the cattle.' Then he added, a little more kindly, 'The ladder's all set for you, and there's a bag hanging on it. You've picked before, haven't you?'

Shirley was too angry to reply.

Both picked in silence for an hour, the labour relieved only when they had to come down to empty their bags into the bushel baskets set out in a row under the wall.

Nature was less sulky than the two self-tortured mortals. Warm air stirred the laden trees, and they whispered without ceasing. Birds, now almost songless but full of argument, flew in and out, the starlings and sparrows in flocks, the pigeons, thrushes and blackbirds solitary or in pairs, tits and finches indiscriminately, but all eager.

An occasional airliner passed overhead, its drone drowning the whole orchestra below, then diminishing and fading out. Shirley looked up at the first one, and saw the tiny jewel flittering in the sunlight against the blue cushion of the sky. She was surprised to find herself still hurt, her eyes moist. She blamed the sudden glance up at the glare, from the cool, close cover of the apple boughs.

'You've nothing to say then, Tom,' she ventured, willing to surrender.

A pause. The reply came when she was halfway down her ladder, conscious of the weight of the fruit, trying to counter the pull that threatened to drag her off the rungs.

'What d'you want me to say, Shirley?'

The words were harsh, but spoken with some feeling. She interpreted this in his favour.

'I don't know, Tom. Maybe that it wasn't just a bit of fun. I told you last night that was how I felt. I'm ready to be serious if you are. But you jumped down my throat when it was all over, as though you blamed me for it.'

'No, it wasn't that, Shirley.'

He had descended too, and they stood close together, emptying their gatherings into the same basket.

'What was it then? Tell me, Tom. We've got to get it right.'

She saw a spasm of bewilderment distort his mouth. It both endeared him to her and distressed her.

'That I don't know, my dear. I'm not blaming you. I'm fond enough, Shirley. I'm not easy that way, and I like to think things out. But this has come upon us so sudden like. Don't that make you uneasy?'

She hesitated. She dared not say what really puzzled her.

'No, Tom. I'm natural enough. I may be

138

quick in this, but I said I love you and I mean it. I've been thinking it over too. I couldn't sleep for it. I've been honest with you. I said I'm no beginner. But no man has meant what you mean to me. That's the truth.'

Silence followed this confession. Shirley stood over Tom, watching him sorting the apples. She saw that he was troubled.

'You don't say anything, Tom. What about last night? I've told you my side of it, and all the rest too. Why don't you say what's on your mind? I can't see any reason to be upset as you are.'

She even knelt down beside him, and put her hand over his on the rim of the basket.

'I don't rightly know, Shirley. I wish I did. Somehow I feel I'm not playing fair.'

'It's somebody else, then?'

She almost wished her question were sincere, for that would have meant a natural complication, one she could understand and fight against.

Tom turned on her roughly, seizing her by the shoulder.

'Don't you say that, Shirley! That isn't fair. You don't believe that, eh? You don't, after last night? I'm not that kind of chap.'

She was too deeply moved to reply. The sense of possession implied by his touching her acted like a declaration, a demand. Tears stood in her eyes. Tenderness hid worse fears.

'I don't mind, Tom,' she said. 'I know what men are.'

'Well, I'm not,' he said fiercely. 'If we're going to have anything to do with each other, you've got to realize that. I've got nothing to say. I don't like being rushed, that's all. I like to think things out; see?'

'Kiss me now, and forget it, Tom. But you've got to treat me fairly. I meant no harm. You should have known that.'

He stared at her; he could not comprehend what she was talking about. She was equally astonished, and relieved, that he had forgotten the incident of her discovery of the dolls' furniture. He was so innocent that she put her arms round him, protectively.

He kissed her, shyly, letting an apple which he had taken up drop back into the basket.

While they knelt clasped together, a warm snuffling came between them, ruffling the lose hair outside Shirley's cap.

Startled, they released each other, and Prince Albert thrust his muzzle between their heads. The Corgi had been at his heels, playfully urging him on, to add to the good company in the orchard.

'Oh, you beauty!' cried Shirley, laughing as she thumped the pony's stout neck with the hand just released from Tom's. 'You'll do, won't you, m'boy? Can't we rig him up to cart the baskets down to the lorry, Tom?'

He got up, and said seriously, 'No, we can't do that, Shirley.' He ordered both the animals to move off, away from the row of baskets.

'Here, Bill! Take him away. Drive him down. Git! Git!'

Gwylliam barked, and pretended to snap at the pony's heels. Prince Albert obeyed with a show of meekness, snorting as he went.

'Better get on,' said Tom.

Shirley showed obedience too.

5

The day continued hot, the sun moving complacently over a cloudless sky. A low hum of wings made a power-house of the outdoor scene: wings of the ephemerids born that morning, to a short energy.

The Burbages, Tom Small and Shirley Kingdom sat silently at the midday meal in the farmhouse kitchen. They were too hot, too air-drunk, to talk. Anna, in her apron, was tired after her busy morning. She longed only to get off upstairs for a sleep on her bed. The droning choir of the outside world penetrated into the kitchen.

Anna leaned back, yawning.

'I can hardly keep awake.'

'You shouldn't have gone down to the

Moxons,' said Matthew. 'The more you do, the more you may. I don't know about him. I think I'll have to get rid of him. We can't afford passengers, Anna. What d'you say, Tom?'

Tom considered this, and looked across at Shirley. She nodded, believing that he had something in mind very much to her mind. But he spoke otherwise: 'I reckon there's a shortage of men here in Sheppey – like the rest of Kent. Even old Moxon gets a job, and there's thousands in our parts like him: don't know a good day's work when they see it.'

'That's an out-of-date sentiment, Tom!'

Matthew rose from the table, and Shirley had no opportunity to speak up where Tom had failed. But she contained her disappointment.

'We're late,' said Matthew. 'That brat of ours will have had her rest, and be halfway home, risking her life on the road. I'm off!'

A moment later the car started up, and left the yard.

'You get along upstairs,' said Shirley. 'You look as though this heat is too much. Those old Moxons! I'll clear the table.'

Anna was grateful.

'I'll come out later, then, and give a hand with the sorting. Good of you, Shirley.'

She disappeared.

'Get you out, Tom,' whispered Shirley.

'This is like it ought to be, eh?' She put her arms round him, to urge him towards the door, but he stood firm, rolling a cigarette and smiling at her. 'Isn't it, Tom? Tell me! Don't you see how life could shape for us, with a home of our own?'

He looked around the large, old-fashioned kitchen and at its shining modern additions.

'It could be so, m'dear. You're full of surprises, Shirley.'

'How d'you mean?'

She stole the cigarette he had rolled, and looked up, silently demanding a light. He began to roll another, making her wait.

'I reckoned you as one of those flighty sort, with that sporting car and all.'

'I suppose it's Dad's reputation, too,' she said, frowning.

He looked up quickly.

'I don't know anything about that. I'm a Tunstall man, and don't know what goes on here.'

'But you've been here a lifetime, haven't you?'

'Not my lifetime.'

'Madeleine's then.'

'What's that? Oh, Madeleine. Why yes, I came just after she was born. She's grown up with me, you might say.'

Shirley looked eagerly up at him, drawing him closer with her hands on his hips.

'Tom! You mean she was born before you

came, before you knew the Burbages?'

He finished rolling the second cigarette, fumbled for his light, and proferred the flame.

'That been worrying you, then?' he said. 'Well, I'm damned. What will a woman think of next?'

She said no more. She was too happy to speak. Only ordinariness, everyday things, the small things, could express her relief. She pushed him off, and began to clear the table.

'I'm washing up before I come out,' she said. 'That poor soul hasn't a scrap of help indoors. She needs a woman around at a time like this. I know I shall.'

Tom walked soberly away, back to the orchard.

Wasps were crawling over the fruit in the baskets, and hovering round that still on the trees. Tom smoked while he picked, and was slowed down by the pests, for he had to scrutinize each apple before lifting it off the twig.

He was not too sweet-tempered when Shirley appeared.

'These damn wasps,' he said. 'Look out while you're picking. There must be a nest hereabouts.'

'They're everywhere, Tom. Down home it's just the same.'

'Where's that, then?'

'You may well ask! We're on the Sitting-bourne road, more like a depot than a home. The house is beside the goods-yard and the garage for the lorries. I keep my run-about there too.'

Tom did not reply. He had set a ladder for Shirley at the tree where he was picking, and she climbed up. He could glimpse her through the branches.

'Nice to pick together, Tom.'

'Aye. I did that thinking it would keep these plaguy wasps off, with two of us at work.'

'Oh, I see.'

They were up and down twice before anything more was said.

'You feeling hot, dear?'

'I'm sweating hot. Properly tired out to-day.'

Shirley laughed.

'Sure it's the heat, Tom? Not a touch of the night before?'

'Look here, girl, you keep your mind off that. We've got work to do. This fruit'll be all bitten if we don't get it away.'

'Oh, well, we were like-minded enough last night.'

The argument was interrupted by Matthew, who greeted them and began to work on a nearby tree.

The heat developed during the afternoon, and a hot breeze came up from the flats

145

along the river-edge. The ladders swayed with the branches, and loose apples here and there thudded to the ground.

'That'll move these wasps,' shouted Matthew. 'Don't feel seasick, do you, Shirley?'

'No, I love it. It's as good as a dance-hall!'

'You've picked on a frivolous young woman, Tom.'

He got no reply. Tom was leaning back from his ladder, to look round. Shirley saw him pull a branch aside. It hid his face from her, while he made a clear view to the gate in the orchard wall. He had heard the click of the iron latch. Shirley heard it too. Then she saw Madeleine picking her way under the trees, holding her arms across her chest, as though hiding something.

'Tom! Where are you? Tom, I want you. I've got a surprise!'

The child had very little on, and was bare to the waist: a skinny elf, golden and brown. Her hair was loose and fanned over her shoulders, nutbrown, lighter than her eyes. Her cries were happy, full of laughter and conspiracy.

'Tom! Come down! I've got something for you.'

Shirley watched her, unseen round the farther side of the apple tree. She saw her foreshortened, standing below and looking up at Tom, her eyes hungry with eagerness.

'Why, Maddy!' he said, his voice shaken.

146

'I'm that busy. Just you wait a bit!'

'Tom, come down at once. You must! You must!'

Madeleine still clasped something, hidden in her arms. The Corgi jumped up at it, and her body shrank away, ignoring him. She did not shift her concentrated stare of entreaty.

'You *must* come down, Tom!'

Shirley heard him chuckling with happiness. She leaned against her ladder, swaying with it in the breeze, and saw him, a shape fragmented by the branches, moving down in obedience to the child's command. She frowned, released a hand to wipe the sweat from her forehead, and felt the salt sting of it.

'Tom, lift me up. I want to show you closer.'

Shirley saw them standing together below. Tom picked the child up, and she clasped her bare arms suddenly round his neck, and held the object hidden behind him.

'Now guess, Tom. It's something I made for you. I made it myself, Tom; I did. Shut your eyes and see what I've made.'

He laughed at the lovely impossibility.

She could wait no longer. Still clinging with one arm half-strangling him, she brought the gift round for him to see.

'It's to hold your tobacco, Tom. Look, I've sewn it, and done the flowers on it too.

147

Nobody helped me.'

Shirley saw him take it, and examine it.

'Why, you made this pouch?' he asked. 'You made it for me?'

He didn't even thank her. The occasion was too emotional, too intimate for that. Shirley looked away as she saw him press the little body against his face, and hold it there for a second or two.

Then a clear voice rang through the orchard, breaking the tension: 'You there, Matthew? Sorry I'm late. Been half round the county today. I should think.'

It was Lady Beverley.

6

Anna overslept that afternoon, and could not go out to the orchard to help with sorting the apples as she had promised. She moved stiffly about the kitchen, preparing the tea-table, with help from Madeleine who had become bored with hanging about the orchard while the grown-ups worked.

After giving Tom the tobacco-pouch, the child lingered under the trees where the ladders were raised. Once or twice she took a surreptitious climb, knowing that she had been forbidden to do so. The motion on the rungs delighted her, adding to the emotional excitement of the little ceremony with Tom.

But she grew weary of this, there being nobody to caution her. Father had gone off up the farm with Lady Beverley to look at the herd. Tom and Miss Kingdom were too busy in the trees to notice her. She joined Prince Albert and made love to him for a while, inventing endearing names and whispering them into his ear, with her arms half-circling his sturdy neck. But he was hot and lazy, and after an initial twitch of an ear and toss of his mane, he subsided into apathy. She left him and returned to the corner whether the apple-picking steadily progressed.

She lay down beside the half-filled basket and munched an apple picked from the latest consignment. She lay flat on her back, the crushed grass tickling her bare skin. From time to time she kicked out into the air, to let her leg fall with a jolt that shook her whole body. It almost hurt, and gave her a satisfaction that began to dispel her sense of emptiness, of reaction after the crisis of bliss when Tom gave her all his attention, and took her up in his arms to receive the gift.

She was thus engaged, in eating and mild self-torture, when Shirley Kingdom suddenly filled the screen of leaves and sky above her. Madeleine instantly shut her eyes, and lay still. Even her mouth, filled with apple-flesh, stopped working.

149

'My word, won't you get a tummy-ache!' said Shirley.

Madeleine took no notice, and lay dead still. She heard the rumble of apples being poured into the basket. Then Shirley spoke again, a little more sharply: 'And sleeping there with nothing on? Better run home and get a woolly, or you'll be in bed with a chill.'

Madeleine did not answer, or open an eye. One convulsive kick upward was the only acknowledgement.

Shirley returned to the tree which she was sharing with Tom, and for the first time since the gift-taking, she spoke to him: 'It's a good job there's another kid coming soon. That small girl needs someone to put her nose out of joint.'

Tom paused, and tried to study her through the tangle of branches.

'You don't like that little 'un, do you?'

'Don't be a fool, Tom. Why should I dislike her? She's not more than a baby. Only there are some nicer than others. I don't believe in spoiling them. It only makes a rod for their backs later on.'

'Maybe,' he said, 'but young Madeleine is not spoiled. She's a brave one, she is.'

An exclamation of disgust came through the tree, and no more was said. The fruit was gradually transferred to the bushel baskets, and branches that had been weighed down with the weight eased themselves, and slowly rose to their normal positions in the pattern of growth.

Meanwhile, Madeleine, her day-dreaming dispelled, rolled away, then got up and wandered towards the house. She saw the lorry in the yard, and inspected it. A woman's handkerchief lay on the driver's seat. The child picked it up fastidiously, thought for a moment, then wiped the handkerchief across the greasy patch on one of the wheels, and put the defiled thing back on the seat.

This was done calmly and innocently. She instantly forgot the incident and went indoors to find her mother, and be dragooned into helping to lay the tea-table.

First Matthew and Lady Beverley came in.

'Hallo, my angel,' said the visitor. 'My word, the sun has got you. And look at this pattern on her back, Anna! Turn round, child!'

Madeleine, flattered by this attention, obeyed, and twisted her head, trying to look down her own back. Everybody laughed, and Lady Beverley patted the shapely little bottom.

'You're a monkey, vain as you please!'

Madeleine gravely handed round a plate of cress sandwiches, while her mother poured the tea. The visitor took two, and was enjoying them, when Tom Small and Shirley appeared. Seeing Lady Beverley,

Tom paused at the door, leaving Shirley to enter alone.

'Come along, show yourself,' cried Lady Beverley. 'Don't I hear good news about you two?'

Shirley turned, and beckoned to the reluctant Tom, who had to obey. But he moved across the kitchen, away from her, and was seized on by Madeleine, who fumbled in his pockets until she produced the new, so-called tobacco-pouch, which she took over to show to Lady Beverley.

'I made it at school for Tom,' she said.

'Why, is this his birthday?'

'No, but I like making things for him. He's my Tom. He gave me Prince Albert. And that's not all.'

Madeleine was ready to become conspiratorial, but her mother broke in.

'Madeleine, don't monopolize! Lady Beverley was saying something to Shirley.'

Madeleine's eyes darkened, and she retreated. The change of mood was not unobserved. The visitor said nothing, but she looked from the child to Tom Small, who had taken his usual stand between the door and the low window, and was thus in shadow. So far as she could see, the man was inexpressive, concerned only with the cup of tea which Anna had taken to him.

Shirley, meanwhile, had seated herself at the table, half-turned away from both Tom and the precocious infant. She approved of the snub given by Anna. She approved also of Lady Beverley's being interrupted.

'You were saying?' she said, as she leaned across to help herself to a sandwich from the plate which Madeleine had set down out of reach.

Lady Beverley observed this, and addressed herself to Burbage.

'You'll have to build another bungalow down there, Matthew, if that's how the wind is blowing!'

Before he could retort, the telephone rang, and he went out to answer it. Everyone paused, trying not to overhear. A robin alighted by the open door and broke into a monologue that caused the dog to lift his head and stare indignantly from his station at Lady Beverley's feet.

Matthew came back.

'That's the doctor, Anna. He's been to the Moxons. Says the poor devil is really ill and must be X-rayed without delay. Wants to know if we can get him to the hospital.'

'What about his wife?' said Anna. 'She's quite helpless, you know.'

'They've got a family, haven't they?' demanded Lady Beverley. 'Though no doubt the public ambulance will have fetched him away by now.'

'It's the wife I'm thinking about,' said Anna. 'We ought to let the daughters know.'

'I'll see to that,' said Lady Beverley. 'I'll call at the bungalow and get the address of one of the girls, and run over there.'

With that, she left, seen off by Matthew. He watched her car move carefully down the drive and disappear. For some minutes he stood, listening to it. Then he went indoors before following Tom and Shirley up to the orchard, to help carry the baskets of apples down to the lorry.

'That's a good friend to us, Anna,' he said, still preoccupied with the picture of Lady Beverley driving away. 'I don't know why she does it.'

Anna, stately with her increasing burden, turned to smile at him. His innocent perplexity was so endearing that she set down the tray of dirty tea-cups, and ran her fingers through his hair.

'Impossible to guess,' she said, as she kissed him. 'It must be just her native goodness. Unless it is that she sees we make a happy team, you and I.'

Matthew, still in a tender mood, responded. Neither of them noticed that Madeleine had come down from her room, and now stood in the doorway from the staircase, watching them solemnly, the glow of her brown eyes almost extinguished in the shadows. When husband and wife relinquished their embrace, their daughter had vanished.

Matthew, thus sustained, set off for the orchard, but stopped at the lorry to let down the tailboard, and make sure that the floor was clear.

He was about to start off again, when a car appeared. For a moment he expected that Lady Beverley might have forgotten something, and had returned. The car stopped near the lorry, and a man got out, to touch his peaked cap politely. He was a police-inspector.

7

Lady Beverley drew up at the new bungalow where 'Doggetts' farm joined and ran alongside the public road. As she got out of her car, another stopped closed to hers. She would have to back a few feet before she could drive off. A young man and woman sat in it. Seeing her, they did not leave the antique, but remained staring awkwardly ahead.

Lady Beverley waited, expecting them to approach her. Then she went on alone, knocked at the front door of the bungalow, opened it, and called, 'May I come in, Mrs Moxon?'

'What d'you want?' was the response from a figure crouched in a chair beside an iron bedstead. The bed was unmade.

'It's what do *you* want, my dear woman. I've come from "Doggetts", on my way home. They've just had a telephone-call from the doctor, telling him about your husband. Sorry to hear about that, you know. All of us sorry. But the thing is, what can we do for you?'

Mrs Moxon eyed her malevolently.

'That's up to them,' she said. 'My husband has paid up regular, and that covers the two of us. I'm entitled as well as him.'

'Oh, you mean the National Insurance? That's another matter. But in the meantime somebody must see to you. I've undertaken to go and fetch one of your daughters. I expect you have made arrangements with your family, for an emergency like this?'

'Don't know about that,' moaned Mrs Moxon, trying to ease herself up, with the aid of a stick and the bed-end. 'None of them ain't at home now. They got their families, mostly down Sittingbourne way, and doing well too. Things come easier to the young people nowadays.'

'All the more reason—' began Lady Beverley; but she was interrupted by the couple who had arrived after her.

They entered without knocking, the man first. The young woman, smartly dressed in a cotton frock, suitable for a palais-de-danse party, dodged round her man and leaned over Mrs Moxon, as though to protect her from the intruder.

'You the lady doctor?' demanded the man.

Lady Beverley ignored this.

'I've come to see what needs doing, and to fetch one of the daughters.'

'We've got our own car, thanks very much,' said the young woman.

'So you are one of the family?'

'The eldest, yes. And we've already been notified, thanks very much.'

She fussed over the mother, who appeared to be indifferent to the solicitude.

The husband now came to the attack.

'No need for charity as things are today,' he said, with an intonation that suggested quotes from a textbook. 'Everything's been set in motion. They let us know from the hospital, and here we are.'

'I'm so glad,' said Lady Beverley. 'But surely neighbours can lend a hand at such times.'

Mrs Moxon interrupted, while easing herself down again into the chair by the bed. Her daughter looked on, not attempting to help her, or to tidy up the bed. '*She's* been down already. Came in yesterday when the old man was about. Seems a long day, it does.'

'Yes, it was Mrs Burbage who asked me to look in. She's worried about you.'

The young husband snorted.

'First time I've heard of a boss worrying over a worker.'

Lady Beverley turned on him. Her beauty disguised her anger, and she sounded almost benevolent: 'It's a long time since Mrs Moxon was able to be a worker, don't you think? She really needs expert care. Perhaps the family should talk it over. I can help there, as I am on the council of several homes for old folk in Kent. Would you let me know if you decide anything? Lady Beverley, at Hothfield.'

The daughter, but not the son-in-law, was impressed.

'*Lady* Beverley?' he said. 'Doing a bit of slumming, eh?'

'Thanks very much,' said the daughter. 'Very nice of you, I must say. Perhaps we ought to talk about it, George. I'm sure Lady Beverley means well. You can't expect Mrs Burbage to keep coming down every day to see to Mother. She's got her own place to look after, like the rest of us.'

'Yes, we'll let you know,' said the husband, offering Lady Beverley a cigarette from a gold-coloured case; 'Smoke?'

Lady Beverley retreated to her car, backed it away from the near-embrace of the other one, and drove off. This manœuvre was watched by the daughter from the window.

'Lady Beverley, eh?' she mused aloud. 'Who is she then? Know her, Mum?'

'One of them nobs,' her husband explained. 'Still poking their noses in, round these country places. They don't know what's happening to them. Someone ought to show her over one of our big shops, or over the river in Dagenham. That'd teach her!'

'Oh you and your politics!' said the girl. 'Can't you leave them out at a time like this? What we've got to think about is who's going to look after Mum. That's right, isn't it, Mum?'

Mrs Moxon did not look up. She trusted nobody in particular, and expected little.

Her daughter went on: 'Jolly good of her, really. She needn't have bothered. And we may be glad of a word from her, if it comes to that.'

'Well, we better take the old girl home with us, hadn't we?' said the son-in-law.

'What, and give up the bungalow?'

Mrs Moxon interrupted her daughter: 'We got no hold here. It's tied with the job, and if your father can't work no more, out we go.'

The son-in-law looked at his wife triumphantly.

'There you are, you see! And you say I talk about politics! It's a bit more knowledge you want. It's the facts of history.'

'I'm thinking about who's to do the looking-after. There's my job to think of, isn't there, and four of us to feed, and do for already.'

'Well, she'll fit in for a bit, won't she, while

159

we have a look round? You got the deep-freeze, haven't you?'

The argument continued, in the presence of Mrs Moxon. She appeared to be unmoved by it. Maybe the shock of seeing her husband suddenly whisked away in the ambulance had stunned her.

At last, it was decided to take her home to Sittingbourne, and to summon the other sisters and the two brothers to a family council. One of the brothers was already at the hospital, and would bring the latest news of their father's condition.

Mrs Moxon made only a feeble objection. She was half-carried to the car and put in beside the driver's seat, where she waited, staring blankly at the windscreen, while the married couple went back to find some garments and a bag to contain them. But there was no bag, so the clothes had to be wrapped in a newspaper. The front door was slammed, and the Moxons thus departed.

Some ten minutes later, Anna Burbage with Madeleine appeared, bringing a hot meal in a Thermos container. The basket, which was filled up round the Thermos with clean towels and sheets, was slung over Prince Albert's broad back. He paced placidly along, content to feel his mistress's hand on the bridle.

Madeleine tied the rein to the garden gate while her mother unstrapped the basket.

160

'It looks quiet,' said Anna, as they walked up the path. 'Lady Beverley can't have taken the old soul away, surely?'

'Perhaps she thinks Mrs Moxon will be lonely at night,' said Madeleine. 'Are they friends, Mummy?'

'I don't really know,' lied Anna. Then she tried to explain. 'You see, darling–' but a second knock at the door brought no response. The door was locked.

'Strange!' said Anna. 'Can it be Lady Beverley? She'd know we need to get in. Perhaps she'll have telephoned by the time we get back. I'll just look in the window to make sure.'

'What d'you want to make sure of?' said Madeleine, peering in beside her. 'Nobody there, Mummy.'

As they left the neglected garden, a robin flickered from one bush to another, and broke into a melancholy song, autumnal and hopeless.

8

'Evening, sir,' said the Inspector. He noted Matthew's surprise. 'Sorry to intrude on you, Mr Burbage, but you may be able to help us in a little matter.'

'I doubt it,' said Matthew. 'Where are you from?'

'Sittingbourne police. We've had instructions to make a few inquiries round our district. It's these lorry jobs. We know some of the boys who are at it, but we want to know more about how they get rid of the loads afterwards.'

'Oh, you mean these modern highwaymen?'

'That's about it.'

'So you're calling on everybody?'

'Well, not quite everybody. We're interested in a few people, mostly in the transport business. You see, after the lorry is stolen, some quick work has to be done about transferring the load before the vehicle is abandoned somewhere else. We're checking up on all the small transport people. The answer may be there.'

He looked shrewdly at Matthew.

'You employ one of them, I think. The same one for all your work?'

Matthew was incredulous. His mind refused to connect the inquiry with Kingdom.

'Yes, but he's done my work for a long time now, and was recommended by Lady Beverley. She's known all over Kent – throughout the agricultural world, for that matter.'

'Do you ever call in at his depot?'

'Never even seen it. Never seen him except on my own farm here.'

'I see. Mind if I glance in your barns?'

'Good lord, no. But you make me feel uncomfortable, Inspector. I'll swear by George Kingdom.'

'I shouldn't risk that, sir. Human nature's very odd and unexpected.'

At this, Tom Small appeared at the door in the walled garden. He carried a bushel basket of apples. Behind him came Shirley Kingdom, trundling a wheelbarrow with two baskets. Seeing the police officer, Shirley stopped abruptly, and Tom advanced alone and unperturbed. He nodded at the visitor, and went on with his own business, dumping the basket on the lorry, then jumping up and dragging it to the front.

Shirley stood, still grasping the handles of the barrow, until Tom looked back, surprised. Then she came slowly forward, her head bent as though in shyness before a stranger. She passed the baskets, one by one, up to Tom, who loaded them beside the first one.

'What's all this, Tom?' she whispered as he stooped over her.

'Eh? Oh, I don't know. Perhaps a parking summons. Or selling tickets for a police orphanage concert.'

The Inspector had not failed to notice the young woman's discomfort.

'Is the driver of this lorry here, Mr Burbage?'

Shirley now spoke up: 'That's me. And I'm helping to pick the load too.'

This interruption interested him still further.

'I see. And you work for Kingdom?'

'I'm his daughter.'

'Ah, yes. Well, Mr Burbage, we'll just have that look round. And these two might come with us to lend a hand. Sorry to waste your time, but you know – these routine jobs must be done.'

From his manner during the walk round the two barns, and up to the orchard, it could be inferred that his inquiry was more than a routine job. He prodded the tightly stacked hay in the Dutch barn, asked Tom to open a bag here and another there, to show him the fertilizers. He kicked the bottom of several sacks.

'Better just look at the stables and cowsheds, Mr Burbage.'

Since the arrival of Shirley and the admission that she was Kingdom's daughter, the officer had become more formal; but he took Burbage aside to explain.

'They're up to all sorts of tricks, sir. You might well find that you're harbouring stolen goods unbeknown.'

'That's a bit romantic, surely,' said Matthew, who was now both uncomfortable and bored.

At the end of the inquisition, the Inspector

spoke to Shirley: 'Do you drive regularly for your father's business, Miss Kingdom?'

Shirley looked from him to Tom Small, but she got no help. Tom stood impassively, rolling a cigarette and studying the job intently.

'I do a bit of everything,' she replied. 'I help at home – I lend a hand here – and–'

'D'you help with the books, the accounts?'

'Oh, no! I don't believe Father keeps accounts. He just carries on from day to day.'

'No?' said the Inspector drily. 'That doesn't make it easy for the Inland Revenue. What about the other drivers: wages and insurance? Does he pay you: regular employment?'

This bombardment flustered Shirley. She frowned, grew red in the face, and stood speechless. It also affected Tom Small. He threw away the cigarette he had just rolled, stepped in front of Shirley, and spoke so sharply that the Inspector turned to him with increased interest.

'She wouldn't know about that, sir. She's worked here, and I know she's straight enough.'

Shirley and Burbage were equally startled.

'I'd vouch for that too,' said Burbage. The gallantry was contagious.

There was a moment of embarrassed silence.

'I see,' said the Inspector. 'Well, you all seem to understand one another. But I won't bother you further for the moment.'

Anna, Madeleine and Prince Albert, returning with the laden basket, joined the party as the visitor was about to enter his car. They made a pretty picture. It appealed to him so much that he returned to greet the newcomers as they joined the others still standing by the lorry.

Madeleine looked up at him, her mouth open, and her brown eyes intent with curiosity.

'Is there another war?' she asked.

He bent his knees and, on the level, confronted her face to face.

'Why, young lady? What do you know about war?'

'Mummy and Daddy were in the last one. They've told me about it. And you're a soldier. Have you come to fetch them back?'

'And what would you do if I did fetch them back?'

'Oh, I've got Tom Small.'

She nodded gravely, to indicate that worthy.

Tom moved half a pace towards her, then stopped. An expression of intense feeling passed over his face. Then it became impassive, blind.

By the time the Inspector looked from the child to him, Tom was rolling another cigarette, but with unsteady hands. Anna saw this, and could not prevent herself from exclaiming: 'Oh, Tom. No!'

Meanwhile, the Inspector, captivated and human, had taken Madeleine by the hand.

'Been for a picnic?' he said, leading her to the basket. She looked up confidingly, and explained why the basket was still full.

'You see, there's no stolen property there,' said Matthew, who by now was rather sore. 'But come in and have a drink before you go.'

He led the way with the Inspector, who had taken no offence at this bitter remark. He was still under Madeleine's spell. She went with him and her parents into the house. The uniform had captivated her.

By this time dusk was falling. Tom and Shirley, with the unloaded pony, returned to the task in the orchard. In silence, the girl lifted two baskets into the barrow, while Tom slung two, pannier fashion, over the pony's back, with ropes which had been brought up with the ladders.

'Why did you speak up for me, Tom?'

Shirley stood between the shafts of the barrow. Tom could not see her clearly, for the shadows were already deep beneath the trees.

'I don't like interference,' he said. 'People ought to be left alone. Damn all these busybodies. We have too much of that. Why don't they let us go our own pace?'

'I don't know about that. It doesn't worry me much. We must have some sort of control.'

He was surprised by this submissive remark. He left the pony and approached her.

'But it's you who are interfered with today, girl! I saw you were upset. That riled me, that did.'

She turned, and touched his arm.

'I didn't know you bothered that much about me, Tom.'

He was offended.

'What d'you think? After what we've had, d'you think I take that lightly? Look here, Shirley, you make me mad sometimes, but what I've had I keep, see? I don't take that lightly.'

She was in love with him, and was crying with a bitter-sweet happiness. His confession was worth more than the worry which had provoked it. She forgot for the moment her father's affairs, and the confirmation of unwelcome suspicions about his activities in a hand-to-mouth business.

She clung to Tom, and he did not withdraw.

'What is to be done, Tom?' she said at last, reassured by his kisses and tenderness. 'I've worried about it for the last year or two. I'm certain he works in with some of these crooks. He'll go off at a minute's notice, night or day, and come home hours later, flush with money and more bluff than ever. He's so easy, Tom. But he'll end up in the courts, and then what do we do: Mother, and the home, and the shame of it? We're not that kind, Tom. Don't you believe me?'

'I'm a free man, Shirley. I go my own way and I have my own values.'

He believed it. He emphasized his belief by repeating it, and embracing her again.

'Look, I stand by anybody who is put upon. I'll stand by you, Shirley. Your old man may be a fool, but he's no crook. He isn't a cruel one, is he?'

'No, he's too easy with us all. He ought to be a bit harder. It would have been better for us girls.'

'You're all right. I've learned that, my dear.'

With that reassurance, they made up for lost time, and failing light. A quarter of an hour later, Tom hoisted the happy young woman into the cab of the lorry and watched her drive away.

Then he turned to Prince Albert, and led him to the stable, and a last feed. While thus engaged, a voice greeted him from the darkness: 'I've come to say goodnight, Tom!'

He felt two small arms around his neck, as he was brushing the pony down.

'Oh, you do smell nice, Tom. You smell of apples.'

FOUR

1

Moxon, the work-reluctant, did not come back to 'Doggetts'. He lay in hospital during the first few weeks of autumn, and his employer heard nothing from any of the family in Sittingbourne. The bungalow stood in its neglected garden, up to its window-sills in weeds; such autumn-thriving growth as thistles, nettle, bramble, and couch-grass. Over all this, the marigolds triumphed, lavishing their gold over the waste of green and the dry copper heads of sorrel.

'Before we start ploughing,' said Tom Small to Matthew, one day after the last of the apples were picked and dispatched, 'we'd best clean up that garden old Moxon left. It'll all be seeding else over our newly-turned soil. Those thistles float for miles.'

'D'you think he'll come back and make a fuss if we go interfering?'

'So long as somebody else does the work, he won't grumble. It's too early to set a row or so of cabbage plants there. He's not likely to be able to tend the place himself, even if willing.'

'He's got a few bags of potatoes up.'

'Aye, but I bet they're spotted. He'll have used any old seed. If we can get into the shed I'll look them over.'

They decided to go down that afternoon, a Saturday in October. It was a gentle St Luke's summer day, timeless in a benignant universe. A swarm of gnats hovered and veered over the colourful vegetation in the deserted garden. Matthew, glad of an excuse to try out a new Land-Rover, decided to drive down with a load of tools, Gwylliam as guard.

'Coming with me, Maddy?'

Madeleine, who had already inspected the shining, new machine, hesitated and finally declined.

'You, darling?' This was an invitation to Anna. But she wanted to rest, after a busy Saturday morning in the house and preparing the lunch.

'Oh, well, I'll go alone,' he said, 'but come down later on if you feel like it.'

'Or you could fetch me about four. I'll fill the Thermos flasks and we can have a last picnic tea out of doors.'

'Oh, this weather may go on for the rest of the month.'

He drove off, pretending to be grumpy, but congratulating himself on being alone with the Land-Rover, as years before he had been alone with the Mosquito, but in a less peaceful setting. He drove on past the bungalow and along the public road towards Sittingbourne. Some mile or two on, he recognized Shirley Kingdom in her sports car, purring along towards 'Doggetts'. Somewhat shamefaced, he turned and followed her, just out of sight. He knew she would have something to say about meeting him on the Sittingbourne road, when he was supposed to be taking the tools down to the Moxons' garden.

Shirley slowed down and stopped when she reached the bungalow – she saw no sign of life. The neglected garden did not much interest her, but the dirty windows and the dirtier rags of curtain made her grimace with disgust.

She moved on, in low gear, and pulled up again when she met Tom Small, leading Prince Albert by the bridle. His other arm supported Madeleine, who rode on the pony in full kit, wearing the velvet cap given by Lady Beverley, and holding the whip, Tom's gift, sceptre-wise with the handle resting on her plump little groin. She had an imperious air, of daydreaming in a world of pride.

'I was coming to fetch you,' said Shirley to Tom. 'I looked in at your place and you weren't there.'

Tom felt Madeleine shrink, startled out of the warmth of her dream.

'Steady, lass,' he murmured. 'You aren't cold, eh?'

'Tom!' said Shirley. 'It's your half-day, isn't it? We've not met all the week. I had the idea of a drive down to Canterbury.'

He looked at her distressfully, half indicating the child who sat beside him, staring blankly between Prince Albert's pretty little ears.

'Didn't you see the Boss down at the Moxons?' he said. 'We're putting in a bit of spare time on that garden before it seeds all those thistles over our ploughing.'

'Most people would want overtime for that,' said Shirley.

'Haven't you heard old Moxon's pretty bad?'

'Sittingbourne's a big place, Tom. And there's been plenty of our own worries to think about.'

'Eh?' he said, frowning. Then, after a moment's cogitation, he spoke to Madeleine: 'Look, Maddy, you ride on down to your father, and I'll be along in a minute or two.'

Madeleine did not move. She grasped her whip more firmly, and scowled at Shirley, as though intending to attack her.

'No!' she whispered. 'I'll wait for you, Tom.'

'Look, lass. Just you do as I say, and tell your Daddy I'm coming along, see?'

'How long *will* you be?'

Shirley was aware of the hostility in those brown eyes. She was half amused, half frightened, but could do or say nothing. This was a matter for Tom and the child to settle.

Suddenly Madeleine surrendered, but with an air that suggested qualifications, and future trouble. She took in the rein dropped by Tom, and touched Prince Albert's round belly with her heels. He walked on, with his mistress, stiff with outrage, on his back. The two adults waited, listening to the tiny hoof-beats on the grit. Tom looked at the pony and its rider. His hands hung at his sides, the fingers working nervously. Shirley watched them.

'I'm not saying anything either,' she said.

'What?' He was still watching the child. Then he added: 'Lot of odd folk about on a Saturday. Cars all over the countryside. 'Tisn't safe for a pony nowadays.'

'Listen to me, Tom. I've not seen you all the week. The police have been in to see Father. I thought it had all blown over since that day when we were apple-picking. That day after our first night.' She turned from the steering-wheel and beat her fist angrily on the door top. 'Oh, Father is a fool! He's got into their hands or something. They've some hold on him, and he has been carrying on with the gang. That's what it comes to.

Now the police have caught one our vans with a load of cigarettes in a yard at Margate. How's he to explain that?'

Tom had seen Madeleine disappear round the bend in the drive. He turned to Shirley, and realized her distress. He was not indifferent to it, merely belated.

'Your mother and the girls?' he asked, reluctant to allow himself to come nearer home.

'All of us,' she said. 'Though I suppose the police won't close down the business. I could carry on there – if I wanted to. But I don't want to, Tom; not now.'

He knew what she meant.

'We'll have to think about that, my dear. But now you go on up to the house and give a hand to Mrs Burbage. She's to get the tea and bring it down to us. Can't do much in a hurry, Shirley. But don't you worry. You've got friends here, see?'

This did not fully reassure her. She leaned out of the car and drew Tom to her.

'Tom, it's not for want of friends. It's you: after what we've shared.'

'Aye,' he said, doubtfully, 'it's been going on since apple-picking.'

She laughed, but with a touch of chagrin. 'Well, don't be so gloomy about it. You're sure that's all?'

He was indignant.

'What d'you mean?'

'Not ashamed of being associated with a jailbird's daughter? That's what I mean.'

He looked down the drive. The pony's footsteps could still be heard, fainter and fainter.

'That's not my way, and you know it, Shirley. I stand by my own choice, see? Now you go on up, and join us at the Moxons' place.'

She was cheered by this.

'How much longer will it be theirs, Tom?'

She started the engine, and slipped into gear, slowly moving away.

'I'd sooner it was ours, Tom. That's how I feel about the whole mess.'

2

Matthew took a bagging-hook and a carborundum hone from the tools in the Land-Rover, and walked up the submerged path, uncertain where to start the attack on the weeds. Even the worked soil where Moxon had lifted his potatoes two months ago was green again. At the corners of the ground, by the hedges, nettles stood waist-high, overtopped here and there by giant thistles already sere and seed-blown.

He decided to work outward from the concrete surround of the bungalow, and was sharpening the hook when Madeleine rode

176

up, looking angry and thundery. She drew up at the gate and stared over it at her father, without dismounting. With her whip she cut savagely at a great strand of bramble that curved out of the hedge. Once, twice, thrice, but it would not break.

'What's the matter with you, young woman?' cried her father, pausing at his task. 'And where's Tom? I'm waiting for him.'

Then, to his surprise, he saw Madeleine lean forward and bury her face in Prince Albert's mane, clasping him round the neck. The whole little body shook with sobs.

He set down the hook and the hone, and walked slowly down the path.

'Why, Maddy? Tell me, what's the trouble?'

But she could say nothing intelligible. Her father, with difficulty, removed her arms from the pony's neck, and lifted her down. But she was protesting, reaching out to Prince Albert, who looked round at her, his great eyes alive with curiosity rather than sympathy.

'Look, Prince Albert is ashamed of you, Maddy! Don't let him see you crying for nothing. Can't you even tell me? Or if I go away, won't you tell Prince Albert?'

She was distraught and could not answer. She struggled out of her father's arms, took the pony's bridle, and stumbled with him to put a few yards between herself and Matthew. There she stood, with her back to him, half hidden by Prince Albert, who waited patiently and selected titbits from around their feet, sniffing at them and raising his lips to take them. Gradually she regained control of herself, but the storm had exhausted her and she leaned against the pony's flank, motionless.

'All right now, old lady?' ventured Matthew. 'Come along and give me a hand. Tie up Prince Albert here to the gate-post.'

He was bewildered, and shy. He could not understand his own child who lived her life so removed from him. He watched her slow reaction to his approach now, and was jealous because of her reluctance.

'Come on, now!' he said, more sharply. 'Don't be a softie. If you don't want to tell me what's upsetting you, you needn't.'

'Nothing's upsetting me,' she managed to say, at last responding to her father's invitation, 'I was just being sad, that's all.'

He looked at the forlorn little figure, but could not understand.

'You can't be sad about nothing, on a day like this. Look, here's a rake. Just you gather up the weeds as I cut them down, and we'll have a bonfire.'

He knew she loved bonfires.

Madeleine made the effort, but not for long. As the minutes passed she flagged, and finally went down to the gate and stared up the lane towards home.

'Hi! Come along. I'm catching up on you!'

She did not heed this, for at last Tom Small came in sight. Instantly her mood changed. The sulkiness, the abstraction, disappeared. She dropped the rake and was out of the gate, running towards him.

'Where are you, Tom? Where are you?'

She jumped at him and made him stagger as he lifted her into his arms.

'Why, I'm here, Maddy. Where else?'

He hoisted her on to his shoulder, and paused at the Land-Rover to select another bagging-hook, and a small two-pronged rake.

'Take care now, mind the blade,' he said.

He saw that she had been crying, but he would not acknowledge it.

'Easy now. I'll set you down. Don't tread on that rake or it'll up and bite you.'

'Silly, Tom! You're silly!'

She was happy now, and dominant again.

Her father had watched this scene from the cleared patch of ground in front of the door of the bungalow.

'Good God!' he exclaimed, as Tom Small came up the path. Then without another word he turned away and attacked the weeds, while Tom took up the job farther away working from the hedge. Neither of the men spoke to the other, and Madeleine, after an attempt to rake the weeds for both, finally attached herself to Tom's labours.

Still Matthew said nothing. After a quarter of an hour he stretched himself, and looked around at the field of battle. The other two were at work. He went out and returned with another rake. After gathering his own cuttings into a heap, he walked down the path again, and out to the Land-Rover. Prince Albert stared at him as he drove off back to the farmhouse.

3

A great swarm of gnats gathered between the two heaps of green-stuff. The low sunlight of the October afternoon touched the myriad wings to iridescence, changing the swarm into a golden veil that veered in a rhythm obedient to an impulse not of this world. Whatever its origin, it affected Madeleine too. After a while, she threw down the rake and took a few skipping steps round the green mound which she had gathered. Tom paused, looking up over his hook, resting on the small rake held head downward on the ground.

'What you up to?' he said.

Madeleine ignored this interruption. Her steps increased to a dance, and her gestures became studied and formal. The expression of eyes and mouth suggested that she was counting. But it might also be interpreted as a mood of ecstasy. The lids drooped over those large brown eyes, heavy with the musical forethought controlling the dance.

'You happy again, then?'

Tom stood upright, hook and hone poised for stropping. He was indulgently surprised. He began to tap the beats of Madeleine's dance, using the hone on the blade. It did not matter that Madeleine again ignored him. He took the display in itself as a reply more cogent, more intimate, than anything the child could have said in words.

She bowed, and with a low sweep of an outstretched arm, scooped up a handful of the fallen weeds. It contained a golden head of marigold, which she selected and held between finger and thumb of the other hand.

The dance grew more formal, more solemn. The gnat-swarm joined it, pulsing and wreathing above the child's dark head, more evanescent than ever, by contrast with this miniature, temporary *religieuse*. For by now the dance suggested some form of worship, with Tom Small as devotee.

He said no more to her, but stood subdued and reverent.

This unforeseen ceremony might have developed further had there been no interruption from the world of every day. A car drove up, and the Moxons' daughter, with her husband, entered the garden.

'Look who's here!' exclaimed the woman. 'What's this, a jazz-session, Bert?'

Madeleine instantly froze. She was the shy, odd child again, who edged towards Tom Small, nervously grasped his trouser-leg, and placed herself half behind him, to scrutinize the intruders. The swarm of gnats retreated, rising like reproving angels to maintain their ritual unmolested.

'What's going on here?' said Bert, addressing himself to Tom Small and indicating the mounds of weeds. 'Feeding the pony on the cheap, mate?'

Tom looked at him, while groping behind to draw Madeleine closer with a protective arm.

'You anything to do with old Moxon?' he said.

The other man did not appreciate this counter-attack: 'What if we are? We don't want no gipsies trespassing.'

His wife spoke up: 'You're the little girl from up the farm, aren't you, dear?'

As Madeleine appeared to be stone-deaf, the woman addressed herself to Tom hurriedly, before her husband could attack again: 'Yes, I'm his daughter. You work here then? So you knew my father? Well, you'll be sorry to hear he passed away yesterday.'

She showed signs of distress, and her husband's aggressiveness withered into embarrassment.

'That's a fact,' he explained to Tom.

'Oh!' said Tom, thoughtfully. 'We were tidying up here for him.'

An awkward pause, during which Madeleine looked up at Tom, either puzzled or awe-stricken.

'Thank you very much,' said the bereaved daughter. 'Very good of you, I'm sure.'

Another silence, over which Prince Albert began to snort and finally to neigh. He was bored, and hated to be tethered.

At that moment, the Land-Rover returned, with Matthew, Anna and Shirley Kingdom. The Burbages entered the garden, followed by Shirley carrying the picnic-basket and a folding chair.'

'Good day,' said Matthew, nodding curtly at the couple whom he had not met before, though he had seen them about the place and knew who they were. He was reminded of the litter deposited by them and the rest of the Moxon family. They knew him too.

'You tell him, Bert,' said the woman, still handkerchief in hand.

'The old man's gone,' said Bert, addressing nobody in particular.

Anna instantly responded. She turned to Bert's wife: 'I am so sorry. I think they were happy here, though.'

'I don't know about that,' said Bert. 'We've

got to settle up his affairs, see?'

'Yes,' said Matthew drily. 'We've not been kept informed so far. Nobody has let us know how Moxon was doing, or about the operation. The bungalow was locked up too, and we could not get in.'

'That's our rights, isn't it?' said Bert. 'So long as the old people's furniture is there? Bad enough having these tied cottages; but we've got our rights even there. Some of you want to learn what's happening in the world. You're out-of-date, you are. Time you woke up.'

Moxon's son-in-law was working himself up into a magnificent indignation. Before he could open his political meeting, however, his wife intervened: 'Now stop it, Bert. If it's Mother you're thinking of, you can't expect her to come back here and look after herself. You've got to be practical. It was the lady here who offered to find her a place in one of those homes.'

'I don't remember doing so,' said Anna, 'but I'll be glad to help Mrs Moxon.'

'Oh, I don't mean you, dear. It was the little lady. Kimberley, wasn't her name? Lady Kimberley?'

'You must mean Lady Beverley. Why, did you meet her here?'

'That we did, the day we took Mother away.'

'Then it must have been you who locked

the house up. I came down again and found she had gone.'

Bert resented this.

'D'you expect us to leave the place open, for anybody to walk in and help themselves? Tied cottage or not tied, that's asking a bit much. Workers in the agricultural industry have been—'

'Bert, stop it, can't you? What I'm anxious to know is who's to look after Mother.'

This touch of realism defeated Bert. He stared at his wife in dismay, then spoke to her, dropping his voice a half-tone, as if he hoped not to be overheard by the rest of those present: 'Why, mate. You can't let the old girl go just like that. We've got a home for her, haven't we?'

The daughter looked from Anna to Shirley, appealing to their womanhood. Her reply was bleak with obstinacy, and a negative patience.

'Well, we won't talk about that here. I'm sure Mrs – er – Mrs–'

'Burbage,' said Anna. 'You may be sure that Lady Beverley will do more than she promised. Would you like me to ring her up at once?'

'Thank you very much, I'm sure, Mrs Burbage. So there you are, Bert, with all your politics. You've got to be human, after all.'

After this, it was simple to make Bert

realize that the Moxons' furniture could be removed without any political principles being abused. Shirley offered to send a lorry next day, free of charge, if Bert would be there to lend a hand. This was accepted, along with a week's wages from Matthew, and the bereaved couple drove away more in sorrow than in anger, after delivering the door-key to Tom Small, who undertook to be there next morning to help Bert shift the furniture.

4

For a few moments the picnic party stood as motionless as a group of statuary. Even Madeleine was still and silent. The sound of the departing car died away, and the only noticeable movement in the universe was the dance of the great swarm.

Matthew broke the spell: 'My God! I'm sorry for that chap! Did you notice the way his wife twisted the facts round? And she's the old woman's own daughter too!'

'Yes,' said Anna, 'but I wouldn't waste much sympathy on him. He's not the one who will have to do the nursing!'

'No, but he's shown a heart! And even to have that old Tartar in the house would be a penance!'

The two men turned to their work with

the bagging-hooks, and soon had the rest of the summer and autumn growth cut down and raked into a single pile. Tom hacked some dry dead wood out of the hedge and started a bonfire. Then he and Madeleine stood by, shaking the loose weeds over the fire, gradually covering it, reducing the flames to a column of smoke that rose straight up, solid as stone, over the roof of the bungalow, to spread into a sun-touched haze under the direction of the cool air wafting up from the river.

Anna and Shirley meanwhile went into the bungalow. It smelled greasy and all too human. The bedclothes on the iron frame were tossed as they had been left when old Mrs Moxon was taken away. No hand had touched the room since that day when Anna had come to tidy up. The grate was full of ashes, and water from a leaking kettle in the hearth had puddled some of the mess into a clot.

'Looks a bit old-fashioned!' said Shirley, wrinkling her freckled nose. 'How do people get a new place into this state? It's a proper slum.'

'Being shut up for a month or more makes it look worse. You know how it is, Shirley, when you've left the house for only a day or two. You come back and it's chilly, dusty, un-lived-in; even on a summer day. Something missing! I suppose it's our own warm selves.'

Shirley was thoughtful.

'It's what the women bring. Men are not the same. A place with only a man in it has just the same feeling: comfortless, grimy. A house wants a woman in it.'

'Well,' said Anna drily. 'It doesn't do to generalize. Mrs Moxon, for example. And I remember the women's quarters in the W.A.A.F. during the war. You'd be surprised, Shirley, at the filth and squalor some of those girls spread around them. I don't know whether it's a matter of character, or the way they've been brought up.'

'*I* know,' said Shirley bitterly. 'There are four womenfolk in my home, to keep Dad in order. Too many cooks spoil the broth there. He goes his own way. Only two of us keep the house going as I'd like it, my oldest sister and I. Joan's so good that she runs the whole family. Mother gave up years ago. You know what I mean? I'm not criticizing. But I think Dad has broken her spirit, he's so easy and hail-fellow-well-met. Prides himself on his good nature. Maybe he's quite right; but it makes the house like a railway station. It doesn't worry Joan. She can cope with it. The other two girls wouldn't know what I'm talking about. They take after Father. So I feel superfluous, especially as there's no lack of money. That's one thing about Dad! But why am I talking so much?'

188

Anna looked at her sympathetically. She saw that there was no need to be sorry for this vigorous, healthy girl, whose clean, forthright person seemed already to be dispelling the squalor of the Moxons' deserted home. She was aware of the contrast.

'I think when someone dies, Shirley, things die round them, don't you? The life of a room goes out too. Let's get out of doors again. I feel shivery. And it's time we had tea. Don't you feel the autumn suddenly? It must be getting late.'

She was right, for, when they returned to the garden, shadows had grown longer and deeper. A coppery haze lay behind the row of elms round the turn of the lane, and the sunlight was powdered with dust-motes.

'Come along! Tea!' cried Anna, while Shirley set the chair for her, and began to lay out the contents of the basket.

Matthew joined them at once, after wiping his blade on a bunch of grass. He stooped over his wife.

'Don't you get cold,' he said, and put his coat round her shoulders. 'Treacherous, so late in the year.'

'Is something happening, Matt?'

'I don't know, dear. Just evening coming on, maybe.'

'Perhaps it's that interior! To think of people living in that misery, when there's no need to. Moxon got a good wage.'

'Far more than he worked for!'

He shouted to Tom and Madeleine, who were still enslaved to the bonfire. Tom was about to come, when one side of the heap tumbled, and flames burst out of the cavity, their fierceness showing that daylight was already on the decline.

'Tom! Come back! Come back!' cried Madeleine. 'It's tumbled down and will go out.'

'How on earth did she learn that?' said Matthew.

Shirley laughed, still busy with the flasks and mugs: 'Ha! That'll be Tom's teaching. Anything to do with nature – birds, and beasts and the elements!'

Matthew bit into a paste-sandwich, and mumbled something.

Tom immediately obeyed the imperious little outcry from Madeleine, who was battling with the fallen debris from the bonfire. He snatched up his fork and lifted the slimy mass of sweating weeds back, padding it down and adding more, to make a firm mound from which the smoke poured, both fragrant and acrid. The column was now less firm. It shuddered in the cooling air as the sun began to sink beyond the orchard and the new saplings, at the other end of the farm. Its top was teased out and flattened. Shreds of the smoke blew down across the garden, adding incense to the picnic ceremony.

'Come along, sweetheart,' called Shirley. 'We shall eat everything up if you don't come.'

Tom was already trudging over to the party, but Madeleine, ignoring Shirley's summons, ran after him, seized him by the hand and tried to drag him back. While struggling with him, she turned her head and shouted rudely to Shirley, 'I don't want any. You can eat the lot!'

Anna was upset. She set down her mug and tried to get out of the folding chair, but Shirley restrained her.

'Don't worry,' she whispered in Anna's ear. 'It's that Tom. She won't part with him. But she'll get used to it.'

Anna ignored this, and appealed to her husband, 'Matt! *Do* something!'

Before he could obey, however, Tom Small lifted the child in his arms, took the rake which she was brandishing so dangerously, and joined the party. He sat down on the kerb by the path, with Madeleine between his knees.

'Now I'd like a cup of tea,' he said to her. She at once jumped up to get it. At the same moment Shirley approached with a mug in her hand to pass it to him. Madeleine cried out, 'No! Me! Me!' and struck the mug out of Shirley's hand. The hot tea splashed over Shirley's stocking, and she cried out, 'Oh, you little demon!' half seriously, half in mock anger.

Matthew had seen the incident, and was furious. 'Get out!' he cried. 'Get out! Go away, we don't want savages here!'

Madeleine stared at the result of her crime, her large brown eyes dilated with an exultant curiosity rather than fear. She appeared not to hear her father, for she was freezing into a cold hatred as she watched Tom snatch a handkerchief from his pocket and stoop to wipe Shirley's leg. Shirley by now was leaning over Tom with her hands on his shoulders and laughing happily.

Madeleine jerked herself round with a violent gesture, and flew down the garden, and out of the gate. They heard her untether Prince Albert, who greeted her with a snickering half-neigh. They heard his hooves clatter on the grit lane, as Madeleine urged him to a gallop up the road to the farm-house.

'Oh, dear, what have I done now?' cried Shirley.

'Done?' said Matthew, 'It's jolly decent of you, Shirley. That little devil!'

'No, Matt. Don't say that,' said Anna. 'It's not so simple. I must go after her; we don't know what she's suffering. I'm not excusing her, but she can't be left alone.'

'Nonsense, my dear girl. She's been a little beast and knows it. An hour in Coventry will give her a chance to think it over. I bet when we get back she'll be as sweet as pie.'

'She's a passionate little thing,' said Shirley. 'Would it do any good if I went up?'

'Certainly not!' cried Matthew, who was still angry and ashamed. 'Forget it! And, Anna, *please* let it go. Let's finish our tea, and we'll keep some to take back to her in half an hour's time. She'll be knocking about the house or the stable, with that saintly pony!'

Anna was only half persuaded, and the peaceful mood of the picnic party was ruined. All four ate and drank in silence, and hurriedly, so that the basket could be repacked and a reasonable departure made.

Shirley devoted herself to Anna, and Tom ignored her. The situation was too complicated for him, and he was not prepared to blame Madeleine. When they left, to return to the house in the Land-Rover, he saw them to the gate, then returned to the company and counsel of the bonfire. He stood there, tending it, as the smoke grew pallid, and the interior crackling heightened. The sun dropped down, and was swallowed up in a ruinous mass of leaden cloud, the first seen for weeks. A wind stirred the elm trees, making their dry foliage rattle.

The temperature dropped sharply, and Tom felt the draught of the air coming into the bonfire. It struck cold to his back, making the heat at his front acceptable. He stood with the fork stuck in the ground beside him, both hands stretched to the warmth. A tongue of flame flickered out and lighted up the thoughtful figure, outlining the furrows in his forehead, and the dogged uncertainty in his eyes.

The clouds rose higher, and so did the wind. From the rattling elms there drifted the cry of an owl. A change of weather was threatening the overlong summer.

5

Tom Small stood in this equilibrium of mental struggle, while twilight gathered round. The squalid bungalow, the neglected garden, thus veiled, became part of the vague beauty of their surroundings. A quarter of an hour after the picnic party had left Tom alone, the bank of cloud rode up the sky, blotted out the evening star, and hastened the fall of darkness.

Tom was still watching the bonfire when Shirley's car stopped, and she came hurrying into the garden. She found him motionless, fork in hand, staring into the mound from which white-hot gleams here and there lit up his figure as from miniature windows. But she was agitated, and did not pause to consider such a picture.

'Tom! Tom! Madeleine isn't there—'

He sprang to life.

'What? But she must be. She can't get away from the farm without passing here. I should have heard her. But is the pony missing too?'

'Yes. There's no sign of either of them having gone home.'

He put on his coat, and set down the fork by the front door.

'Then she may have got out. Prince Albert would take that layered hedge down below, where we've sown the oats.'

'Yes, but where would she make for, Tom?'

'I don't know, girl. But nothing must happen to her, see? Nothing must happen!'

For a moment he was lost in panic. He stood clasping his hands and shivering in the night air.

'Look, Shirley; have you got a torch in the car? No? Then drive me down to my lodgings. I've got one in my shed. We can't let anything happen, Shirley! Why did he frighten her like that? The Boss, I mean.'

'It's only when you're around, Tom. Just as though he's jealous and wants to remind her who is her father.'

Tom looked at her angrily as they hurried down the path.

'What's that?' he said, refusing to understand. But Shirley was afraid to repeat her accusation. She was still unsure of him. Her flash of insight was followed by bewilderment. Only her good nature, warm and sensual, saved her from resentment. It made her wise enough to say nothing while she drove down to the main road and along to the coastguard cottage. By this time darkness was almost total, with the wind increasing from fitfulness. Only a smell of the warm earth survived as a reminder of the belated summer day.

Shirley drew up by the heap of ballast off the road, opposite the cottages.

'Look, Tom! Look!' She pointed to Prince Albert, tethered to a gate-post in the hedge behind the stones. 'What does it mean?' She was frightened now. 'She hasn't gone down to the river, Tom? She can't have!'

He did not answer. He was out of the car and running up the garden and round the side of the cottages. Shirley switched off the car lights and followed him. She saw his dim figure racing up the garden to the shed.

They stood side by side, while he called softly, 'Maddy! Where are you, Madeleine?'

Only the wind answered, rattling the hard leaves of the pear tree overhanging the shed.

'I'll get the torch,' said Tom. He unlocked the door, went in, struck a match, lit first a candle and then the mantle-lamp.

The torch was on the bench under the window.

'Tom! What's happened?'

Shirley pointed to the broken window-pane, and the broken toys. A hand had come through the window and smashed the bedstead, sofa and chairs. They were beyond repair.

Tom stood at the bench, with his back to her, his head sunk in his shoulders. He picked up one fragment after another, putting each down again gently. He seemed to be awe-stricken.

Then he went over to the still unfinished doll's house, out of sight of the window. It stood with its front wall opened, all the tiny rooms exposed. He gravely shut the front, and stood for a moment contemplating the little house.

'That's not like you, Maddy,' he said quietly, speaking to himself.

'Tom, she's cut herself,' said Shirley. 'On the glass.'

A few drops of blood on the bench were still wet. The cut must have been made while she was at work. But it had not frightened her, or deflected her from her purpose.

Tom picked up the torch.

'You staying here?' he asked, staring at Shirley with blind eyes.

'Don't be a fool, Tom. I've got no feelings. We must find the kid, that's all. She can't be far away.'

She followed him out of the hut, and the

wind buffeted them both. The candle was blown out as the door swung back, and the flame of the lamp shot up in a glare of red smoke. Shirley ran back and turned down the flame, leaving half the mantle sooty.

'I'm coming, Tom,' said Shirley. He had disappeared behind the shed, and she groped her way after him. At the foot of the pear tree lay Madeleine, sound asleep from exhaustion after the outburst.

Tom stood over the tiny figure, diverting the beam of the torch so that it should not startle her.

'All that time, Shirley,' he said, his voice hushed by sadness. 'Ever since her father drove her out. What's she been doing, eh?'

Shirley meanwhile picked up the sleeping child and pointed to the scratch on her arm.

'Nasty, Tom. We must clean that up before we take her home. Go into the old woman and I'll bring Madeleine down. We want hot water.'

Tom took the child from her. 'I'll carry her,' he said. 'If she wakes up–!' He nodded his head.

'Look, Shirley,' – as she followed, steadying him with a hand on his arm, and holding the torch in the other – 'you've taken it properly, properly. There's none to blame maybe. But he shouldn't have driven her to it, Shirley.'

'I'm thinking of Anna, and in her

condition too,' said Shirley. She was more sure of herself now, and of her victory. 'We must stop her worrying.'

'I meant them for Christmas, the house and the furniture. But I'll have to start again now. It'll be for her birthday; I work that *slow.*'

'But why did she do it, Tom? Little devil, with that temper!'

'Don't you ask; don't you question it, see? She's got her reasons maybe, and we ought to know, you and me!'

'Whatever are you talking about, man? A baby like that? You shouldn't harbour such thoughts! You make me feel ashamed of you – ashamed of myself too. I never heard such nonsense.'

She shook his arm so angrily that the child stirred, moaned, and in half-waking moved in Tom's arms consciously and put up an arm, to clasp the flesh of his neck in her fist.

'Easy now, Shirley, you're fretting her. Don't you say things like that. Leave it alone, see?'

'But where do I stand? I've got a right now, after what we've had together.'

He did not question that, because they had reached the back door of the cottage.

Mrs Weston greeted them: 'What's going on up there? I heard something a while back, and thought it was cats; but I didn't venture out. What is it, Tom? Who you got there? Somebody hurt, or – why, it's the little Burbage girl.'

'A bowl of boiled water,' said Shirley. 'She's scratched her arm on something, and it may have been a rusty wire.'

Tom looked at her swiftly, gratefully, knowing she had entered a conspiracy of silence with him. He sat down inside, between the door and the sink, with Madeleine on his knees. She woke, fretfully, and looked around her.

'Where's Prince Albert?' she demanded. 'I rode here; nobody at home. I wanted to find you, Tom.'

'But I was with you at the bonfire, Maddy!'

She frowned, confused by facts.

'No, you left me. I lost you there, Tom, at teatime. You went away, didn't you?'

'No, Maddy. It was you who went. You rode off on Prince Albert. I thought you'd gone home, so I went back to the bonfire and piled it up for the night. We'll go and see tomorrow.'

She could not understand, and sat upright on his knee, puzzling this thing out. Then Shirley appeared, with a towel and the basin of water. Madeleine instantly turned in to Tom and hid her face in his coat. He felt her draw her whole body into a knot when Shirley tried to take her hand and sponge the scratch, where the blood had congealed in a long line of red cord.

'No use,' said Shirley in despair. 'I can't do a thing right. Here, Mrs Weston, you try.'

The old woman meekly took the bowl and sponge, and the child submitted without a murmur. As she worked, Mrs Weston muttered something about nursing, and her experience as a midwife.

'You don't have to fuss them,' she said. 'There, duck; no harm done. I'll put a wind of lint round it, case it breaks out again. Whatever was you up to, you young limb? Past your bedtime, too!'

Tom still ignored Shirley's distress. He had only one concern: 'Must get her back. You drive her up, my dear, and I'll bring the pony.'

But Madeleine would not have this. She clung to him savagely, too desperate even to cry.

'Oh, well,' said Shirley. 'You'd better humour her. I'm thinking of Anna. I'll drive on and tell them she's safe. You can bring her up on the pony. That may calm her down. Another few minutes out of bed won't matter after all this.'

She went off. Madeleine immediately became reasonable. She thanked Mrs Weston and trotted off with Tom.

'It's dark,' she said. 'Where's the moon? Is it behind the wind?'

'Aye, that must be it,' he replied, marvelling at her indifference to recent events. The torchlight made a moving circle down the path in front of them, and led them out to the road and the lay-by where Prince Albert awaited them. He gave them his usual snuffling welcome, a faithful sound, patient and unquestioning.

When Tom lifted Madeleine on to the saddle, Prince Albert turned and made his way homeward to 'Doggetts', with Tom walking slowly beside him, and the fairy of torchlight mopping and mowing in front, as though moving backwards, making obeisances on the way.

Tom glanced from time to time at the little figure, as it moved so demurely to the rhythm of Prince Albert's gait. He put a hand on the back of the saddle, and felt the pressure of the child's buttocks on his knuckles.

'Are you there, Tom?'

She was half asleep again, her words dissolved in drowsiness.

'Yes, I'm here, Maddy.'

Tom spoke from a great depth of gratitude. He did not understand; but he could recognize his fortune. 'How did you know about that furniture?' he ventured. 'I never told you about that job, Maddy.'

'I always know, Tom. I know about you beforehand.'

'Heigh, girl! What's that? You monkey!

Don't you say things like that to me.'

'But you asked me, Tom.'

He was nonplussed; but the gratitude remained, and it was touched with wonder, a religious wonder.

Prince Albert missed a step, or trod on a stone. Madeleine was jerked forward, and Tom's hand instantly grasped her by the small of the back. The touch gave him an index to his emotion.

'Why, Maddy, you're a funny one!'

His voice was husky, almost broken.

'That was Prince,' she said; 'I wish I could ride him all night. If I did, where would we be tomorrow morning?'

He thought about this seriously, glad to escape from the intensity of his feelings.

'You got to get over the bridge,' he said. 'Then it depends where you want to go.'

'Oh, it's where Prince Albert wants to go. He knows everything, Tom. That's why you gave him to me, isn't it?'

His mind hurried past this metaphysical suggestion.

'Well, I reckon he'd turn southwards, Maddy, away from roads, and buildings. He'd take you into the hills.'

'That's where you were born, Tom.'

'So it is, Maddy, so it is. I hadn't thought of that.'

'I did, Tom. I think of everything you've told me; and you told me Tunstall was up there in the hills. We could go there one day, couldn't we, like this, you and I and Prince Albert: nobody else.'

That last qualification was made with great emphasis, each word punctuated by an admonitory shake of the head.

Tom was lost in confusion. He half resented the claim, and the guilt it woke in him. He could not speak, and the small cavalcade moved on in silence to 'Doggetts'. When they reached the house, Madeleine was asleep, held limply upright by Tom's left hand.

Anna came hurrying out, but was forestalled by Matthew, who put out an arm to prevent her from lifting Madeleine down.

'She's too heavy,' he ordered. 'Let me.'

He thanked Tom severely, and carried the child indoors.

'Oh, Tom, how did you know where she was?' Anna was weeping. 'I imagined all sorts of dreadful things.'

'I don't rightly know,' said Tom. 'That's just about it. I don't rightly know. It works that way, I suppose.'

'What does, Tom; what does?'

She was so eager that she clasped his hand on Prince Albert's bridle.

He shook his head. He was quite at a loss.

'Better get the pony bedded down,' he said. 'And you've no need to fret, Missus Burbage. She's come to no harm, beyond a scratch, and old Ma Weston bound that up. I'll get along now. Good night.'

He led Prince Albert away to the stable, and Anna saw them both disappear. Only the circle of light from the torch flickered along the flagstones. She waited until he switched on the light in the stable. Then she went indoors, surprised by her own calmness after the recent search and alarm.

6

Shirley came to the stable while Tom was feeding Prince Albert. She found him about to hang up the saddle and harness. He held the small accoutrements and fondled the leather. The action irritated Shirley.

'What's that for?' she demanded.

He looked up, like a sleep-walker.

'Eh?'

'Why are you cuddling that saddle? Can't you forget it?'

'I don't know what you mean, girl.'

'I don't really know, either.'

She hesitated, turned away, and savagely plucked out a handful of hay from the rack above Prince Albert's head. She offered it to him, and he turned his head to study her with interest. His big eyes shone with an oily gleam, reflecting the light of the naked electric bulb. Then he took the hay, wrinkling up his lips and showing his teeth.

'He likes me more than his mistress does.' She repeated the bribery, while Tom hung up the saddle and turned to watch her. 'More than you do, maybe,' she added.

She put up her hand to pull another tuft of hay, but Tom seized her arm and made her face him.

'You women aren't fair. That's what it is!"

Shirley regained confidence.

'I don't know about that. There's been plenty of provocation, Tom. Did you ask her why she did it? Did she tell you?'

He shook his head.

'That's not it. She's true enough, Shirley. She hasn't changed all this time. Since I came here when she was new-born, she's been that way.'

'What way?'

He evaded this, shaking his head sadly, like a man defeated.

'What I mean is, you want to push on so fast, Shirley. I don't know what this means, see? You come along, and that little 'un straightaway turns to this devilment, obstinate like. What have we done that she understands, and hates us for?'

Shirley looked angry, but she did not release herself. Indeed, she pressed against him defiantly. 'That's what I want you to answer. It's your responsibility, Tom. You've got the kid worked up in some way. I don't understand it. I'm a fool, I expect. But I'm straightforward, and I've been straight with you. I love you, and that's natural, isn't it?'

Suddenly she began to weep, and as suddenly stopped herself. Her tears turned to caresses, and she pressed her lips to the side of his neck, murmuring, 'Tom! Tom! You know that! I don't care what happens, so long as you know that. And don't you care too? Weren't you happy that first night, down by the river, and all the others?'

He forced her back, and she stood against the manger, close to the pony's head.

'I told you, Shirley. I told you all that. And I know you better after tonight, the way you took that bit of trouble. But things aren't that simple. That's what it is. They don't seem to add up.'

Shirley contemplated him more calmly.

'I know what it is, Tom. You want kids of your own. I'm ready for that too, when we're married. I'm not flighty, though you thought I was, didn't you? I'll bring that up against you one of these days.'

This did not dispel his dilemma. He stared blankly past her at the manger, and did not see Prince Albert lean towards her and snuggle his nose under her breast and armpit.

'Now, greedy!' she said, releasing herself from the pony's embrace and plucking another handful to offer him. 'You're all alike, you men.'

She had been out of her depth, and wanted to get back to security. 'Do I sound coarse? Do I shock you, Tom?'

Prince Albert had dragged her cardigan, and exposed her shoulder. Tom's reply was to stoop and rub his chin over the smooth skin. She flinched.

'For God's sake, Tom! Wait a bit. Get me away from here first.'

He stepped back to let her move. Prince Albert looked round, ready to say something; but lacking the equipment, he fluffed and huffed and whinnied a little, making that do as an accusation of some kind, to suggest that his friends were deserting him.

'He seems to understand, anyway. Prince Albert,' said Shirley, as she pressed the starter-button of the sports car. Tom said nothing all the way back to the coastguard cottages.

'If I left the car here all night would it give the game away?'

Shirley said this as she leaned across Tom to open the near side door, though he could have stepped over it. The wind was now fitful, and the young woman put up a hand to control her hair, which was blowing up and over her face. The other hand went to Tom's chin, to detain him while she sought his mouth with hers.

'Tom! What have you done to me, to make

me love you like this? I've never known it before. It was just fun before. Don't you see? I'm desperate; I'm not a jealous person. I've no right to be. But I could easily be, Tom. I could, and I don't know why. It's not just ordinary–'

He broke away impatiently, imprisoning her hand and forcing it back against her breast.

'Don't you say things you'll regret,' he said roughly. 'I don't break faith with people, man or woman. That's how I'm made. I've got few friends, but the Boss and his wife are among them.'

Shirley bent her head and kissed the hand that still pressed hers away from him.

'And the child too?' she whispered, venturing rashly. 'You're her slave too, aren't you?'

He released her, and leaned back, staring up at the noisy branches of the elm tree above the lay-by. A flurry of leaves touched his face, and settled in the car and over Shirley's hair and dress. But he did not notice this impersonal caress.

'Tom! What is it?' She was alarmed at the result of her bluntness.

'I was thinking,' he responded slowly. 'I haven't reckoned to be any man's slave, Shirley. I've got my skill and I can work where I like. No, I can't be called a slave.'

'But you haven't explained about the

child. You always evade it.'

'But there's nothing, girl, nothing! I don't understand you. We all have our feelings, don't we? And where's the harm? You've got yours, and I don't understand that either. What d'you see in a chap like me, old enough to be your–'

She stopped him passionately, seizing him by the shoulders and shaking him. 'Oh, you fool! Don't I know you then? You're not so old that way. You don't fail a woman. No, it's I am the fool, to have gone so far. But I don't care, Tom! Tom darling, I don't care a damn. I can give you a child, whether we're married or not. And it'll really be yours, this one: not just a fairy, fancy thing. It'll be your flesh and blood. Do be real, Tom; do be sensible.'

'You don't mean–?' he said.

'No, but I'm ready to. That's where I stand. I want you, and kids of my own, *our* own. And a home away from all that extravagant mess at Sittingbourne. A steady man, see, instead of Father. I'm too like him, and I don't trust myself. Look where it's leading him – and I want to get away from it, since I've known you, Tom.'

A shower of leaves, mysterious in the darkness, rattled down like tinsel, driven by the increasing wind. A few drops of rain fell too.

'You'd better have the hood up,' said Tom.

He spoke tenderly now. He was still at a loss; but her confession had shaken him.

They put the hood up together. Then Tom reached over for her woolly coat and put it round her shoulders. Before she thrust her bare arms into the sleeves, however, she drew him to her, where they still sat side by side, and he no longer resisted.

'Tom, shall we risk it?'

'What, the car being seen in the morning?'

'If you like: and the other as well. I'm ready, Tom. I trust you, though I don't understand you.'

'Drive down to the river, where we went that first night, Shirley. There's none about there; and there won't be with the night turning rough.'

7

Madeleine was neither repentant nor unrepentant. For a week after the outbreak, Tom watched her shyly, waiting for a sign. He wondered if she had confessed to her parents, and he was relieved to see no signs of that either.

Work for him and school for Madeleine kept them apart. And the break in the weather added to the unintentional estrangement. Wind and rain, with a savage drop in temperature, brought late autumn thundering over Sheppey. Overnight in mid-week, the trees were half-stripped of their green leaves, and roads, paths, fields and woodlands lay carpeted ankle-deep in foliage whose colour changed almost hourly under the rough chemistry: all autumn in a day.

Tom and Madeleine met only in the afternoons, at the midday meal in the kitchen, or in Prince Albert's stable. The pony missed his freedom and exercise and was restive in the stall. One day he nipped Tom's arm while being groomed.

Madeleine was looking on, and saw the bared teeth and Tom's spasm of pain.

'Oh, wicked! You wicked Prince!' she cried. Something was released, and the shyness vanished. She turned to Tom and seized the bruised arm with her small hands. She examined the marks of Prince Albert's teeth, then put her lips to them, sucking and murmuring at the same time.

Prince Albert looked on, amused but demure again. Then he turned back to the feed of oats which Madeleine had recently tipped into the trough.

Tom sat on the stool, looking down on the neat little head bent over his arm. He felt the wet warmth of the succouring lips. And deeper down, he felt the strange, half-terrifying stirrings of the devotion which had lifted up his life since he first came to 'Doggetts'.

Outside, the wind whistled round the stable eaves and flung up straws and wisps of hay above the floor. The upper half of the door crashed home and half the dim afternoon light was cut off. Still Madeleine clung to Tom's arm, now with a touch of fierceness.

The stable grew lighter. Matthew had opened the door, and stood watching this strange little scene.

'What's going on?' he said.

Madeleine spoke first, but was unintelligible because her mouth was still covering the bruise on Tom's arm.

'Easy now, lass,' said Tom. 'He's done no harm.'

He looked up at Matthew, and nodded confidentially, indicating the child.

'Her pony wants a job of work, Boss. He's fancying himself, with nothing to do here. Just nipped my arm, he has: pure devilment.'

Matthew listened to this without conviction. He took hold of his daughter and lifted her in his arms, away from her ministrations to Tom Small's mahogany-coloured forearm. He shook her, half playfully, half angrily.

'Look, young woman. Just you take him off and exercise him. A bit of fresh air will do you good, both of you. Saddle him up, Tom. And then you get along, Maddy. Ride him round the top meadows under the wood. You'll get the breeze there.'

His boisterous mood was accepted by Madeleine without question, but Tom turned dogged, as though resenting something implied in Matthew's pose of heartiness. He saddled the pony, led him out into the yard, and stood there waiting, indifferent to Prince Albert's head-tossing and other signs of eagerness.

Matthew carried Madeleine out and dumped her heavily on the saddle.

'Daddy, that's rude. You should let me mount properly.'

'Well, for once you can drop ceremony. Just get along; I'm busy and want Tom's help.'

'But aren't you coming with me, Tom?'

Matthew slapped Prince Albert's rump, and the indignant pony moved off more slowly than he wanted to, as a protest against this offence to his dignity.

'Go on! Get away with you. And don't come back for an hour.'

She moved off, turning in the saddle to have the last word: 'How shall I know without a watch? Tom, you must come and find me in an hour's time.'

The two men watched her leave the yard, and heard the clatter of Prince Albert's hooves cease suddenly as pony and rider left the cobbles and entered the field beside the orchard.

'That sounds soft,' said Tom. 'I've just been grooming him too. He'll come back spattered all over.'

'Good job we've got our ploughing done,' said Matthew. 'Nothing but rain ever since. We're paying for a good summer.'

They stood irresolute. Matthew was struggling with something which he distrusted himself to say. He decided against it, and turned instead to more tangible matters. Tom at once dropped his air of dogged defensiveness.

'Look, Tom. I didn't want to discuss it in front of the child, for I don't know how things stand. But Anna and I have been talking about the Moxons' bungalow. The point is, if you want to marry, you're welcome to it. I'd take on another chap who could have your lodgings with old Mrs Weston.'

Tom looked past him, and up at the tumbling clouds. Then he busied himself with rolling a cigarette. His lips were pursed in sympathy with the nicety of the job. He said nothing.

'It's that way with Shirley, isn't it? So Anna tells me.' Matthew was anxious to help him. 'Of course, we'd have to redecorate, though Moxon wasn't there long. They've made a pigsty of the place, but we can soon remedy that. It's got everything for a married couple. The fact is, Anna has taken a liking to Shirley Kingdom and would welcome her as a neighbour.'

Tom lifted an eyebrow: 'I've nothing against her, either.'

Matthew was irritated by this indecision: 'Well, what are you dithering about? Is it that father of hers, and the trouble with the police?'

It was a lucky hit that stirred Tom at once. 'I don't worry about him. No, I don't! If she's in for trouble of that sort, I'd stand by her no matter what. She's sound enough, Shirley. A good girl, that.'

Matthew plunged: 'There isn't another girl in mind, Tom?'

Tom walked away for a few paces, then turned back and spoke almost threateningly at his employer: 'Look here, Boss. I've been with you for a long time, "Doggetts" means something to me. We've got it into good shape together, and we don't owe anything to old Moxon for that. But I don't reckon to talk about my feelings, see? I've got my feelings, but that's my affair. I don't talk about it. Maybe that's why I've not married sooner.'

Matthew, equally shy and inexpressive about such matters, tried to bridge the gap; but the effort made him stammer, and brought the blood flushing to his already well-filled cheeks.

'I'm not pushing you, Tom. We've been

good friends all along, and you're not an easy chap to understand. You say so yourself. It's not my idea. But it's obvious you lead a lonely life – Anna says so. That may be why you concentrate on–'

But he dared to say no more. Tom looked dangerous. Like most reticent people, he was capable of threatening latent power.

At that moment of deadlock, Anna appeared across the yard at the kitchen door, followed by Mr Kingdom, Shirley's father. The couple walked towards the two men, Kingdom talking volubly and gesticulating.

'Well, Tom,' said Anna, by way of greeting. She saw at once the position, or the lack of it.

Tom nodded to her curtly, and at Kingdom who was still almost a stranger to him. The older man eyed him.

'Oh, so you're the boy, are you? You got on well since we first met, eh?'

This was not calculated to tame Tom Small, and he might have escaped had not Anna touched him with kindness.

'Has Matthew mentioned the bungalow, Tom? I know what Shirley thinks about it. She'd be happy there, and I'd love to have her there.'

'That's about it, son,' said Kingdom. 'I didn't reckon to lose my girl. She's a good hand in the business is Shirley: strong and can hold her own, without being rough like.

But I don't stand in her way. If that's what she wants, let her have it, I say. So does her mother.'

The last was added as an afterthought. Tom and Matthew were still mere spectators, maybe glad to be relieved.

Anna took over: 'Mr Kingdom does building work too, and he has offered to decorate the bungalow.'

'That's right. It'll be my wedding-present. Make a proper love-nest of it, and fill the kitchen with gadgets. A young woman wants all those things nowadays. No need to be a slave to the sink. I'll put my chaps on to the job straight away, and be glad to.' He clapped Tom on the back. 'Better get Shirley up, to say what she wants done, eh?' He wheezed with sly laughter, and Tom stepped back as though to get out of the range of this familiarity. 'Be a good excuse, eh, lad?'

Tom realized suddenly that he had not seen Shirley since that stormy night of reckless abandonment down by the river. He had been wholly concerned with the possible consequences of Madeleine's outbreak. But there had been no consequences, and he could turn with relief to the offers now being made by the Burbages and Shirley's father. He was not averse to a home of his own. And looking at it that way, he was likely to be content with the young woman too.

Waking from this short daydream, he turned away to look up the slope, and saw Madeleine standing in the saddle, and Prince Albert galloping in miniature fury over the top field, rounding up the herd into the shade cast by the copse. He walked away without another word.

'Well, I'll be damned,' said Mr Kingdom. 'What d'you make of that, Mrs Burbage? I'd better send the girl up, to sort him out a bit. It's her choice. Takes all sorts to make a world, eh?'

8

Autumn stormed savagely into early winter, and by mid-November some of the lowest ground by the river was waterlogged. Between the furrows of ploughed land left fallow, long ribbons of steel-blue water reflected the clouds.

The relationship between Shirley Kingdom and Tom Small became publicly accepted, so far as they had a public. Tom, however, had not consented to visit her home, and was still a stranger to her mother and three sisters. She showed no eagerness to introduce them, though one Saturday afternoon she called for Tom at the coastguard cottage, and presented her eldest sister, Joan, who sat rather drably in the back of the sports car. They drove into Sittingbourne for tea at a cake-shop, but stopped to look over the bungalow and plan the re-decoration.

Although it had been empty since Moxon died, it did not smell damp. Rain had blown in at a metal casement left on the latch, but so had the cleansing air. The living-room was fresh. A good fire in the rusting grate would quickly make things cosy.

Joan Kingdom, at first shy of Tom, soon took to him. Her silences matched his, and they understood each other. She was some years older than Shirley, but the two women shared a family likeness and in an un-demonstrative way were good friends. They shared also a liking for a tidy house with everything well run. Joan, even in her physical appearance, had evidently resigned herself to fighting a losing battle at home. If she ever had anything like Shirley's vigour and heartiness, it had long since dwindled away into patient resignation. She wore spectacles, and that made her look older still.

They stood about in the empty rooms. The Saturday sounds of the outside world hardly penetrated the silence and hollow-ness. A quiet drizzle, the aftermath of another windy night, kept up a hushing sound, close to the windows and down the chimney. It did not detract from the latent cheerfulness of the modern building.

'Dry as a bone,' said Shirley, looking hopefully at Tom. 'We'll make it nice, Tom. You won't know yourself once we're settled in.'

'When's that to be?' asked Joan. She had a wry outlook on the play of circumstances.

'There's nothing to stop us,' said Shirley.

Joan looked sad. 'No, I suppose not. But I'll miss you, Shirley. Thank goodness that business with the police has blown over.'

'How long ago is it?' asked Tom. 'Six or seven weeks now, eh? But I reckon they're in no hurry.'

'What d'you mean?' said Joan. 'You don't like it?'

'Who would like it?' Shirley demanded. She wanted to protect Tom from so direct an inquiry. Assured now of the greater issue of her relationship with him, she reckoned to condone his minor reluctances.

'Well, there's no need to worry,' said Joan. 'That business at Margate! They agreed that Dad's lorry had been taken without his knowledge, and that's the end of it.'

'It's like Dad not to tell us,' said Shirley. 'I don't suppose he's given it a thought, my dear. That's what he's like, Tom. He'll never grow up.'

Tom was in a genial mood, and this good news increased it. He entered into the discussion about colour-schemes, and even looked grateful when Shirley suggested that

221

he would need a workshop of his own behind the bungalow.

'No room indoors for you to do your carpentry,' she said. 'You know, Tom dear, it'll be like your shed; only it'll be your own.'

'What a pair,' added Joan. 'But shouldn't we get along? Oh, look!' She had gone into the kitchen. 'Dad's men have already got their clobber here.'

They joined her, and stared at stepladders, tubs of distemper, planks powdery with whitewash, jars full of brushes.

'Something happening at last!' said Shirley.

The thought made her so happy that, ignoring Joan's presence, she planted a kiss on Tom's leathery neck, and hung on to his arm, beaming with ecstasy: 'Oh, Tom darling!'

He took it coolly, and led the way out to the recently dug garden, the scene of that picnic on the day when the weather broke.

'That's another cloud lifted,' she said to him, as they drove down the lane to the public road to Sittingbourne.

The relief affected Tom by making him expansive. He even consented to look at window displays in the furniture shops, though as a craftsman he had some scathing things to say about the factory-made suites and bedsteads.

'If I'm settling down for the rest of my

life,' he confided to Joan, 'I'd like to make my own home. It might be rough but it would last.'

'And be cheaper,' said Joan. She studied him fondly, having taken his remark as the sign of a steady character who would be a good husband to her sister.

'You're not Robinson Crusoe, Tom,' said Shirley. She laughed and shook him by the arm: 'It would take years. Why, how long did you spend on that toy furniture that kid–'

She stopped abruptly. Tom had snatched his arm away as though stung by a wasp.

'What's that...?' said Joan. But her curiosity was swept aside by a new interest.

The Burbages overtook them, and stopped.

'Ah!' said Matthew. 'Beginning to line the nest, Tom?' He had been more friendly towards Tom since the marriage with Shirley was openly talked of.

'He says he wants to make his own furniture!' said Shirley, who had been congratulating herself on being stopped in time from spoiling the conspiracy of silence about Madeleine's outbreak. But she was frightened by the reappearance of the spectre as Tom shrank from her. Her teasing words were meant to cover that fear.

'I didn't know they taught him carpentry in the Sappers,' said Matthew. 'Well, we're going into the shop, aren't we, Anna? The old pram has stood around in the sheds for so long that it's become a hen-roost. We've got to buy a new one. Moral, Shirley! Don't leave too wide a gap each time!'

Shirley purred, but Anna, already conscious of her bulk, was embarrassed by Matthew's remarks.

'We'd better get along, Matthew,' she said coolly. Then she explained to Joan Kingdom: 'We've had to leave our little girl on her own. She refused to come into Sittingbourne. Her pony, according to her, hasn't been well, and she insists on nursing him. We can't see anything wrong. But it doesn't do to cross her where Prince Albert is concerned, does it, Tom? He's the centre of her world.'

'She's a spoilt little brat,' said Matthew. 'I'd have dragged her here by the hairs of her head if I had my way. But fathers don't count!'

With that he convoyed Anna through the dangers of the swing-doors. For a moment Tom stood frowning. Shirley watched him, in such a way as to try to conceal her vigilance from Joan.

'Coming, dear?' she said.

'That's a funny way to talk of young Maddy,' said Tom, half to himself. Joan heard this, however, and was amused by his obtuseness.

'Why, that was fond enough, Tom. That

was an anxious father talking.'

Tom looked at her with suspicion. Then, he relented, stepped between the two sisters, and moved off with them.

During the following week Matthew Burbage went away with Lady Beverley to a cattle-show in Hampshire, and Tom was left in charge of 'Doggetts'. The days were short and he was too busy to look in at the bungalow to inspect the work in progress. Shirley came up on the Wednesday afternoon and reported that nothing had been done as all the workmen had been called to a rush job in Gravesend. She said her father had promised to make a start next week.

'Well, that's all right, Shirley; we don't need to fret.' He said this in front of Madeleine, who was helping him slice up mangolds in the barn, when Shirley arrived. 'You don't seem very eager,' she said, mortified by his lack of enthusiasm, and also by observing that he always showed this lack when Madeleine was present. She turned to the child, almost angrily: 'He doesn't, does he, Madeleine? If you were getting married, wouldn't you be eager?'

Madeleine's brown eyes studied her impersonally. 'It depends–' they then contemplated Tom '–who I was marrying.'

'Don't you talk that way,' said Tom, twirling the wheel of the cutter noisily. 'You don't need to talk about marrying, Maddy.

That's for grown-up folk.'

Madeleine was contemptuous. She tossed two turnips into the trough of the cutter. She might have been a *sans-culotte* attending the guillotine.

'I need to talk about everything,' she said. 'You don't mean that, Tom. You don't say that to me at other times.'

She had turned her back on Shirley, to emphasize the meaning of this last remark.

Shirley walked out of the barn, to avoid losing her temper. Madeleine, alone again with Tom, instantly changed. 'Shall we give some of this to my Prince?' she asked. As she spoke, she put in her hand and took up a mass of the yellow pottage. Tom stopped the wheel with both hands, dodged round the machine and snatched the child away. 'Ha! Don't you do that, Maddy! Don't you do that! It might have had your hand off!'

The mash dropped from Madeleine's hand, which Tom had taken in his own, to examine it for possible injury. His anxiety unmanned him. He was breathing hard and, in his relief at finding the mischievous limb untouched, he pressed it to his cheek. The impulsive gesture caused Madeleine to respond, maybe in remorse. She hugged him fiercely.

This was the picture to which Shirley returned after her quick effort at self-control. In the dim light of the barn she saw

Madeleine in Tom's arms, a dab of wet mangold on his cheek, and his head enveloped in the child's embrace.

She stopped at the door, stepped back, hesitated, then made a gesture of utter bewilderment. After that, she drove away, forgetting her intention to call in on Anna who was alone in the farmhouse, and to offer to spend the next two nights there, until Matthew's return.

Her distress lasted over the rest of the week. She told herself that she was angry, disgusted. But she knew this was not true. She had to face her trust in Tom, and this strange, new sensation that grew stronger than her desire for him. It was so much more personal. It made her want to sacrifice herself, rather than to possess. And this was a power alien to her, though she recognized it dimly, at the back of her consciousness, as similar to that which acted through Joan, and made her serve the graceless family with undemanding devotion.

To find it in herself frightened Shirley. It created a new dimension and she dreaded where it might lead. But she surrendered when she found herself driven back to find Tom.

She drove over on Saturday morning to the coastguard cottage, thinking that as the day was wet Tom would have returned after the morning's milking was done. But Mrs

Weston told her that he was still up at 'Doggetts'.

'The Boss comes home today, m'dear, and Tom is waiting up there to report.' Then she turned to something more interesting: 'How they getting on down there with your new place? He don't speak about it. Indeed he's not uttered all the week. Never known a man so silent. Might be a ghost in the house, moving about that quietly. Not exactly moody, mind you. Just quiet; wrapped up in hisself. I got to know his moods by now, but he used to worry me at one time. Thought I'd upset him, or he didn't like his meals. You never know with these single men. They get so taken up with ideas. But Tom ain't one of that sort. You couldn't find a more accommodating fellow. Make a good husband, he will. I always said, it's a lucky girl that gets him. And he's useful round the house. Mind you, Miss Kingdom, he can't be– But there, I'm not the one to talk. You must know his little ways by now, and you set no store by them, I dare say.'

She watched Shirley drive away westward to 'Doggetts', then realized that she had been standing talking in the rain. With a gesture of disgust she turned and went indoors, while wiping the raindrops from her wrinkled cheeks with her apron.

Shirley drove slowly along to 'Doggetts', half afraid to arrive because of the unpredictability of Tom's mood when she got there.

She was both eager and reluctant. Love for Tom Small was sharpening her nervous intelligence, and refining her robust manners.

She drove into the muddy yard at 'Doggetts', prepared to ignore the week of estrangement from her lover. She was surprised to see one of her father's vans standing by the stable door. It was empty, except for some planks, a ladder, and two tubs of distemper. Kingdom stood by the lorry talking to Tom Small.

Shirley climbed slowly out of her car. She was both worried and annoyed. It was impossible to greet Tom first, thus to ease that particular anxiety. She could see that her father was flushed and breathing heavily, as though he had been drinking. But he was not a heavy drinker.

'What you doing here, Dad?' She spoke casually, trying to cover up her fear.

'Looking for you, lass. See here, that Gravesend job is the devil, everything at sixes and sevens. I've had to rush over and collect this stuff which we left last week at the bungalow, so that the men could start work on Monday. I know you're in no hurry there. Now I want you to take it in to Gravesend and deliver it at the job. I must use your car and get back to the office, for I've got a couple of chaps coming in to see me this morning and I *must* be there.'

He was flurried, and evasive. Shirley hesitated, trying to see beyond this obvious bluff. She turned to Tom, eager to meet him halfway over the embarrassment.

'Where's Madeleine, Tom?' she asked, with that purpose in mind.

To her relief, and joy, he responded kindly, moving closer to her.

'She's gone down on her pony to meet her Dad. He rang up last night, says Mrs Burbage, to tell her he was setting out at six o'clock this morning while the roads were clear. He should be home any time now.' He paused, then added shyly, though tenderly: 'You all right, me dear?'

Shirley could not speak. She felt the rain trickling down her face, but it was a baptism of restored happiness.

'Sorry, Tom,' she whispered at last.

'You don't reckon to be sorry, Shirley. What are you talking about?'

Kingdom broke in impatiently.

'Look here, you two. Time for that later. I *must* get this stuff over to Gravesend, see. Get you along, girl. I'll come in later and pick you up there. I don't want the lorry back at the yard over the week-end, see? Leave it at Gravesend on the job. I'll come and get you there.'

'No need for that,' said Tom. 'I'll fetch her in our Land-Rover.'

'Eh?' Kingdom eyed him suspiciously. 'But what about her own car?'

'I'll bring her home. But we want to take a look round the bungalow garden, you see.'

Kingdom was disconcerted again.

'Oh, for God's sake! On a day like this? No, her mother wants her as soon as she can get back. Explain why later, Shirley.'

He was so nervous that, having filled his pipe, he knocked it out again, wasting the tobacco down the stable wall. He was about to say more, but a car hooted at the junction of the drive and the public road, where the bungalow stood, out of sight from 'Doggetts'. 'Hey! What's that?'

'It'll be the boss,' said Tom, calmly. He was content to wait for Shirley to explain what this excitement could mean. 'Young Madeleine will be trotting up behind, you'll see.'

The car was heard coming up the drive in low gear. It appeared. It was a police car.

Tom glanced quickly at Kingdom, his future father-in-law. He looked at Shirley. He was aware that, behind him, Anna had appeared at the kitchen door, to greet her husband. She remained there surprised by what she saw, and afraid to approach.

'Why, Mr Kingdom,' said the Inspector. 'Good morning to you. I thought we were to have a little talk in your office this morning?'

'That's so, Inspector,' said Kingdom. He was calm now, and inclined to be jocular. 'I

231

had an SOS from an urgent job on a shop in Gravesend. Wanted more gear, and all I could muster was waiting on the farm here, in the bungalow where you drove in, for a start on Monday. So I had to rush over and collect it. My girl here is taking it along to Gravesend straightaway. You better get off, Shirley. Those chaps are losing time all this while.'

'One minute, Miss Shirley. Before you go, I'd like to know what connection you and your father have with this outlying farm here. I recollect I had to come up some months ago and look round. You were here then, you remember?'

Shirley smiled at the Inspector, and took Tom's hand.

'That's simple enough,' she said; 'Tom Small works here, and we're to be married. Father is re-decorating the bungalow for us.'

'Oh. I see. Congratulations, I'm sure.' The Inspector paused, then looked shrewdly at Tom. 'So you're to be one of the family, eh? Do you know anything of the transport business? You take any hand in it?'

'No, none,' said Tom. 'I work full time here, and live down the road at Mrs Weston's.'

'I see. So you wouldn't know much of what goes on outside the farm?'

'Nothing in particular,' said Tom. 'I've got my own interests. I do a bit of woodworking.'

He looked stupidly non-committal, standing there beside Shirley, sombre against her healthy buoyancy. The Inspector studied him for a moment, almost indulgently, then turned to Kingdom, who was refilling his pipe, closely attentive to it.

'But you'll have heard, Mr Kingdom, of more van robberies at Tilbury Docks? Now one of your lorries came over the ferry from Tilbury to Gravesend the very day a van loaded with export cigarettes was snatched from a pull-up. It was going into Tilbury, and the driver had stopped for a cuppa before entering the town and the docks. Know anything about that?'

'Aye,' said Kingdom, surrounding his head with a cloud of fragrant smoke as he lighted his pipe; 'read about it in *The Kent Messenger*. Bit rough on the driver. They're always suspected of collusion.'

'Yes,' said the Inspector, drily. 'About ten thousand pounds' worth there, I'd say. We found the empty van next day down a lane near Billericay. Quick work that – well planned, the switchover of the swag, eh?'

Kingdom looked at him blandly.

'That's what I feel. And I've had a taste of it. You remember my lorry last summer, used for that very purpose and abandoned at Margate? My driver left high and dry in a road-halt café at Birchington. That was the same thing: cigarettes.'

A pause, during which the Inspector watched Mr Kingdom, while Tom Small and Shirley stood side by side, waiting for they knew not what, but fortified by their silent reconciliation.

'Yes,' said the Inspector. 'And in view of that affair last summer, we'd like to make sure that you're not imposed on again. It might look odd if another of your lorries was commandeered. Can you account for the movements of them all during the last few days?'

Kingdom could. He counted off his half-dozen lorries on his fingers, and located each vehicle as though he had memorized their day-books.

While this was in progress, Matthew Burbage drove into the yard and pulled up near the kitchen door. Anna opened the car door, eager to greet him. He looked across at the company gathered in front of Prince Albert's stable, and questioned Anna about it while he was kissing her.

They approached arm in arm. Anna's anxiety, like that of Shirley, was allayed by the reassurance of love.

'Morning, Inspector,' said Matthew. 'What, another visit? I've just driven back from Hampshire: a long run in the rain. Can I help?'

'Well, Mr Burbage. Good morning, Mrs Burbage. It looks as though everything is straightforward. You saw there had been more highway robberies at Tilbury? We just want to check up on the transport which might be available to help the thieves. They snatch where it's most handy, as Mr Kingdom here knows to his cost. They borrowed one of his lorries last summer, and left it at Margate.'

He paused again, then signalled to his driver.

'Well, we'll be getting along. How's that little girl of yours, Mrs Burbage?' He carefully averted his gaze from Anna's swollen belly.

'She rode down to meet her father,' said Anna. 'She ought not to have missed him.'

'I didn't see her,' said Matthew. 'But here she comes. Hi! Where were you, Maddy?'

Tom Small turned from Shirley and was the first to meet the child. She was walking gravely beside Prince Albert, balancing a square parcel on the saddle.

'I've found something wonderful, Tom,' she said, as he took the pony's rein from her hand. She repeated her words with added excitement as the little cavalcade stopped in the path of the Inspector, who had already stepped forward to join his car.

'I missed you, Daddy. I saw the front door of the bungalow open, so Prince Albert and I went in. And do you know, the back kitchen is full of parcels: hundreds and hundreds of parcels. Look, I've brought one of them to show to Tom, because that's where he's going to live. Are they presents, Tom?'

The parcel was clearly packed and labelled for export to India.

'We won't undo it now, my dear,' said the Inspector, taking it up and reading the manifest label. 'You go with your mother and get ready for lunch. Father will come with these other people down to the bungalow with me, and we'll decide what is to be done with the – the presents.'

He drew Matthew aside.

'This is unfortunate, sir. Especially in view of–' he nervously indicated Anna's promissory condition. 'You understand? The goods are found on your property, as a kind of clearing-house. I'm afraid it will mean an appearance in court when the case comes up. You are sure you know nothing?'

'Good Lord,' said Matthew. 'This is absurd. I've been away for some days. I must get some advice, I suppose. A costly business, whatever happens. Of course I know nothing, nor my man Small either. He's as straight as a die. I thought Kingdom was; he's worked for me honestly, and he came recommended by Lady Beverley. You know her. Everybody in Kent knows her.'

'Yes, Mr Burbage. Don't take it too hard. This chap's no criminal. He's just an easy-going mug out for an easy profit. But it means a stretch for him: eighteen months at least, I'd say, for receiving.'

'The damn fool. But it smears us all. That girl of his, too. Sorry for her. We've found her a good sort; just the wife for Tom Small.'

The Inspector, as Anna walked away leading Madeleine firmly by the hand, turned to the rest of the conference, his manner instantly formal: 'Now then. I'll ask you to accompany me to the bungalow, all of you. Hitch that pony up, my lad, and come along.'

He took Kingdom and Shirley in his car, and Matthew and Tom Small followed. Neither spoke.

There was too much to say.

FIVE

1

Anna and Matthew lay in bed, too disturbed to sleep. They talked in undertones, half ashamed of their mutual anxiety. The rain drummed on the roof. It had been falling steadily for three days, since the police came and arrested Harry Kingdom.

'It's no use worrying,' said Matthew. 'I tell

you it's no use, especially at this stage in your career.'

'Don't be disgusting, Matt. I'm not one of your prize heifers.'

They could not laugh off their worry, however.

'You know what I mean, Anna. It's quite serious if you upset yourself, with less than two months to go.'

'I know, Matt. Frankly, I was so frightened the other day that I thought I was about to give birth on the spot. The infant dealt me such a kick that I thought it must know what was happening. Could it have? Couldn't the subconscious begin working before birth? When does it all begin? Oh God, what a mystery everything is! And on top of it all, we have to contend with these idiotic accidents of everyday life. At the moment I feel I can't cope.'

'You don't need to,' growled Matthew. 'Leave it to the men.'

'Now you're being idiotic, Matt. It's not funny. I'm worried about you, as well as about Maddy. Did she know what she was doing? I mean, if you look at it one way, she has behaved like a precocious little monster: jealous and vindictive. It's as though she really hates poor Shirley Kingdom.'

'Well, it's you are saying that, Anna. I'm usually accused of taking the strong line with the kid, especially over her dealings

238

with Tom Small. But you can't possibly believe she was deliberate over this business. How could she know what was involved? It's absurd!'

Neither was convinced, one way or the other, and they lay silent, their thoughts muffled by bewilderment and worry. The drumming of the rain became a threat.

'Shut that window, Matt. I'm sure the wet is coming in.'

'Everything's coming in,' said Matthew, as he groped his way to the window and closed it. 'No, it's dry here. We're safe for once. It's coming straight down, and no wind. What a winter! Nothing to be done about it. We're just being carried along, old girl, at this stage in our affairs. The fields will be sodden, and the pasture sour. One good thing, our land slopes up to the wood, and the cattle can get some shelter there during the day. And we've got a good store of winter fodder, though I wish we'd clamped those mangolds higher up. I'm thinking of floods. That could happen, you know.'

Anna was only half listening, though her common sense told her that Matthew's fears were justified. But all farming problems were dwarfed by the menace of this trouble with the police.

'Matt, tell me honestly. Does it mean that you will be caught in this business? It looks so ugly. The stuff was found on your premises. What proof have we?'

Matthew left his bed and sat down on hers. He put an arm under her shoulders and half lifted her: a protective gesture.

'Look, darling. You must believe in justice. I do. I may be bumptious and a clumsy fool. But I trust the law. I'm English enough for that. Good God, that's all we've got left to distinguish us in this bloodthirsty modern world. We're no longer top dog. But the politicians and the gangsters still have to respect our Common Law. *You* know I'm innocent. *I* know I'm innocent. The proof is in the truth of it, and be damned to circumstantial evidence.'

'But won't we be ruined in the process of proving that innocence?'

'Look, dear. It's a statement of facts. And who would benefit by implicating me? Kingdom wouldn't. And who else is there? Didn't my own daughter help the police?'

This last remark was overheard by a small figure in pyjamas, who had appeared at the open door of the bedroom, unnoticed by her parents.

'I didn't, Daddy, I didn't! I wanted Tom to open the presents while I was there.'

'What are you doing, wandering about in the middle of the night?'

Matthew picked her up, and carried her over to his bed. He wrapped the eiderdown round her and himself, and sat with her facing her mother, who switched on the bedside lamp and raised herself laboriously to contemplate the lumpy pyramid of humanity.

'I don't like the rain,' said Madeleine; 'it makes a drowning noise.'

'We've got to put up with it, Maddy. We are safe under our good roof, you know. Think of that, and go back to bed and sleep. I'll carry you there.'

'Yes; but, Daddy, if I go to sleep, how shall I know about Prince Albert?'

'How do you mean, Maddy?'

'How shall I know if he is drowning? And what will Tom say?'

Anna reached out to touch the forlorn little object under the quilt.

'But his stable is higher than we are here in the house, Madeleine. So if there was any danger, we should be warned first, and Daddy would run out with you, to take Prince Albert up to the wood, along with the cows.'

Matthew was chilly and impatient. The mention of Tom Small had diluted his sympathy for the small night-walker.

'What's all this talk about drowning? Forget it! Come along now, back to bed. What's a drop of rain? Isn't it wintertime? Nearly Christmas! Think of that, Maddy, and forget everything else. Count up the presents you might have in your stocking.

And you, Mother, you go to sleep too, while I carry this horrible brat back to her bed.'

When he returned, some minutes later, he found Anna still sitting up, with the light on.

'She all right, Matt?' Then she added, 'No, it can't be possible.'

'What can't be possible?'

'It's obvious that she didn't realize. She still thinks the parcels were wedding-presents for Tom Small. And this must mean that she is becoming reconciled to the idea of the marriage.'

'Good heavens, what are you talking about, Anna? Can infants have feelings about such things? It sounds indecent to me. The whole lot of you are crazy. Go to sleep!'

Anna said no more. She switched off the light, lay down, and tried to compose herself beneath the continued muttering of the rain over the world outside the warmth and comfort of 'Doggetts'. But she could not sleep, and she knew that Matthew was awake too.

After submitting thus for over an hour, she turned and reached across in the darkness. Her hand encountered Matthew's. The telepathy of distress was at work.

'You're quite sure, darling?' she whispered.

'Of course. But even if I weren't, Anna, I know you're there.' Then he added drowsily: 'Tom Small's a bit of a damn nuisance, isn't he?'

2

Daylight was reluctant next morning, and the rain still tumbled recklessly out of the sky, tossed about by a fitful wind blowing down the river, tainted with London smoke.

The family was at breakfast when the police car appeared in the farm-yard. Matthew saw it through the streaming window: 'This is it, Anna.'

She was attending to Madeleine, who was still worrying about Prince Albert, and had suggested that she had better not go to school, 'in case'.

'Now hurry up, dear. Finish your milk, or you'll be late. And Daddy too.'

Matthew's remark had cut across this habitual conversation between mother and daughter. He saw Anna flinch, then steel herself not to exclaim or to look round. He knew she was frightened. As he rose to open the door he touched her, closing his fingers on her shoulder. He took no notice of Madeleine, who had paused, the glass of milk suspended, to stare at what was happening.

Matthew invited the constable into the kitchen and Anna turned to offer him a cup of coffee. Pleasantries were passed, and complaints over the weather and the horrors of winter. The constable glanced once or twice at the child, embarrassed by her scrutiny.

At last Anna broke the spell.

'Come, darling. We shall all be late. If Daddy is to take you to school, we must hurry.'

She hustled the child out of the room, looking back at Matthew imploringly.

'Well, sir,' said the constable. 'I'm afraid I have to serve this summons. You know all about it, of course: just a formality, I hope. The magistrates at Petty Sessions will want to ask a few questions when this chap Kingdom appears on a charge of receiving.'

Matthew took the papers.

'But look here, my daughter is five years old. She can't appear in the Courts. Not her too!'

The constable froze, self-protective.

'Sorry, sir. That's how it is. But you can depend—'

The reassuring words were interrupted by Tom Small. He came in through the back door, leading from the scullery and the dairy beyond. He stood for a moment, glowering dumbly at the constable sitting hatless and diffident at the table opposite Matthew.

'What's that?' he said. His tone was aggressive and clumsy. It came from a figure hunched up with nervous anger. The constable swung round, recognizing such hostility almost with relief. Here was a familiar situation, more easy to handle.

'Who's this?' he demanded.

'My foreman,' said Matthew. 'Tom Small.'

The constable picked up his helmet, as a badge of office, fumbled in his large wallet, and produced a paper similar to that handed to Matthew.

'I was coming to that, sir: about to ask you where to find him. Look, Mr Small, this one is for you, to appear also on December the second along with others concerned.'

Tom advanced like a cat stalking a sparrow. He took the paper, and then spoke over it: 'That's all right. But you don't have that young 'un in court, see? That wouldn't do her any good. I reckon the Law don't allow that. She won't make anything of all that.'

The constable was indignant.

'That's not your business, mate. You've got your orders there. Just stick to them, or you'll find yourself in trouble.'

Tom Small was trembling. The blood drained away from his weather-beaten face. He stared at the constable savagely, as he struggled for words.

'See here,' he began; 'she ain't to be bothered. She don't reckon–'

'Now, Tom!' said Matthew, rising from the table and stepping between him and the constable. 'This is my affair.'

'Aye,' said the constable. 'What's he worrying about...?'

'Nothing at all, officer. You were about to tell me something when he came in. Listen to this, Tom. It may reassure us. I don't want Madeleine dragged in any more than you do.'

'No, sir. I was going to suggest – mind you, it's only my opinion, speaking from experience – that as principal witness the little one will have to be questioned, but it won't be in public. One of the magistrates will see her outside the court, and her evidence will be taken down, so to speak.'

An awkward pause, while Tom Small digested this. He was still not reconciled, but the threat of violence died away. He folded up the summons and put it in his pocket.

Then he spoke, his voice small and far away over many fields of rumination: 'That makes it different, maybe. But she don't have to be scared.'

'We're all scared, man,' said Matthew with some irritation. 'Don't you think I'm scared; and Anna, which is more important? What about your young woman too? How is she feeling about it? Doesn't that worry you?'

Tom frowned, and shifted his feet as though feeling for firm ground.

'That ain't the same. We've got ourselves

to answer for, maybe. Maddy ain't that knowing. She's got to be kept out o' this.'

By this time the constable was inclined to be indulgent, thinking him to be slightly touched in the head.

'I'll be getting along, sir.' He nodded in the direction of Tom Small. 'It'll be all right on the day. They handle everybody very human like.'

Before he could leave, however, Madeleine came in, ready for school with her satchel under her mackintosh making her a gnome-like little figure. Her face was shaded by the hood, but it shone out again, a flame of happiness as she pushed the hood back, to greet Tom Small.

'He's here, Mummy! Look, Tom has come back! Tom, where *have* you been since Saturday?'

She ran to him and held up her arms. He stooped, oblivious of the three adults.

'That's all right, Maddy.' His voice was husky with strong feeling. 'Don't you fret yourself.'

She reached up and touched the leathery cheeks.

'Oh, Tom, I missed you. Where have you been?'

He could not answer. He stepped back and nearly collided with Anna who had followed the child into the kitchen. She too was prepared for the rainy journey.

'You're not taking her, Anna?' demanded Matthew, in surprise.

'Yes, today I am. You're busy. I'll hear about it when I get back. Is the car ready?'

She withdrew, leading a reluctant Madeleine, who had clung to Tom passionately and now left him staring after her like a man in a trance.

The constable observed all this, spellbound.

'Well,' he said at last, after mother and daughter had gone. 'Better be getting along too. So that's the little lady, eh? Proper character, she must be. Good day sir.' He did not care to acknowledge Tom Small again. Here was a situation outside his scope.

3

It was true that Tom had absented himself from 'Doggetts' since the arrest of Harry Kingdom on the Saturday morning. Nor had Shirley seen him. She had been occupied with the disastrous effects on her family at Sittingbourne, while Tom had shut himself away in his retreat in the garden of the widow's cottage.

On the night of the serving of the summonses, however, Shirley drove up, and found Mrs Weston in the front room of the cottage.

'Thought you'd be up before long,' said the old lady. 'Knew it was you when the car stopped. Where've you left it, under them trees out o' the worst of the rain? I don't reckon to have seen a day and a night like this since my old man went; and that's a time ago. What are we coming to? The river will be up if we ain't careful. So what comes now, my dear? He's up the garden there, thinking his thoughts: silent as ever. Might as well have been born deaf and dumb, for all the use he puts his tongue to. But he's a deep one, though he tells you nothing. I'm not criticizing, mind you. A kinder codger never breathed. I'll say that for him, as you should know too. Oh, it's a sad business, my dear. I feel for you, indeed I do. I feel for you both.'

Shirley was not put about by this flood of sympathy. She settled the shawl about the old woman's shoulders, hand-persuading her back to the wicker chair by the fire.

'Were you listening, Mrs Weston?' she inquired, indicating the radio-set.

'Nothing to speak of. Sooner have a *real* talk. There's flesh and blood in it. Sit you down.'

Shirley obeyed, though she was impatient to find Tom.

'He ain't been to work, you know,' said Mrs Weston. 'Properly worried, I am. He'll lose his job if he goes on like this. Can't think what's got into him. If you don't mind my speaking of it, my dear, I'd say he has no cause to worry about your father's doings. They are not your responsibility, are they? And you're an honest-to-God young woman as any man could cherish. You're fond of him, ain't you?'

Shirley understood this straight talk, and she wept. Her tears flashed in the firelight, and unashamedly she dabbed at them with her handkerchief. She answered in kind: 'I'd cut myself to ribbons for him, Mrs Weston. And I'm not without experience. I've looked around a bit. But he's different, as you know. You've seen it too. I don't know what it is; and, oh God, what a lover! Nothing wrong with him there. You don't mind my saying that? I'm not ashamed of it: and you're old enough to understand. You won't think I'm fast.'

She wrung the handkerchief in the effort to express further and deeper thoughts.

'But it's this kid where he works, Mrs Weston. That's something beyond me. A five-year-old, but passionate and fixed on him. I don't know. It's as though he's hypnotized by her. What is it all about? I've nothing against the child, not even jealous. How absurd if I were: a kid of that age. But she hates me all right. Properly frightens me sometimes. D'you know, I left one night last autumn, after apple-picking, and found that she'd taken a hanky from the seat of my car, smeared it with grease from the axles, and thrown it back on the seat. I saw her walking away after that trick, though she thought nobody was about!'

'I can't believe it,' said Mrs Weston, 'the little limb!' She eyed Shirley gratefully. Confidences of this kind were meat and drink to her. Then she added: 'It happens that way sometimes. You never really know where you are.'

They were silent after this, and Shirley's distress revived, after being allayed by a moment's gossip. She made her excuses and left Mrs Weston.

The rain drummed on her mackintosh. There must have been a moon behind the clouds, for she could see the path, and the vague shape of the hut, with the lozenge of the lighted window, a dim green through the curtain.

Shirley stood at the door, too nervous to knock. She was breathing heavily, and waited there, to calm herself. She felt the odd raindrops flicking against her face, and was grateful that by this dilution Tom would not see she had been crying.

Then her natural and generous recklessness took command. She pressed the latch, intending to walk in. But the door was bolted.

'Tom! Tom!' she called. 'I'm drowning.

Let me in.'

She heard him move; heard the bolt drawn. Tom opened the door a few inches and peered out blindly. Then he saw her.

'Anything wrong, Shirley?'

'Don't keep me standing here. I'm not your wife yet. Here, take this off me.'

She had almost forced her way into the hut, and now turned with her back to him, to be relieved of the streaming mackintosh. Tom took it and shook it outside the door. Then he came in, dropped the garment on the floor and faced Shirley.

'Anything wrong!' she said. 'That's one way of looking at it!'

'Well, it's not that bad, my dear. The summons came this morning, and the policeman said she won't have to give her evidence in court.'

Shirley stared at him. Then she stepped back, and held out her hands over the Valor stove. She didn't want to look at him. He was something beyond her belief.

'So that's all is worrying you?'

Then she began to laugh, with an edge of hysteria to it.

'I don't see anything funny,' said Tom. 'They've no call to bring young Madeleine into this.'

Shirley turned on him savagely.

'Oh no, she's had nothing to do with it! She took no chance to break up things

252

between you and me. Oh no! The innocent little angel!'

Tom flushed, and stood obstinately withdrawn.

'Well, can't you say something? You've left me alone since it happened. Three days of hell, wondering what next, and where to turn. Now all you're bothered about is this damned kid's – oh, I don't know what! What's it all mean, anyway? And where do I come in? You take what you want and leave me to it when I'm up against something too big to handle alone.'

She gave way to the anger and despair which had been accumulating since the beginning of her intimacy with Tom. His detachment enraged her, and before she could stop herself she seized him with one hand and struck him across the mouth with the other. Blood gathered on his lip and trickled down his chin.

'What's that for, Shirley?' he said. He put out a hand as though trying to grope through a thicket towards her. 'You don't believe I'm that easy, my dear?'

This reaction to her violence defeated Shirley. She was so bewildered that she knelt down on the floor and buried her head in her arms, neither weeping nor raging: just utterly defeated.

Then she felt Tom's arms round her, his hands persuading her face up to his. The salt taste of the blood from his broken lip added to the agony of his kisses, and she responded, repairing with her mouth the damage done by her hand.

They knelt there, clasped together, wordless and thoughtless, for some minutes.

At last, Shirley recalled why she had come to seek him out.

'It's no use, Tom. We always quarrel. And now you've cause to be ashamed of us Kingdoms. I didn't mean to hit you like that. I'm just like my father: I just blunder on. And look where it's landed him. I should drag you down too. We don't mix, Tom. I must go. I'm not your kind. Better to face it now than later on.'

Tom tried to silence her by caressing her and rousing her desire, but she pushed him away, rose to her feet, and began to tidy her hair and clothes.

'I mean it, Tom. Everything is against us. Now this business makes it clear. What's the use of fooling ourselves? I love you all right, I know I love you – but it would do you no good. I can see it now. I'm not blaming you. I'm not blaming anybody. That's no help!'

Her renunciation was not accepted. Tom, sensing that she was about to escape, moved to the door and stood there. He too was struggling with something larger than himself. But he could hardly find the words.

'You don't mean all that, Shirley. You say

254

too much. Let me speak. Look now, do you think I'll let you go? Don't I know you, after what we've had together? That's man and wife, to my way of thinking. I don't let that go. And I stand by that. You want a man along with you over this trouble. You talk about love. I don't rightly understand that. I just go where I belong.'

He stepped nearer, kicking the mackintosh aside with one foot.

'And you know where I belong, Shirley, after what we've done.'

These last words were whispered. He might have been thrusting the world away. The manner, and the gesture with which he approached her, broke down her defence. She put her hands to her face again and let herself be taken into his arms.

Tom groped behind his back and shot the bolt home.

Shirley woke at daybreak, to the sound of drips falling from the gutterless roof. The hut was still dark, and the curtain drawn. The front of the doll's house stood open. She saw another set of miniature furniture half completed: the sofa, the bedstead, in their respective rooms. Tom was still asleep, breathing gently, one arm heavy across her thigh. She lay, reluctant to disturb him, while queries and bewilderments resumed their masquerade around her defenceless mind.

Tom's three-day retreat to think out the meaning of the recent rush of events roused neither comment nor complaint at 'Doggetts'. Matthew had been hard-pressed, but he was thankful for the extra work because it prevented him from worrying about Anna, and the forthcoming ordeal of the Petty Sessions. The two threats interacted. Anna was frightened, and this disturbance was no help at this stage of her pregnancy.

One morning, a week before he was to appear in court at Maidstone, Matthew woke to find the bedroom heavy with a cold fog. Rain, which had poured down unceasingly for many days and nights, had stopped. The silence was positive: no drumming on the roof, no clucking of water in the gutters. Every object in the room, and in the world beyond, seemed consciously to be soundless, aware of its icy insulation.

Matthew shivered, and turned to Anna. She was sweating.

'What is it, old girl? You all right?'

'Don't speak to me. I can't bear any more, Matt.'

'Come now: that's not like you, darling. Nothing to worry about. I keep telling you that, so why don't you believe me? You know as well as I do what the facts are. Nothing else wrong, is there? You've very hot. I'd better ring–'

'Yes, I think you had.' She began to weep, and Matthew was alarmed at so uncharacteristic a demonstration.

'Now look; just ease off, or you'll upset everything.'

'Almost six years is too long between them, Matt. I don't believe I can do it.'

'Oh, it's that!' I can't think what – but the other affair is nothing, my dear. I thought you were on to that again. Now just lie still, and I'll ring the doctor.'

'He'll say we're fools, but you'd better fetch him. I'm not sure of myself. Something is happening; I can hardly breathe!'

Matthew hurried downstairs to the telephone and spoke to the doctor, who was just getting up. This was 'Doggetts" first contact with the outside world since the arrest of Harry Kingdom and the report in the local newspapers. Matthew spoke shyly, half expecting to be treated like a guilty schoolboy.

The doctor could not have been more friendly. On hearing of Anna's feverishness he said he would come at once, and told Matthew meanwhile to give her a cup of tea and an aspirin. He also said that he would warn the nursing home that the bed there might be required prematurely: 'But don't

257

worry; and don't let her worry.'

The friendliness steadied Matthew's nerves. He stood for a few moments by the telephone, immobilized by thankfulness. Then he went through to the kitchen, riddled and filled the Aga stove, and set about making tea.

'Daddy!'

Madeleine stood at the kitchen door, still struggling with her dressing-gown. 'I heard Mummy crying. It woke me up. I don't like it. I've never heard her cry before. Oh, Daddy, what is the matter?'

Matthew pulled her to him, tied the cord of her gown, and turned down the collar which was sticking up under her hair.

'Now don't you start!' he commanded. 'I can't have two of you at it. Mother's got a tummy-ache, that's all. And it's a bad tummy-ache.'

Madeleine studied him severely, her large brown eyes still glistening with tears.

'Is that why she's angry with me?'

'Angry with *you*? What are you talking about? Mother is *not* angry with you.'

'Yes she is. She has been all this week, since I brought up Tom's wedding-present on Prince Albert's back, and the policemen took it from him.'

Matthew groaned.

'Oh, forget it! All that's over now.'

'No it isn't, Daddy. I heard Mummy

yesterday. She was talking on the telephone to somebody. You know, the old lady who gave me my riding-cap, and who you went away with last week.'

'Yes, Lady Beverley. And you'd no right to listen. That's as bad as peeping at keyholes.'

Madeleine ignored this bit of moralizing.

'Well, Mummy said to her, "What about the child?" and I know she meant me because she was looking at me when she said it, and I read her thoughts.'

'You did *what*?' Matthew glared. He disapproved of these precocious remarks that dropped too frequently from her. He associated them with the uncanny attraction towards Tom Small. Madeleine went serenely on, her trouble dispelled by her explanation of it.

'I read her thoughts. Is it true, Daddy, that I shall have to stand up and tell the policeman again what I found at the bungalow? Why do they want to know about Tom's wedding-presents?'

By this time the kettle was boiling, and Matthew had a good excuse for breaking off the inquisition.

'Look here,' he said, 'Mother's not getting up yet, so you can make yourself useful. You lay the breakfast for us, and then get yourself bathed and dressed. I'll have to ask Tom to take you to school this morning, because the doctor is coming to see Mother.

That'll be all right, eh?'

'Tom taking me?' she said, incredulous with joy. 'Oh!' she drew a deep breath, and found no words.

'Yes, I thought so,' said Matthew mysteriously. 'But that can't he helped. And mind you don't make yourself late. Now find the tea-cosy for me. I'm going up to Mother. You'd better not bother her again this morning.'

'I didn't go in, Daddy. I heard her crying and was afraid to go in.' Her lips trembled.

'Don't start that over again. Leave things to me and look after yourself.'

Left alone, Madeleine stood frowning. She was always puzzled by her father when he talked her down and avoided her questions. She began to lay the table, and put three, not two places.

The fog thickened, and Gwylliam barked outside the back door, voicing his disgust. Madeleine opened the door and he crept in, his coat saturated, the beads of fog festooning his furry ears. She was about to shut the door when she heard somebody moving about in the yard.

'Tom! Tom!' she cried, and ran out. Gwylliam, creeping into his basket, sighed, turned, and dutifully followed her, giving a miniature yelp of expostulation.

Tom, about to disappear into the dairy, heard the cry. He halted, turned, and peered through the fog towards the house. He saw Madeleine in dressing-gown and slippers racing towards him, floundering through mud and puddles.

'Eh! What you up to? Look at your feet.'

She was too excited to hear.

'Oh, Tom! I got up early because Mummy is not well, and Daddy has telephoned for Doctor Bray. And I've laid breakfast for us. Come along, you can help me. Tom! Why did you stay away three days; were you ill too?'

Even had Tom been quick-witted enough to deal with her questions, he would have been prevented by her physical attack, for she had leaped at him and was clamouring so fiercely with her arms round his waist, that he was thrown back against the door-post.

'Steady now, steady, m'dear,' he pleaded, stooping over her to rescue the skirts of the dressing-gown from the mud. 'A fine mess you'll be in. And it's cold, Maddy. You don't reckon to be out in this weather. What are you thinking of?'

She still could not listen. She pressed her face against his leg, working her nose into the hard muscle with a fondling motion, accompanying this emotional extravagance with little cries and moans of happiness.

Tom was so perturbed by this that he picked her up in his arms.

'Hold me tight, I'm cold,' she com-manded, and sealed this order by rubbing her cheek against his, and whispering, 'I love you, Tom, don't I? I love you so.'

He held her firmly; this was his only means for responding to her ardour. He could not repress it. He dared not, for it meant something to him larger than he could comprehend. It was a religious ex-perience, and just as elusive.

'You love me too, don't you? You do, Tom, yes, you do. I feel it. And you gave me Prince Albert, didn't you? Let us go and look at him; just for a minute.'

'No, Maddy. You'll catch cold. It's a bad morning – this fog and frost. Look, the puddles are skinned with ice. We don't want you ill.'

'No, I mustn't be ill, for I'm to go with you and Daddy to tell the policeman about your wedding-presents.'

'Eh? What's that you say? My wedding-presents! You mean the parcel you brought up on Saturday? Oh, that's a fine game, I can tell you! Proper bit o' mischief that was. Here we all are, as a consequence of that, standing in the police courts in a few days' time, and I don't know what. They was no wedding-presents. That was a bad business, Maddy, and you should know it, and be kept out of it.'

Her response to this so surprised and

disconcerted Tom that he nearly dropped her. She might have fallen had she not been clinging still, with her arms round his neck.

'And does Shirley have to be kept out of it too?'

Her relentless pursuit of poor Shirley made him angry.

'Look, Maddy. You just leave her out, see? Shirley has no grudge against you. That's mean, that is.'

Madeleine tightened her grasp, and again fondled him with her cheek. Her hair swung loose and flicked his skin.

'No, Tom,' she whispered. 'Don't put me down. Let us say good morning to our Prince Albert, and give him his breakfast first.'

Her persuasive pleading won. Tom carried her along past the dairy, the length of the yard, to the pony's stable. A stamping, shuffling and neigh of impatience greeted them. Tom released the child, who now directed her caresses at the pony. He received them more placidly than had Tom. His moist nose sniffled up and down the figure of his mistress, searching for the expected lumps of sugar. But they were not forthcoming, and he tossed his mane contemptuously.

'Proper old conscience, ain't he?' said Tom. 'Takes all and asks for more.'

'You're not to say things about him, Tom.

He's my Prince.'

Tom poured a small measure of oats into the trough, and Prince Albert stretched his neck past the endearing supplications of the two small hands still caressing the rough coat.

'There, you see how much he cares!'

They both watched him, Madeleine having retreated, to take Tom by the hand, leaning against him. He rested the wooden measure on her shoulder, unconsciously drawing her close to him, and she as unconsciously responding. Their happiness was complete, with the rest of the world forgotten.

It could not last, however. Gwylliam, who had seated himself at the threshold, mournfully patient, suddenly yelped and ran back down the yard to greet his master, who came out of the house to search for his daughter.

Before he could call, Tom spoke to Madeleine.

'That'll be your Dad. Now you're in for trouble.'

'And you, too,' she cried gleefully. 'Oh, Tom, what have you done!'

'You blaming me, are you? That's another score. Maybe she was right!'

'Who was right, Tom?'

But Matthew had located them, and he shouted through the fog: 'What's on, there?

Where's the breakfast? D'you know the time, Madeleine?'

He glared at Tom, but said nothing, as the couple returned to the kitchen, with Matthew walking behind like a warder.

'Better have something with us, I suppose,' he growled. 'You'll have to take her in to school this morning. The wife not up to much, and I've called the doctor. I must wait in for him.'

The comfortable smell of frying bacon filled the kitchen. It challenged the cold, metallic odour of the river-fog. Tom took over, cracking the eggs into the pan while Matthew made the coffee.

'Made a damn fine mess of her dressing-gown,' said Matthew, eyeing his daughter who was twirling the handle of the coffee-grinder. She was too intent on this task to heed her father's attack on Tom. Nor was Tom impressed.

'Missus been fretting herself, has she?' he asked. 'No good to her at this time. Not her way, either. She takes life as it comes; that's her way.'

'What d'you expect? A thing of this sort isn't an everyday matter. A nice mess she and I are landed in, between the lot of you. This damn fool Kingdom, trying to make a quick penny, and see what comes of it! I thought we were settling down nicely, with you and Shirley taking over the bungalow and being handy together. What about her, poor girl?'

Madeleine looked up at him as he towered above her, waiting for the ground coffee. An innocent voice inquired: 'Will she go to prison too, Daddy?'

Both men started, neither of them prepared for the unaccountable outbreaks of consciousness in this child: naïve one moment, cunning the next; cunning and seemingly vindictive.

Matthew seized her by the hair.

'What are you talking about, you monkey? What do you know? Wedding-presents indeed!'

She was out of favour with Tom also. He was so shocked that he misfired with the last egg, and broke the white of it over the edge of the pan, on to the hot-plate, where it hissed and solidified into a slab of porcelain. Tom was not prepared to attack her in front of her father, however. He said nothing, but prodded savagely at the browning albumen with the knife, to scrape it from the hot-plate.

Breakfast was eaten in silence. As soon as Madeleine had finished, Matthew ordered her upstairs to dress for school. She disappeared demurely. Tom avoided her appealing glance at she passed him. He was sulking because he was so helplessly enslaved.

'What d'you make of that?' said Matthew.

Tom was about to reply when the doctor appeared.

'God! What a morning, Burbage. Just your luck, and mine too. Whenever there's a happy event, you can bet on a day like this, even if the birthday's in June!'

Dr Bray was about Tom's age, thickset and bound in the habits of his profession; but still capable of personal interest. He had delivered Madeleine, and remained an absentee friend of the family.

'I gave her the aspirin and she's quiet now,' said Matthew. 'A cup of tea first?'

'No, I'd like a look at her. Come on up.' He dropped his coat on a chair, and went to the sink to wash his hands.

'Morning, Small. Didn't notice you there. Man of few words, aren't you. When's the wedding? I heard about you and Shirley Kingdom. Nice girl that! Does a good job in the Red Cross in Sittingbourne. That's how I know her. Rough family, but plenty of dough.'

Tom looked furtively up. He expected some reference to the news paragraphed in the local paper. But Dr Bray said nothing. His shrewd eye was kindly enough. Tom Small was on his panel and he had known him since first coming to 'Doggetts'. But he did refer indirectly to the scandal, as he followed Matthew out of the kitchen. He put a hand on Tom's sensitive shoulder.

'It's cabinet-making with you, Tom, not fretwork.'

His joke pleased him, and he chuckled with Chestertonian humour all the way to the foot of the stairs.

When he and Matthew came down again, Small and Madeleine had driven away.

'Sorry for that good chap, Burbage. Just about to marry, aren't they?'

'Oh, he's able to look after himself. Odd character, in some ways.'

'How d'you mean? I should say a cut above the usual run of humanity. Clean living, reads a bit, fastidious too. Clever with his hands. I should say he thinks with his fingers. Some people are made that way; most surgeons, perhaps, though I'd get slapped if I said so in public. How's that precocious imp of yours? Still saying wise things? Nice little handful. But a brother or sister will keep her in hand. A good engine needs a good brake.'

Matthew hesitated. He was susceptible, after the intimacies upstairs and the reassuring words offered by Dr Bray. He could do with some more.

'You know she's the one who blew the gaff over this business; and here I'm landed with a sticky situation. Stolen goods found on my premises. It's all over the country now. Even the London papers have reported it.'

'So what, Burbage?'

'You never know. It's all outside my experience. What proof have I got, though? I try not to let Anna see I'm worried, but I am worried, damnably worried. And that's not all–'

Here he hesitated again. He was wading out of his depth. But he decided to go on. Dr Bray was putting on his coat, and would be gone in a moment.

'Madeleine's a problem too. She's fixed on my man Small. It's uncanny. He gave her that pony for her birthday, and the three of them together make a tight triangle. This girl he's marrying is worried about it as well. Madeleine, of course, won't let her break in.' He told the doctor about the abrupt question at the breakfast table, flashing out like lightning from the child's stormy brain. He added: 'Tom Small is all right. I'll swear to that. But the whole business drives me up the wall. I'm not a jealous father, but one wants things to be natural.'

Dr Bray studied him for a few moments, and collected his hat and disreputable bag.

'Look, Burbage. Leave it alone. Growth puts these matters right. You've got plenty to be thankful for, including a sensible and healthy wife. Anna's a bit nervy: combination of the kicks from within and the recent one or two from outside. It's a pity they have come at the same time. Now I must face the

269

fog. Phew! It stinks of East London! G'bye, Burbage.'

Matthew watched him dissolve into the fog. He stood looking down the drive, and heard the drone of ships' sirens from the estuary. The bare larches set as a wind-shelter stood ghost-like, sodden and black from the week of rain. Frost was whitening them, and the fog draped them with mournful veils.

Matthew heard Anna calling him from the bedroom, and he turned back into the house.

'Does he say that to every woman on his panel, Matt?'

'Does who say what?'

Anna was sitting up in bed, smiling as though congratulating herself.

'Does he tell them that they are as healthy as a Flanders mare, and as tough? That's what he said to me. And he reckons it will be another month yet, which makes things quite normal. That should be some time after New Year. Funny time to be born, poor lamb.'

'There's a good precedent.'

'How d'you mean?'

'Well, what about Christmas, in the year nil A.D.?'

'Oh, that's so obvious that I didn't think of it.'

They were laughing together, their confidence in their good luck and their mutuality restored, when a car hooted up the drive.

'No! Not more police?' cried Matthew before he had time to prevent himself from lapsing into anxiety, and betraying the fact to Anna.

'You'd better go down,' she said. 'But don't get obstinate. Let things happen.'

He kissed her; then kissed her again, and went downstairs leisurely, summoning up confidence by an effort of will.

'Matthew!'

It was Lady Beverley's voice – silver alloyed with blue steel.

'Who's at home?'

Matthew met her at the door.

'Ah! A bad penny this time! What on earth hasn't been happening since we got back last week? Is it a week? Seems like a month!'

She talked her way through to the kitchen, where Matthew poured a cup of coffee.

'Look, I expect you're worrying your guts out over this business. And I'm the one who brought it. Didn't I introduce Kingdom, the fool? But he's no criminal, Matthew, he's just–'

'Someone else said that to me, Lady B, I can't think who!' Matthew wearily passed a hand across his forehead. 'Oh yes, it was the police-inspector himself, the day they arrested Kingdom. Bit of a shock, you know – the booty found on my premises – and

271

found by my own daughter.'

Lady Beverley still refused to sit down, or remove her old tweed coat.

'Do I hear her upstairs? All going well? What, signs already?'

Matthew managed to edge in the information that the doctor had just gone, after a reassuring visit. Lady Beverley took this like an express train netting a mail-bag. She paced about the kitchen, her beauty damped down by the clinging fog, but made more endearing thereby. Matthew, in spite of his preoccupation with Anna and the police-court case, stood admiring the elderly beauty: the exquisitely moulded features, the quick, darting eyes, the slight stammer that gave an individual emphasis to every phrase.

'It's this business of your daughter, Matthew. That's why I've crawled over through this fog. Thought I shouldn't arrive until lunchtime. The funny thing is, I'm deputizing on the Bench that day – or rather I should have been – but I've said it's impossible because I'm a friend of the family and heavily involved as I employ Kingdom and first recommended him to you. But I've undertaken to take the child's evidence out of court. There will have to be two of us, and a stenographer, and somebody representing the Court. So she won't be embarrassed, the little devil!'

'You're right, Lady B. She's a bit too much for us sometimes. Something uncanny about her.'

'Don't talk rot, my dear. Nothing uncanny at all. She just wants a spanking occasionally. Jolly good slipper! Sounds old-fashioned, doesn't it? Don't say I'm a moron; I'm not. But all livestock is the same in its early stages. It wants first go at the trough, and will tread the others down in order to get there.'

'That's sounds simple enough,' said Matthew, so seriously that Lady Beverley took him by the arm and shook it vigorously.

'Now don't become over-civilized, Matthew. You're making heavy weather of the whole thing. Let's go up and have a word with Anna, since she's still intact. After all, it's a simple enough matter. The child has only to tell us how she went down on her pony to meet you, found the bungalow door open, and went in, as any infant would, to explore while waiting for you to turn up. And there she found the stuff which she thought was presents for the bridal couple. It was only putting two and two together. She just wanted to be helpful, by bringing up a sample of the goods, knowing both bride and groom were up at the farm.'

'I hope you're right,' said Matthew lugubriously.

'Well, what else, my dear man?' said Lady Beverley, leading the way upstairs.

5

Nobody had been down to the bungalow since the police removed the packages of export cigarettes, under the supervision of a Customs Officer concerned in the Drawback of Import Duty on goods re-exported from the United Kingdom. The bungalow stood under the early-winter weather, naked to the rain, after being stripped by the builder's men in readiness for re-decoration. The cleared and autumn-dug garden was bare also, seen through the leafless quickhedge to be taking already a film of arsenic-tinted green over the clods.

The police had lost interest in the place, for there was no question of further investigation. Kingdom had told the whole story, which he would repeat in court. The keys having been returned to Matthew, the owner, he passed them to Tom Small, the future tenant. Harry Kingdom's foreman-builder held the duplicate keys, for admission to the job which had already been delayed for more than a week.

The reconciliation, if it could be so called though there had been no open quarrel or broken engagement between Tom and

Shirley, set the latter to some practical purposes again. Her father being held by the police, she took charge of the transport and building business. She no longer worried, though under summons, since being re-assured of Tom's affection and his claim to stand by her. She rounded up the work-sheets, and saw to it that the job on the bungalow was put in hand at once.

'Damn it all,' she explained to her sister Joan, who warmly supported her, 'one job's as good as another. Not everybody's getting married and housed on the strength of it. I'm doing this for Tom as well as for myself, and doesn't he need a home!'

She said nothing about the possibility of her being caught up in the machinery of the law as it ground exceeding small in its direction against her father's crimes.

The weather changed during the four days before December 2 when the Petty Sessions were to open in Sittingbourne. Everything was peaceful and serene, as it can be in a northern winter, between the ravaging extremes. The sun rose in the south-east, over the reaches of the estuary, across the bar of the Kentish downs, and threw a ghostly warmth all day, to sink beyond Sittingbourne and the wooded heights farther back, down a sky of melancholy splendour, smoky and dusted with falling curtains of frost.

Nothing dried out; but the landscape took on colour again, and a definition of solid shapes. Light was triumphant for an hour or so round about noon, before it began to wither out of earth and sky, westward into the premature sunset.

Shirley drove up from Sittingbourne in the afternoon of the day before that of the Sessions. She stopped at the bungalow first, parking her tourer on the now-marked spot close to the hedge where it curved away from the lane.

As she got out of the car, she saw, almost at her feet, a patch of adventurous primroses, half a dozen blossoms, in full flower. She stooped and picked them, and sniffed greedily at the faint, aureolin perfume.

'Well I'm damned,' she said. 'Fancy that!'

She stood, tears in her eyes, looking at the flowers so fragile in her sturdy hand, and was startled when Tom Small spoke.

'What you got there, something precious?' he said, approaching from round the car. 'Why that's early, my dear. Primroses, eh?'

Shirley turned and offered them to him, putting them into the buttonhole on the lapel of his coat and kissing him almost with desperation.

'Does it mean good luck, Tom, good luck tomorrow?'

Tom was touched by her ardour.

'Why, girl, you don't want to worry about

276

that. I don't know that I greatly blame your old man, even if he is found guilty. But he may get off with a caution, or a fine. All depends on his lawyer. They may say he was not receiving, only carrying on his trade of transport. Mind you, I reckon it ain't worth the risk, a game like that. He did well enough without it, surely, the carrying business, and the building?'

'Oh, don't talk to me about it! I don't feel so kind as you, Tom. I've had to live with that happy-go-lucky caper all my life. Don't you play me up that way when we're together, will you? I can't believe you will, you're steady, Tom.'

Tom looked at her solemnly.

'I don't know about that, Shirley. I don't reckon to think about my own goings on. If you start that you don't know where you are. Proper womanish game, that is.'

They stood in silence for a while, contemplating the building and garden which were to be their home.

'What brought us both here like this, Tom?'

He grinned, and opened the little gate in the hedge.

'Maybe this bit of sunshine. Makes you think of getting ready for next year. Good to have a bit of ground to work – a bit of our own.'

Shirley put her arm round him.

'Yes, and you'll have your own place behind there, sweetheart. I'll come down the garden sometimes and visit you there. We must put up a curtain too!'

They both laughed, stopped walking and exchanged kisses.

'Mind the flowers, Tom; don't squash them,' she whispered. 'They're to bring us luck.'

They disappeared inside the dwelling, after Tom had fumbled in his pocket for the key.

'They've made a start, you see. I chivvied them up now I'm managing the business. That was all nonsense about the job in Gravesend. The boards and materials are all back here. Look, they've put a coat on the bedroom walls. Would you believe that old couple could make the place so filthy in a year or two? I don't want to remind myself of them. Ugh! Horrible!'

She turned to Tom again for reassurance, and they stood clasped together, so lost to the world that they did not hear the thud of Prince Albert's hooves on the turf along the laneside as Madeleine came seeking Tom.

She saw Shirley's open car, and stopped dead. After a moment's thought, she dismounted, and tied the pony's rein to a gatepost, beyond the cottage garden. A double-trunk holly tree hid Prince Albert from sight, both from the bungalow and the garden beyond the hedge separating it from the meadow.

Madeleine laid her head sorrowfully against the side of the pony's neck, and murmured to him, incoherently, a stream of words that might have been an apology. Then she put her hand, palm downwards, on the flat expanse between his eyes.

'Wait for me, Prince Albert. Wait here for me,' she said, more distinctly. She moved away, one or two paces, still facing him and studying him with the intensity of a person taking a long farewell of some beloved being or object.

Prince Albert remained passive under this drama. He was content to stand in the almost horizontal morning sunlight, that found its way under the foliage and berries of the holly tree. Plats of sodden grass and dry sorrel reached almost to his belly, and he need hardly lower his head to find a welcome mouthful. He was already munching when Madeleine turned and crept along the turf under the hedge.

She halted beside Shirley's car, and stood staring at it, her fists clenched. One set of knuckles went to her mouth and she bit at them so fiercely that the pain made her snatch the fist away with a gesture of anger. She peered over the door, meditated some mischief, thought better of it and turned away, her fists still clenched and her eyes stormy with trouble.

She lingered for some moments, supporting herself by leaning against the gate, which Tom had left open when he led Shirley to the bungalow. Something was tormenting the child, for she appeared to be at the point of sinking down at the foot of the gate, exhausted by the struggle raging in her mind.

She shivered, though the sunshine showered over her through the leafless trees across the lane. The sun was approaching the belt of winter mist round the lower sky, but it kept a little warmth, sufficient to bring out a few gnats that hovered above Madeleine's head. They were helpless fairies and could not comfort her. She moved on, treading silently on the dug ground beside the concrete path.

The bungalow shone before her, its wall and windows glowing with the false warmth. The two front rooms were lit up by the penetrating rays, and as Madeleine crept nearer she saw the two figures of Tom and Shirley, clasped as one.

As though adding to, or at least confirming, her own torment, the child stood staring for some moments. The lovers did not move. They made no sound.

At last Madeleine broke from the trance. An expression of ugly maturity contorted her features, and she turned away with bowed head, moved furtively to the gate, and, once outside the garden and under the shelter of the hedge, ran back to Prince Albert. As she untethered him she began to sob and had to pause before she could mount, so shaken was she by despair and misery.

The ride up to 'Doggetts' gave her time to control herself, and the tears were replaced by a calmness that set her mouth into an un-childlike line of determination. She felt Prince Albert's broad back and flanks between her thighs, and the sensation added to her confidence and sense of power. She tugged at a fistful of his unruly coat, and he flinched, tossing up his head in protest.

'You beast! You beast!' she said, leaning over and hissing the words close to a furry ear. But he was indifferent to this. She might have been addressing somebody else, over his head.

He got no more attention that afternoon, neither grooming nor petting. His mistress unbuckled the saddle, dragged it roughly off his back, fastened his halter to the stall, and shut the stable door.

She found tea laid, and Father reading the newspaper beside the fire, while Anna filled the pot.

'Ah! Here you are then? I've been hunting for you, Maddy. Been for a ride?'

Madeleine could not speak. She nodded

grimly, and silently obeyed her mother's command to wash her hands at the sink. While she was out in the scullery, the parents looked at each other.

'Don't you fuss now,' whispered Matthew. 'Leave it to me. Looks as though she knows what's coming tomorrow.'

'I don't like it, Matt. It's not fair to the child.'

'Well, she did poke her nose in, after all. I've talked things over with Lady Beverley, and she assures me it's just a formality. Maddy's only got to tell them what she found, and what she did that afternoon. Simple enough.'

'But you know what she is. And all this business with Shirley Kingdom and Tom?'

'Now, don't complicate the wretched business, darling. It's bad enough as it is. It seems to me obvious that the funny little soul has reconciled herself to the fact that Tom and Shirley are getting married and that it won't affect her.'

'I hope you're right!' She called through to the scullery: 'Come along, Madeleine. Tea's poured.'

'Now you'll see, Anna. I'd better tell her what's to happen tomorrow. It's a good moment, while we are all together, at home here, nice and quiet and ordinary.'

Madeleine returned, and her mother snatched a hairbrush from the dresser and drew it through the silky head of hair. The child submitted to this delay and then took her place at the table. She said nothing, and her face was expressionless.

For a while, the meal proceeded, though with pleasure only for Matthew. He was determined to have no nonsense.

'Well, Madeleine,' he said briskly, pushing back his cup and saucer and reaching across the table for Anna's packet of cigarettes. 'You know we have to go into Sittingbourne tomorrow. They want to ask us what happened that day when you brought up the parcel from Tom and Shirley's bungalow.'

'It's *your* bungalow!'

'Yes, but they will live there soon, when they are married. That'll be nice for you, as well. I'm glad because Tom will be nearer to his work; and Shirley will help Mother.'

He turned to Anna for support, but she could not bring herself to offer it. She concentrated on pouring herself another cup of tea. She looked strained, still tired after the recent false alarm.

'Been down there since?' asked Matthew, as innocently as he could.

'No!' said Madeleine. Her frown was dangerous.

'Oh, I see. Well, tomorrow they will want you to tell them how you rode down there on Prince Albert, went inside and–'

'Didn't take Prince Albert inside. I let him

outside, by the gate, so that you could see I was there when you came home. I went down to meet you.'

Matthew studied her.

'No need to make heavy weather of it, Maddy. Just tell them that tomorrow, nothing more is expected of you.'

'Who is *them*?' she demanded sourly.

'Oh well, I'm not sure yet. But they will be nice people, ladies and gentlemen. You know what to say, don't you?'

Matthew and Madeleine looked at each other suddenly. It was a challenge, and Matthew knew it was a hostile challenge. Silently, he appealed to Anna, but she would not take sides. She may have been too much concerned with the dawning relationship to be made with the newcomer at the threshold of their family life.

'Doggetts' was active early next morning, for the milking had to be done before the family drove into Sittingbourne. The last argument the night before had been over Anna, whether or not she should accompany the others.

'I can't be left her alone,' she pleaded, 'wondering what's going on. I can sit at the back somewhere, and I shan't be called. Much safer for me, after all, rather than being by myself here, everybody gone into Sittingbourne.'

So she rose early too, and groped clumsily

about the house by artificial light, calm and reassured now that she was taking part in the unusual affairs of the day.

That day was slow in dawning. The sun appeared at about eight o'clock from behind the Kentish hills, which had an ominous gloom about them. The gloom rose with the sun, and gradually overpowered it. By the time the family left 'Doggetts' at nine-thirty, daylight had receded into a damp twilight, and rain began to fall, at first hesitantly, but gathering momentum and a long-distance rhythm.

Tom Small was picked up from his lodgings, and he sat in front with Matthew, having said nothing. He greeted the Burbages with a grim nod, nervous and awkward. As he opened the car door, he looked sharply at Madeleine, who sat beside her mother, withdrawn and taut. She ignored him, and stared ahead through the windscreen. He looked surprised, almost hurt, but did not speak. The rain, the gloom, the human silence, combined to a setting for the coming ordeal, ripe with unpleasantness, or something even worse.

Nobody appeared to be interested in the proceedings at the Police Court. Two or three newspaper reporters sat there in abject boredom. The rest of the public was seedy enough: the Clerk of the Court, the officials and the policemen matter-of-fact, ridden by routine. The Burbages were directed by a constable who appeared incomplete without his helmet. They found Shirley already there with her father and the younger daughter. Both young women were nervous, clasping their gloves, swallowing convulsively from time to time. Harry Kingdom sat squarely, a daughter on either side of him. They might have been merely the ornamental arms of a comfortable chair in which he was relaxing. He nodded in a friendly way to the Burbages and to Tom Small.

The beehive-murmur of voices dropped a tone and died away when the magistrate entered and took his place on the Bench. He was an elderly, bleak-looking person, non-committal. But his conducting of the first case was startlingly in contrast to this negative manner. Counsel had been briefed, and he handled both police and lawyer with speed and sympathy. The prisoner, accused of rape, was turned to after prosecution and defence had been heard.

A vague, depressed young man advanced. The magistrate studied him for a moment, then spoke: 'I may want a word with the alleged victim, but' – and his gaze drifted over the court to the back, where the Burbages sat – 'I am not happy to go further with this case in the presence of children. Is it necessary?'

The clerk whispered to him, and he

appeared to be replying with some emphasis. The result was that a constable approached and suggested apologetically that the child and mother should retire to the waiting-room until recalled.

As Anna rose, her condition was immediately apparent, whereupon the constable gently took her by the arm and steered her towards the door. An air of religious ceremony entered the court. The magistrate removed and polished his spectacles, and a sigh of devotional fervour rose from the public benches.

Matthew was in an agony of embarrassment; Tom Small sat frozen, betraying nothing. Nobody could have seen his rapid glance aside, after the small figure of the child who had caused this early interruption of the proceedings. A bead of sweat trickled down Tom's temple, but he did not put up a hand to wipe it away. Another followed, and still he sat, rigid.

Two or three minor cases followed: parking offences, traffic lights, defective brakes.

Then the road-robbery case was called, and its complications began to unwind. Witness after witness appeared, and at last the particular aspect of the robbery in which Harry Kingdom was implicated came up for examination. The magistrate had been darting about amongst the evidence like a terrier in a warren of rabbits, sharp and lethal.

Suddenly, he subsided, after committing three men for trial at the County Assizes. He leaned back, looked at Harry Kingdom in the box, and smiled. Tension in the court relaxed, and some whispering was heard while the magistrate leaned forward again to glance at the papers before him.

'It appears that you have pleaded not guilty on the grounds that you were merely acting in pursuit of your usual business as a transport agent and common carrier, Mr Kingdom. Can you enlarge upon that? Can you tell us, for example, what took place when you picked up this consignment of goods, and why you did it personally? I would like, also, to know something more about an earlier case, when another of your lorries was found abandoned at Margate, after a similar theft. Have you a regular connection with the organization that promotes these highway robberies? I fear that I sound more romantic than I intend.'

Harry Kingdom had been too jolly, too confident of his own and other people's good nature, to take steps to defend himself. He began to talk confidentially to the Bench, but was cut off after a while, when the magistrate said that he would like to hear about the disposal of the stolen goods after the police had approached Mr Kingdom.

Another whispered conversation between

the Bench and the clerk was held, while Kingdom stood blandly in the box, still confident of his powers of persuasion. He had forgotten his earlier confession, which had not yet been brought up. It seemed as though the police were still dragging their net.

An officer left the court, and the magistrate ordered Mr Matthew Burbage to take the place of the accused in the box. Kingdom winked loudly at Matthew as they passed each other, but he was in no mood to respond. He was worried about Anna, and enraged by the whole humiliating business.

To his surprise and relief, however, he found himself being handled with sympathy almost apologetically. It was apparently accepted that he was the victim of what might have been called a practical joke, had it not been so serious a matter.

'The carrier habitually works for you, and is also, I understand, by way of being a builder and decorator who is at present fulfilling a contract to re-paper and paint the interior of a tied cottage or bungalow on your farm, to suit your employee as tenant, who is shortly to be related to the accused. An embarrassing situation, Mr Burbage, is it not?'

Matthew agreed, and felt so guilty that he looked it. This appeared to be in his favour, for the magistrate went on: 'The accused, however, began to work for you upon the recommendation of a lady known throughout the county, who is a Justice of the Peace. She lives, however, farther away from Mr Kingdom than would be advisable if she is to be knowledgeable about the whole of his activities. Kent is a spacious county.'

Nobody dared to laugh, the personality of the Bench had by this time grown impressively.

'There is this matter, however, of the impending matrimonial connection between your employee and the daughter of the accused.'

'*A* daughter, Your Worship,' interposed the counsel briefed by Burbage.

'Is that relevant?' asked the magistrate, raising his eyebrows at this, the first plea put in on Matthew's behalf.

'Definitely, Your Worship. It implies a much looser connection. The young lady is one of a large family, and with large families the members usually go their own way.'

'Usually? But these are unusual circumstances. I would remind you of that.'

'Quite, Your Worship, but I point it out.'

'Thank you. But I am impressed by the fact that, for a week before the goods were secreted on Mr Burbage's premises, he was away on business in another county.'

The magistrate paused, to have another whispered conversation with the clerk.

He resumed: 'I understand that meanwhile a statement has been made by Mr Burbage's infant daughter, the child who found the bungalow door open, entered the premises, and discovered the parcels of cigarettes packed for export from Tilbury Dock. The exporter and the Customs Officer have since identified the goods. The statement has immediately been made by the child in the presence of a Justice of the Peace, of officers of the court and of her mother. I would like to thank Mrs Burbage for her co-operation in what is always a delicate matter: I refer to the evidence of young children. We have to bear in mind that such evidence is not given upon oath, and that by its nature it tends to be – to be fluid. On the other hand, we must not forget that it has been said, and said with authority, that "out of the mouths of babes and sucklings..." Yes, we must bear that in mind.'

The magistrate leaned over and took from the clerk a sheet of paper brought in by one of the unhelmeted policemen. He read it, and a frown of perplexity added to the austerity of his features. He snatched off his spectacles and wiped them, before re-reading the document.

'I would like to ask the daughter of the accused to step forward: Miss Shirley Kingdom.'

Curiosity rustled through the court-room, as Shirley stood up, looked about her nervously, smiled wanly at Tom Small, tucked her handbag under her arm, and walked to the witness-box. She took the oath.

'Are you aware, Miss Kingdom, what the nature of this statement by the child is likely to be?'

Shirley murmured indistinctly. For once she was frightened.

'A little louder if you please. I want the court to be sure on this point.'

Shirley was even more flustered. She gave the appearance of extreme guilt and of having been found out. Her face flushed, and she had to clear her throat before she could speak. She looked round despairingly until she sighted Tom Small. Her appeal to him was obvious to the Bench and to the public, but Tom sat haggard and stony, staring into space. He had nothing to offer her.

Thus left to fight alone, Shirley suddenly regained courage. She turned to the Bench, and spoke out clearly: 'I've no idea. You never know what that child will do next.'

'Is that an impartial statement, Miss Kingdom?'

'So far as it can be, Your Honour.'

This caused a sensation in court, and Burbage's counsel was seen anxiously consulting the solicitor.

'That is an enigmatic statement. However, here is the child's report. I need not read it in detail. The gist is that she did not enter the bungalow at once. She first saw the accused drive up in the lorry, followed, Miss Kingdom, by you in an open car. She watched you and your father unload the packages and carry them into the bungalow. She says you both appeared to be in a great hurry. That last has a circumstantial ring about it. You were in a great hurry. And after that you drove up to the farm-yard, leaving your father to follow later.'

Silence: while everybody in the court watched the blood mount in Shirley's neck and cheeks. She visibly became possessed by anger: open, healthy anger. She half turned from the Bench, and looked first at her father, and then at Tom again. But Tom did not see her. He was bowed, elbows on his knees, and his head hidden in his hands.

'What have you to say to that, Miss Kingdom?'

The magistrate spoke quietly, severely, but Burbage's lawyer smiled, and gave his client a reassuring nod. Matthew needed it.

'I would say, Your Honour, that this is the same child that once found a handkerchief of mine on the driving seat of my car, smeared it in dirty grease from one of the brake-drums, and threw it back on the seat for me to find.'

Further sensation, increased by Tom Small's interruption. He suddenly leaped up, and addressed the Bench, while one of the constables by the wall moved forward, intending to restrain him.

'That don't hold, sir! Young Madeleine is not that way! She's–'

'Sit down, you fool!' hissed Matthew. 'Leave it alone!'

This intervention by the child's father had more consequence than Tom's. It certainly interested the Bench more. The magistrate looked shrewdly from Tom to Matthew, then back to Shirley, who stood momentarily neglected in the witness-box.

'We must not take into account all this emotional display. I want to know the facts. I am concerned with what happened on that day, in connection with this theft.'

He turned upon Shirley.

'Now, Miss Kingdom! Do you mean that this child has some animus against you? Is it possible in an infant of five years of age, that she could direct and maintain so consistent a bias against an adult?'

The barrister whispered in Matthew's ear, 'Oh, lovely! Lovely! He's steering the boat superbly!' But Matthew was in no state to be reassured. He was humiliated by this public parade of his family affairs, both those disclosed and more threatened. He

294

was enraged by Tom Small's stupid simplicity, and Shirley's vindictive recollection of a childish act of mischief. He could see no deeper motive there; and would not see.

'That is what I mean,' said Shirley. She had now gained courage, and stood up in command of herself and of the court.

'Then you are prepared to deny the accuracy of this child's statement? Remember that you are on oath, Miss Kingdom, and that you were observed to be in a hurry,' he consulted the document, 'and that you drew out from behind the lorry and drove up to the farm-yard. These are very specific statements, Miss Kingdom.'

Shirley looked at him.

'They are both lies, Your Honour.'

'Come, come, madam. We must have proof of that.'

Shirley hesitated for a moment. She was still very angry. Then she looked at Tom, who sat white-faced beside Matthew, clasping and unclasping his hands. He would not look at her.

'I would like to ask Mr Tom Small and my father to prove that.'

'Very well. Step down, Miss Kingdom, and I will call Mr Tom Small.'

Tom was prodded by the solicitor, who sat between him and Matthew. He rose, looked around like a trapped animal, then took the stand. Before the magistrate could address

295

him he lifted an arm and brought it down with a cutting gesture, and called out in the tone of a mortal in solitude, trying to break the threatening silence of a ravine, or a cavern. His voice rang hollow, tortured, round the court-room: 'She don't need to be brought into this! She wants to be left alone, young Madeleine!'

The magistrate studied him with curiosity, and a titter from the public was instantly hushed.

'Will you take the oath, Mr Small,' he said quietly.

After this formality the magistrate continued: 'We will turn to another matter. Can you recall the moment that morning when Miss Kingdom drove up to the farmyard? Did you see her arrive?'

So long as Madeleine was not being discussed, Tom remained calm and soberly dignified.

'I did.'

'And how long was it before her father followed her?'

Tom frowned, in perplexity.

'But he didn't. He was up there already, talking to me by the stable door. I'd been seeing to Prince Albert.'

Laughter in court.

'Prince Albert?'

'He's the pony, the pony I gave to Madeleine.'

'You appear to be deeply attached to the young witness, Mr Small; if she may be called a witness.'

'Ah,' said counsel, mouthing satisfaction at his client.

'So you affirm that Miss Kingdom came up after her father, and not before, as this statement implies?'

Tom nodded. He could not bring himself to put it into words.

'I see. That will do, Mr Small. I will now recall Mr Kingdom. Will you confirm, Mr Kingdom, this statement that you were already up at the farmhouse when your daughter arrived there that morning?'

Harry Kingdom looked kindly at the Bench, and took a benevolent survey of the people in the court, including his own party, before replying.

'I do, Your Honour. And what is more, I did not take the stuff up to "Doggetts" that Saturday morning. I took it up after dark on Friday night. All I did that morning was to load up some tools and planks left at the bungalow by my workmen a week earlier. Oh yes, and I tidied up the packages in the back kitchen behind the paint pots and dust-sheets. Can't think how the youngster found them. She must be pretty sharp.'

'She certainly appears to attract much notice,' said the magistrate drily. He then sent Kingdom down and turned to the court.

'It is plain that, as not infrequently happens with evidence from young persons, the play of imagination has triumphed over facts. We cannot accept this statement. I am satisfied about that, and I must repeat that it is regrettable for your daughter to have been brought, Mr Burbage. I hope you will make that point with her mother. It is obvious, too, that the accused has acted alone, so far as the reception and conceal-ment of the stolen goods is concerned. Not you, your employee or Miss Kingdom herself is implicated. Please step up, Mr Kingdom.'

He looked drolly at Harry Kingdom, who returned to the witness-box, not quite crestfallen, but somewhat hard done by.

'You are committed for the next Assizes, on bail of five hundred pounds. This result being upon your own confession, I have no more to say. We will take the next case.'

The three other men more directly con-cerned in the robbery were kept in custody. Harry Kingdom, after looking appealingly at his daughter, joined the Burbage party. It was hardly a united party. Matthew was still smarting from the publicity beamed upon his private life. He led the way out to the lobby where he greeted Anna, and ignored his daughter.

'So we've got a liar in the family!' he said, loud enough for Madeleine to overhear.

'Matthew, don't! We've had enough for one day. Please get me home.'

Anna took Madeleine protectively by the hand, and began to walk out. But the child was reluctant. She looked back, searching for Tom Small, and appeared to be unaware of the scene in court caused by her statement. Her father's angry outburst left her untouched. All that she resented was being hustled out into the street and away to the car-park before Tom Small appeared.

The Burbages had gone before Tom left the court. After the case was concluded, he sat huddled among the public, his coat-collar up about his ears. Harry Kingdom went through to the lobby with his younger daughter. Shirley waited at the door, trying to catch Tom's attention and to beckon to him to follow. But he could not or would not look round.

'Come along, Miss, either in or out, we have to shut the doors.'

Shirley silently appealed to the constable to fetch Tom out of his trance.

'He's upset,' she said. 'Can you tell him we're waiting?'

A few moments later Tom came out into the lobby, and would have walked through to the street had not Shirley taken him by the arm.

'What's wrong, dearest?' she said.

He stared at her, hostile and frightened.

'That don't signify,' he murmured, as though the words were drawn through a furnace of thought.

'For God's sake, Tom, stop it? Can't you let it go even now? It's all over, and the kid hasn't had to face the music, though she nearly had us all in for trouble. I'll bet her father gives her what for over this!'

He looked at her coldly.

'I'm leaving, Shirley. Sorry, but I'm leaving it all.'

Shirley did not understand. She tried to take him by the arm, to get him away from the crowd, and from her father and sister who were standing near the door to the street. Harry Kingdom had lighted his pipe, and was looking around in the most friendly way. He saw Tom and Shirley close together.

'Ah! The love-birds. Come along there, we want a drink!'

'Oh, shut up, Dad,' said the girl. 'Can't you see they're having trouble?'

'What's the trouble? I'm the only one in trouble, and look at me! Well, let's go, and leave them to it. I'm dry after all that palaver.'

They had disappeared when Tom, followed by Shirley, left the building. The pair stood irresolutely in the rain. Shirley struggled with her umbrella, the cord caught in the spokes. Tom watched her and did nothing to help until she appealed to him irritably. He took it, opened it, and passed it back to her.

'What d'you mean, Tom – leaving?'

'I'm doing no good there, see? No good. It wouldn't do, Shirley. It wouldn't make anybody happy if we lived at "Doggetts!. I've got to work this out. Maybe I'm not made for being with womenfolk. You see what it would be if we lived there as man and wife. You better let me go, Shirley, much better. You wouldn't understand young Madeleine.'

'Understand her! Well, I like that, Tom Small! She does her damnedest to land me in jail, and I stand up and tell the truth. Is that unfair? Haven't I tried? You're mad. That's what. I could do with a brute, but I won't take this. You break my heart, that's all. But I'm going too. We can both go. But where to, God only knows. So good-bye. If you think better of it, you can seek me out, if I'm still there; but I may be gone too. There's room in the world.'

She went off weeping, no unusual sight to be seen outside a police court. Tom watched her merge into the muddy crowd, under the ever-increasing downpour of the rain. He shivered, pulled his coat about him, and moved off, to the nearest pub.

Though the threat of prosecution was lifted from 'Doggetts', the family it sheltered was unhappy.

On the morning after the proceedings in court, Matthew went downstairs to make a pot of tea as usual. He was clumsy from lack of sleep, for Anna had been restless, and in her physical distress she magnified the significance of Madeleine's conduct. She had the notion that Matthew would never forgive the child, never trust her again.

On this assumption Anna spent much of the night pleading and arguing, and worked herself up into a nervous distress that frightened Matthew. He too was in no mood to be goaded, for there was much truth in Anna's anxiety. He was very angry with Madeleine, partly because of the publicity given to the child's malicious statement; still more because it was so obviously connected with this emotional bond between her and Tom Small.

The bond had for Matthew something menacing about it, beyond his comprehension and sense of the fitness of things. He would not allow himself to acknowledge more, and worse, possibilities. He could not even bring them to the level of his conscious mind, to present them to Anna as a justification for his disapproval of the child's strange attraction and loyalty. All he could say, again and again during the night, between the breaks in Anna's uncharacteristic pleadings, was: 'I don't understand it; I just don't understand it.'

He would say no more. He did not even condemn the child, or try to justify his coldness towards her.

It must have been in the early hours that Anna suddenly cried out, her voice broken with hysteria, 'You're jealous! It's that! You're jealous of Tom Small and his devotion.'

Both were silent for a while after that. It was as though Anna had released a demon who instantly surrounded the house, drumming with sinister fury at the windows and on the roof. Both were afraid as they listened, though they knew it was the rain which had not ceased since it returned with yesterday's sunrise.

Matthew tried to escape from the fear by turning to something practical: 'Listen to it, Anna! We shall be under water if this goes on much longer. I'm thinking of the herd. Tom and I will have to get them out tomorrow and improvise a shelter up under the wood. It's a good sixty feet above the house up there.'

'What about the pony?' said Anna.

'Oh damn the pony! That's her look-out. She's so devoted to it, she had better see to it herself.'

'Matthew, be reasonable. She's only five.'

'She might be thirty-five, the way she behaves – and after that show she put up yesterday.'

'Don't start that again, dearest.'

'*I* start it! I've said nothing so far. I've nothing to say, except that I don't know where to look. What are we going to do when the news spreads? It'll be in all the local papers, you bet. Our daughter – a public liar! Well, let's forget it, and try to get a bit of sleep!'

The tension was so acute, and the love underlying it so strong, that both gave up the struggle and slipped away into fitful sleep, while the rain continued its muffled drumming on the fabric of the house.

Madeleine, the cause of all this distress, slept peacefully. She had dealt her blow, and was released, until the next occasion that might threaten her devotion to Tom Small, and his to her. Her parents were so bewildered, almost awe-stricken, by her offence that they had said or done nothing after getting home from Sittingbourne. Punishment, if any was possible, would have to be part of a long-term policy. They had stood aloof for the rest of the day, treating her as a stranger, with stiff politeness which appeared not to affect her secret triumph.

While Matthew was making the tea, Madeleine appeared, creeping into the kitchen like a kitten ready for play.

'You up, Daddy?' She stood fastening the cord of her dressing-gown.

'Yes, I'm up,' he answered grimly. 'I hope you've slept at any rate.'

'Yes. Is it still raining?'

'Sounds like it.'

'I must brush Prince Albert, though. I didn't do it yesterday.'

'No, you were too busy yesterday.' The irony did not penetrate. She was thinking.

'No school today, so I can give him a good run. Tom will help me groom him, and he's promised to polish the saddle.'

'Tom won't, young woman. Tom will be more than fully occupied helping me put up a shelter in the top field. I can assure you of that. The only attention Prince Albert will get will be from his owner.'

'But Tom helps to own Prince Albert. He gave him to me.'

'We won't go into that. All I can tell you now is that Tom's services will not be available. Is that clear?'

Madeleine did not reply. She went to the back door and opened it. The chilly air made her shudder. 'Oh, Prince! He'll be so miserable.'

She was truly worried, a forlorn little figure reluctant to shut the door because the gesture cut off Prince Albert from her. Then she cheered herself by saying: 'But Tom will see to him. He always does, every morning when he arrives.'

Tom, however, did not come that morning. At first, Matthew lost a quarter of an hour, lingering about, waiting for him, as the routine of milking was so much simpler with four hands at work. Matthew had to set about it alone, and the job was not made easier by the weather. Rain still fell, tumbling out of an icy mist. Forecasts on the radio said that the Thames level was rising, and that farmers in East Anglia and the Fens were unable to plough, and were anxious about their autumn-sown wheat.

Anna insisted on giving a hand with the milking, though her bulkiness made her slow. Madeleine darted about between her parents, making herself useful. Nothing was said about Tom Small's absence, or about yesterday's events.

The milking done, Matthew took the churns down in the Land-Rover to the stands at the end of the lane, beyond the bungalow, at the angle with the public road. He found the rain-water standing there, pitted with the downpour from the invisible clouds above the mist.

He backed the Land-Rover to the stand and unloaded the churns. The only warm element about him was his rising temper.

'Hell! Where's that damned fellow!' he cried aloud, startling himself into the decision to drive on to Small's lodgings.

He found Mrs Weston on the look-out.

'Packed a bag and gone, he has, Mr Burbage. Paid up everything, and says he'll write about his bits and pieces up the garden. Proper upset, he seems. Can't think what's took him after yesterday. Of course, that limb of yours means a lot to him, and the idea of having her up in court seemed to put him out proper. Been brooding about it all the week, he has. But now it's all over, you'd think he'd be relieved, even though his young woman's father is for it. Serves the fool right, I say, monkeying about with other people's property. You don't know what's your own, today. Wasn't like that when I was a girl. How's the missus? False alarm, I hear it was? It goes that way sometimes. We're not machines, after all, though you'd think we were, to see the way they handle hens nowadays. It goes against nature, it's not Christian.'

'But where has he gone, Mrs Weston? I was expecting him at work today. I've had to do the milking alone. My wife can't stoop about much these days though she insisted on–'

'Bless you, it'll help things along.'

Matthew, shy of intrusion into his private life, backed away. Mrs Weston's voice followed him out to the road: 'He might have been a tramp moving off, that uncertain he was. But he ain't one to let you down, provided he ain't ruffled. I reckon he will go back where he came from – Tunstall. No shortage of work on them fruit-farms.'

Matthew drove back, to face the job of putting up, single-handed, a shelter of hurdles and bales of straw for the cattle. He stopped, however, at the bungalow, for a lorry stood at the gate. Harry Kingdom appeared at the front door, and gestured welcomingly to Matthew.

For a moment, Matthew was tempted to drive on; then the audacity of this irrepressible character touched him to a mood of sardonic humour. He opened the gate and walked slowly up the garden path, watching for Kingdom's next move.

'Time we got this job through, Mr Burbage. Shirley been on at me this month past. Can't wait to be married, that girl! I've got a couple of men at it now, and the love-birds will be in the house inside a week, if they're so disposed.'

He did not even look sheepish. He might have been granting Burbage a favour.

'I see,' said Matthew, still uncertain how to handle him. 'But the trouble is, the bride-groom has walked out. Funny situation, isn't it?'

'Eh? Walked out?' Kingdom frowned. 'That's a nice tale! What about my girl? He can't play fast and loose with a woman of that spirit. What's she got to say about it?'

'You should know, Kingdom. I don't. We've not seen a sign of her, nor of him, since we left the court yesterday. Isn't she at home?'

'No. Rang up and said she was sleeping at her friend Sally's house. I took that for a tale, but didn't fuss, as she's getting married. Well, they must have gone off together, to be quiet like after yesterday. Don't blame them. Feel a bit shaken myself.'

'Yes, you have reason to be.'

Kingdom looked at Matthew impishly.

'Between you and me, Mr Burbage, I've been a damn fool. Too easy-going is my trouble. Fact is, I wanted to make a bit extra to help Shirley make a start. But now I've burnt my fingers.'

'Was that your aim before, when the lorry was found at Margate?'

'Oh, that!' He waved his pipe in the air, to brush away the irrelevance. 'But you coming in out of the rain?'

'No. I've got to do something about my cattle. This weather looks like staying, and the flood warnings were out on the radio this morning. My sheds are low-lying, and if the water rises one night we shall be in trouble. I wanted Small to help me fix up something temporary at the top of the farm – hurdles and bales of straw. Just been down to find him – but he's gone!'

'Gone?'

'Paid up his rent and departed. Landlady says he is properly upset; but so are the rest of us. We've you to thank for that, Kingdom. Doesn't that occur to you?'

'Well, I don't know about that,' said Kingdom, thoughtfully. 'Seems to me I'm the one to be upset, seeing as I'm the only one of our lot who is committed for trial, and likely to be given a stretch.'

Matthew gave it up.

'Oh, well, there it is! He's left the farm. I've got nobody, and your girl has lost a husband, it seems. Nor am I going to the expense of decorating this place.'

'It's costing you nothing, Mr Burbage. I said I'd do the job as a wedding present, and by God I will. I'm not so certain as you are that this chap Small has gone for good. I hope she'll get him and make a man of him. Always thought he was a funny customer.'

'That won't do,' said Matthew. 'Better for you not to be seen around "Doggetts" after what has happened. I'm not too pleased about that, you know.'

'Don't take it hard, Mr Burbage. I was pushed to it, you see. Bit of a panic, really. When the police said they were coming round for a talk, I knew they'd look round my yard; and I had the stuff there overnight. That was the Friday. Yes, that's right, the

Friday. Without another thought I ran it up here and came up intending to get it away next day – but everything happened too quick, as you might say, and not a soul to help me. It would have been all right but for that youngster of yours!'

He looked reproachfully at Burbage, and relit his pipe, turning to the shelter of the porch.

Matthew had nothing to say. He retreated, as Kingdom called after him: 'This job can wait then. I'll bring my chaps up and give you a hand with them shelters.'

'Well, thanks, why not?' said Matthew. Then he drove on to the farmhouse, convinced that he might as well get what he could out of the absurd situation.

He went straight to the barn and hauled out the bales of straw. While he was doing this Kingdom's lorry rumbled into the yard, and the three men got to work on the hurdles stacked beside the barn. With the material aboard, the lorry and the Land-Rover splashed through the lower meadows up to the wood, followed by the Corgi, and Madeleine on Prince Albert.

'Ah! There she is, the young devil!' cried Kingdom. 'The lady that let me down!'

She studied him solemnly, the rain dripping like a veil from her mackintosh hood.

'Where is Tom Small?' she demanded.

'You better ask my girl Shirley, m'dear.'

311

She sat there on Prince Albert's back, huddled and tragic, suddenly aware of the fullness of her loss. Matthew could not bear the spectacle.

'Look here, Maddy. Mother's all alone in the house, and you've no need to be out in this weather. Just you go back and lend a hand indoors. Off with you!'

He watched her ride down the field and through the gateway to the lower meadows. Then he turned aside, uncomfortable, perplexed.

'Oh, hell!' he said, and joined in the labour of the team. The workmen thought he was referring to the weather and the job.

'He's right!' said one of them, with fellow-feeling.

Madeleine did not obey her father. She halted in the farmyard, and sat battling with herself for some moments. Then she shook Prince Albert's reins and the miniature couple moved on through the rain. They passed the bungalow and turned left along the main road until they reached the coast-guard cottage. Madeleine hitched Prince Albert to the gate-post and went up to the door. She turned the handle, peered in, and called. Old Mrs Weston appeared.

'What, another of them?' she cried. 'Why, your Dad's just been along. You looking for the same thing, I daresay? Well, Tom Small ain't here, and ain't likely to be. So there, young woman. And whose fault is that, I wonder?'

Then she saw the misery in the child's face.

'Why, bless my soul, you look proper upset, my ducky. Just come along in, and give me that dripping cape. Ugh! What a day, and more to come. We shall all be driven out of house and home yet. But let's make the best of them while we can. Come and sit by the fire and tell me all about it, while I cut you a slice of cherry cake.'

Confirmation of the news was more than Madeleine could bear. She appeared to be broken by grief, and allowed Mrs Weston to take the mackintosh off her and to lead her to a stool by the high steel fender before the stove. The tears gathered and fell. Slow sobs shook her as she sat bolt upright, trying in vain to control herself.

'There, duck, there. Don't you take on so. I shouldn't have told you that sharply. Silly old fool I am, maybe he'll come back tonight, who knows. Look, lovey, my cherry cake. Just you try that as you fancy.'

Madeleine gulped, shook her head in thanks, took the plate on to her lap, and fingered one of the cherries, working it loose absent-mindedly, still convulsed in her sorrow.

Mrs Weston was about to urge her again, when someone knocked at the door.

'Bless me, did you ever know?' muttered the old lady. She opened to Shirley Kingdom.

'So you've got her here?' demanded the newcomer.

'Just this minute, my dear.'

Mrs Weston made explanatory grimaces and gestures, to indicate the state of mind of the small figure by the hearth.

By the time Shirley entered, however, a complete change transformed Madeleine. Grief was stifled by defiance. She was stuffing the cake into her mouth, nearly choking herself in the dry effort to chew it. Her eyes rivalled in heat the fire into which they stared so resolutely, in the determination to ignore the intruder.

But Shirley was resolute too. Desperation made her merciless.

'Well, are you pleased with yourself this time?'

Her voice was rough, with an overtone like that of her father.

'You've got your way, with your mischief. That's what you wanted, isn't it?'

Madeleine did not look round.

'Go away, please,' she said quietly. 'Go away.'

'That's just what I am doing. Right away! Out of this madness. And much good may it do you!'

Then Shirley turned to Mrs Weston,

distraught with rage.

'Good God, look at me! Talking like this to a kid! I must be as crazy as the rest of them. Well, it's over. Tom's gone. He walked out on me at the Police Court yesterday – not a word of explanation. Just left me standing, and all on account of this little–' she glared at Madeleine's rigid back and the crumbled cake. 'No, it's useless! I know it's not on Father's account. Tom isn't that sort, and he said so when the trouble first blew up. I won't talk about it! I won't. What's the use? You can't deal with her that way. The mischief's done. She hasn't landed me in prison. She's done worse than that.'

She turned to Madeleine again, less angrily, but with a depth of mournfulness that penetrated where rage had failed. '–And what has Tom got out of it? Tell me that! What has Tom got? You've upset his life worse than you've upset mine. Isn't that enough for you? Think that over when we're both gone. Tell it to your pony, the Prince Albert he gave you!'

Shirley was weeping now, openly and helplessly. But she had broken down the child's resistance, for Madeleine suddenly let the plate slide to the floor, spilling the cake crumbs over the rag-mat. She was bent double, her head hidden in her arms, and again the deep sobs racked her, body and soul.

Mrs Weston followed Shirley to the door.

'Better not stay, dear,' she said kindly. 'But you know he's left his tools and books up there in the shed. Not like him to leave them behind for good. You see, love, it'll work out. Just you get along out o' this weather, and wait for things to happen.'

Shirley, unable to speak, nodded and sniffed, then turned and kissed the old comforter before departing.

Mrs Weston went back to Madeleine.

'Now, lovey, you too! What a commotion! I'll tell you something. That doll's house he's making in secret. I know you've seen it – well, ducky, it's up there still! So Tom Small can't have gone far, can he? Now you think about that as you get along home to your mother. Just you remember that, my little sparrow.'

7

Mrs Weston's advice to 'wait for things to happen' was given emphasis during the rest of December and the opening weeks of the New Year of 1953. Nature took a hand, dwarfing the individual drama by her huge stagecraft.

This began with a lull in the weather up to and over a Christmas which was almost seasonable. 'Doggetts', however, did not make the most of this concession. Anna, in her final month of pregnancy, was apprehensive and nervous, a condition so out of character that she irritated herself by the unfamiliarity.

She said one day to Matthew, by way of apology after snapping at him over some household chore, 'You don't realize how horrible it is not to recognize myself. I don't mean in the mirror, though that's bad enough too. But I'm saying and thinking things quite unlike me. It makes me feel quite wicked – and at a time like this too, when I should be looking forward, and grateful for what we are about to receive. That's it – saying my Grace!'

'Well, the confession is like the real you, darling,' said Matthew. He was all tenderness again, the smarts and resentments forgotten. 'Not much longer now. It looks as though we are settling down once more, now we've got over Christmas. Pretty grim for us this time, wasn't it: no help yet on the farm; nothing but mud and toil; you as you are, living in the near future, and–?'

'Well, what are you going to say about Madeleine?'

They looked at each other helplessly.

'What can I say? Like a ghost about the place, since the row. I can't understand Tom Small. He must have a will of iron underneath that placid manner. Otherwise, how could he walk out and leave that luscious piece he was about to marry?'

'All men aren't like you, young man!'

They both laughed, and at once realized how hollow was their indulgence, even in the verbal approach to love-making. 'Doggetts' might have been a monastery for the past month, and now they recognized the fact.

'We can do nothing, Matthew. Best to leave her alone. After all, she's got the pony, who may be the cure as well as the cause, in this infatuation. Have you noticed how she has devoted herself more than ever to Prince Albert since Tom left? It's as though the animal stands for something beyond our comprehension. And really, as far as I can see, he's rather a dull little creature; not very responsive, like our Corgi. He just goes his own way, at his own pace. However, he belongs to her; but she behaves as though Prince Albert is all she's got. We don't count.'

'Come, Anna, you're being morbid. What d'you expect the kid to do? Maybe she's a bit scared of you, all swollen up. I am too!'

'You're being coarse again. I'd better go off now to the nursing-home, if I'm so repulsive—'

'Repulsive! You dear idiot!'

The conversation died away in endearments and infinitely tender caresses which not only reassured them of their marital good luck, but again pushed the problem of Madeleine, the third party, into the background.

But there the problem remained, personified in Madeleine's elusiveness, her thinning cheeks and ever more prominent brown eyes, her lack of interest even in the anticipation and excitements of Christmas.

After that colourless, dispirited Christmas the rains returned. A cold snap was followed by gales from the north-east, and day after day of rain, steady rain beating on the roof, on the land, on the whole world. If there was a pause, then the wind blew again, rough and heavy with soddenness, smacking against exposed surfaces and knocking the breath out of all living creatures, breaking down resistance to the further armies of the rain marshalled over the Low Countries and the wider plains of northern Europe. The Thames Estuary was like a drowning mouth forced open to receive the flood.

By the end of January there was indeed a flood. Every high tide became a menace, armoured with a leaden sky, heavy beyond human control. The Isle of Sheppey lay under perpetual twilight, an evil twilight, cold and metallic.

The holidays came to an end, and now it was a question who should take Madeleine to school every morning. Matthew had been struggling on alone with the milking for two months, and still could not find help. Madeleine's wan face could not make him forget that she was the cause of his lack of hired labour. He was so exhausted that his temper suffered, and this added to the child's misery. She developed bouts of vomiting and a stomach-cough. That solved the question of the journey to school. Dr Bray looked her over, and prescribed rest at home.

'Keep her warm, Burbage. Nothing radically wrong, I think. It's my belief she's worrying. That recent business may be having a delayed action. Pity, that!'

He looked at Matthew shrewdly, noticing the signs of overwork and emotional strain.

'Seems to me that Mrs B is the best of the bunch at the moment. Nothing wrong with her at any rate. Wonderful how nature works.'

'Nature's working a damned sight too much in these parts,' said Matthew savagely. 'I'm having to face it alone. Tom Small shows no sign of coming back, and we've not heard a word from that young woman of his, whom he's left in the lurch as well. So we've lost four pair of hands!'

'Are you blaming the child for that?'

Matthew was too indignant to reply, but Dr Bray was able to complete his near-correct diagnosis from the scripture of resentment on Matthew's face.

'Leave it alone, Matthew,' he said, unprofessionally. 'If I get a chance, I'll find a chap to lend you a hand. I see hundreds, you know.'

The medical advice was not a cure of souls, however, and no help turned up. Meanwhile, the course of nature went ruthlessly on, both in Anna and over the countryside. The drama intensified. Madeleine behaved as if she were awaiting a message, and were attempting to signal to another world. She lost weight, and the fervour of her questing gaze grew brighter. Attempts to keep her indoors, away from Prince Albert's stable, resulted in bouts of sullen despondency that defeated her parents. Neither of them was in a condition to put up a responsible fight against her.

From time to time she responded to Anna with a kind of reproachful ardour that was more disconcerting than her long periods of complete indifference. She ignored Matthew, or looked at him over a barrier of grievances.

Such was the emotional condition of the household at 'Doggetts' on the morning that the radio gave out the flood warning. The coast of Norfolk was already in danger, it said, with abnormal tides driven in by the north-eastern winds down the North Sea.

The warnings were repeated at midday,

with the news that the Essex creeks were submerged and the mud cliffs of North Kent were being washed away.

'Anna, I must get the cattle up to the shelters. It's no longer safe to leave them in the byres at night. Heaven knows how it will affect the milk.'

Rain ceased in the afternoon, but a heavy mass of cloud was lumping over the sky before the wind from the North Sea. Anna insisted on helping. She could at least stand in the background to prevent the cows from breaking away. Matthew wrapped her in an old Service mackintosh, and stationed her, with a stout ash-plant in hand, near the house and the drive down the lane.

With Madeleine to support him nearer the byres, he brought the cows out. They had been shut up for over a week during the violent weather, and now they stood, heads lowered to the wind, lowing and suspicious. For some minutes they refused to move. Then the Corgi summoned up his inherited wisdom, and began barking and snapping at their heels. They turned and began to trek through the first open gate, up to the higher meadows.

One cow changed her mind, however, and, wheeling suddenly, bolted down the yard. Anna ran across to intercept her. At that moment, the cow swerved, with a low swing of her head, and knocked Anna over.

Matthew had not seen this. He was beyond the gate, dragooning the herd through the first meadow, with the Corgi working to and fro in a frenzy of excitement. No human cry could reach more than a few yards because of the steady roar of the wind in the bare elms.

Madeleine heard, however. She had broken away from the teamwork, to bring Prince Albert out of his stall, intending to take him up with the cows to the safety of the shelters for the night. As she brought him out to the yard, she saw her mother kneeling in the mud, and received her cry of alarm.

She left the pony and ran over to Anna.

'Mummy, what are you doing?'

'Nothing. Help me up. The brute barged into me. That's right. Oh, look, I'm mud all over! No, nothing wrong. I don't think so. Feel a bit awkward, sort of twisted. But you run and bring the animal back. She's gone down the lane.'

Madeleine ran back to Prince Albert, and mounted him, clasping his bare back firmly between her knees. Anna saw her trotting off, and then returned to the house. She felt giddy, and rather sick.

Madeleine did not have far to seek. The cow was lumbering back up the lane, and the child could see the cause of this retreat. Where the lane curved, on its way to the bungalow and the road, lay a sheet of water.

She let the cow pass her, giving it a slap on the rump to speed up the return journey to the herd. Then she rode on to the water's edge.

'Look, Prince, look,' she cried, leaning over so that her head was beside the rough ear into which she was speaking. 'It's a flood!'

The water fascinated them both. It was moving towards them, pushing a thin lip of foam nearer and nearer. A pulse flickered through it, adding to its depth every few beats. It was a living creature, crawling forward, with that snarl of foam dribbling over the dry land. Then it paused, and seemed to retreat, only to come on again, inch by inch.

In the open centre of the lane, the surface of the water reflected the sky, a leaden gleam smeared with oily lights, a pavement of metal.

Prince Albert was the first to be frightened. He backed one or two paces, his hooves clattering. Then he sniffed with outstretched neck, and terror widened his eyes.

'Prince! Prince!' whispered Madeleine, catching the fear from him. 'Back! We must tell Daddy.'

She turned him, and he broke into a trot, then into a gallop which caused her to cling flat to his back, both arms round his neck.

But he recovered confidence when he reached higher ground in the second meadow, and the flight dropped to a steady trot that brought pony and rider somewhat more stylishly to the herd, which was now feeling its way suspiciously into the improvised shelter, persuaded by Matthew and the Corgi.

'The flood, Daddy. It's coming up the lane! I rode down to bring the cow back, and she must be here by now. The flood stopped her, I didn't. And Prince Albert was frightened too.'

'Oh well, we expected it. But where's Mother?'

'She fell down. The cow knocked her over and she fell in the mud. So she's gone indoors again.'

The effect of this news electrified Matthew, after his indifference to the announcement of the coming of the floods.

'What?' he shouted. 'Don't you understand? Look here, Madeleine, just you get these animals in and close the hurdles. Look! Here is the way to tie the string; and then pile a bale or two of straw outside the hurdles. I must run down to Mother.'

The last of these commands was shouted as he ran down the field under the lee of the hedge. His voice gradually sank into the uproar of the wind rushing through the hedge. He soon became invisible also, for the poor afternoon light was failing.

Madeleine stared after him, then turned to the pony: 'Don't be lonely, Prince. Don't be sad.'

She struggled with the hurdles after the cows were safely inside the corral. First one string, then the next, and at last the heavy bales of straw. The job was done. She was free to hurry back to the shelter of home. But she lingered, spiritless. Darkness was creeping up the meadows, and down from the rushing clouds. She felt the rain begin to fall again, and she turned up her face to it, took the icy sting of the heavy drops. The Corgi had followed his master.

A soft muzzle nudged Madeleine. Prince Albert wanted to return also. Or maybe he was aware of her misery. He snuffed at her wet mackintosh, and thrust his head between her arm and her side.

'Oh, Prince,' she murmured. 'You can't come. You must sleep up here, with the others. Good night, Prince. Be good now.'

She tied him up behind the corral, under the protection of the hedge, where it was heightened and strengthened by a bank of mossy earth.

He whinnied after her as she left. She made her way slowly, reluctant to leave him. He cried after her again as she closed the lower gate. Then he gave up the protest, and all she could hear was the wind, and the subdued lowing of the cows.

Still under the fascination of these strange events, Madeleine did not go indoors. She had to take another look at the flood water. It seemed to be seeking her too, for it had crept onward, and was still on the move, spreading out on the eastward side over the lowest field, where Tom Small had sown wheat in the autumn. By the last of the daylight, Madeleine could see the spikes sticking up out of the shining water, like black needles, thinning out as one by one they were engulfed.

Meanwhile, Matthew ran down the farmland and reached the house breathless. He found Anna sitting in the kitchen, her feet on the fender and the wet raincoat lying, thrown down beside her.

'What's this? What's happened?' he gasped.

Anna was calm, but her voice sounded withdrawn. She smiled wanly: 'Nothing! It's nothing, Matt. The clumsy creature knocked me over. Look at your old coat. A nice mess! I've just been sick. It's only pressure, or something. Feel a bit odd. After all, it's nearly due. Or is it overdue? I never trust dates.'

She made light of it, but Matthew didn't. He was thoroughly frightened, and in his keyed-up state he wanted to act at once.

'Wait, dear, wait. Where's Maddy? We

can't leave her out. I sent her after the cow.'

'Yes, and she followed it up the meadows. She says the floods are rising and have reached us. That's good news too! I don't care what you say, I'm going to telephone to Bray.'

Five minutes later he returned from the hall.

'It's broken down, Anna. We're cut off.'

They looked at each other. Then Anna eased herself up, approached him, and clasped his thin face between her hands.

'Look, you two. Yes, Maddy as well. You're both becoming thin as rakes. What a pair to live with! Don't take things so hard, darling. We've everything to be thankful for. Look! Year after year it has come right. Why shouldn't it now?'

Gradually she comforted and reassured him. Madeleine came in as darkness finally closed over the stormy outside world, and she found tea ready, the Corgi coiled on the hearth-rug, and the friendly smell of buttered toast enriching the warmth of home.

The renewed confidence spread from the parents to the child, and she returned, for the couple of hours before bedtime, almost to her former self.

'I won't come up with you tonight, Maddy,' said Anna. 'It's those stairs. That old cow must have knocked the breath out of me.'

So her mother and father kissed her good night and she went up alone to her room. While she was undressing, the electricity failed. She groped her way to the head of the stairs and called out.

'Coming, old lady,' shouted Matthew; and he appeared up the stairs, lighted candle in hand, his shadow bobbing and bowing beside him along the wall.

The novelty delighted Madeleine, who had never before seen candlelight indoors. She clapped her hands, and slapped at Matthew's shadow as it leaped above the top of the stairs.

'Look, Maddy. I want your help. I'm anxious about Mother. I'm going to get her to the nursing-home in Sheerness while the going's good. We may be cut off by the morning. I must leave you in charge here. You will be alone; but I'll be back as soon as I can. After that, we shall have to do all we can to look after the livestock. First thing tomorrow morning, mind you! We'll open that clamp of mangolds and cart them up to the top, above water-level. And as much hay as we can. It'll be hard work, Maddy, so you go off to sleep quickly. Is that all right?'

Madeleine stared at the candle-flame. It was shaped like a spearhead. Little whiffs of smoke leaped from its tip every time it flickered in the draught. Gouts of wax trickled down the candle. The darkness, the wind, the winter universe threatened that flame. But it shivered and revived.

'Yes, Daddy. I'll go to sleep until you come back. Is Mummy very ill?'

'She's not ill at all, Maddy. But she shouldn't have fallen down. That's what I'm anxious about. So I *must* get her safely away, don't you see?'

He kissed her good night, and put the matchbox from his pocket into the candle-stick.

'Blow it out when you're in bed. If you have to get up, here are the matches beside you. Now you'll be all right?'

She knew that he was eager to get away, and she said no more. Matthew looked back as he left her room, and saw that she had already jumped into bed and drawn the clothes over her head. So he switched on his hand-torch, crept back and blew out the candle-flame.

Downstairs, he told Anna of his plan to get her to safety immediately, and to his relief she agreed, though her acquiescence made him doubly anxious.

'Hurry up, my dear. It'll have to be the Land-Rover; the car may not get us through. Once we get round past the bridge we're safe.'

Anna too was frightened. She was in pain, and this could have only one meaning.

Matthew brought down the packed suitcase. He wrapped her in a car-rug and tucked her in beside the driver's seat.

'That's fine, eh, love? Don't you fret about a thing. Maddy's like a grown-up, isn't she? Wise little bird, and it's just as well at times like this. Makes up for her other funny ways.'

'Don't criticize her too much, Matthew. We ought to understand her more. I often feel guilty about it. Perhaps we love each other too much, and keep her out.'

'Now don't talk rot, my dear girl. Go easy for once. Now then, off we go, and time too. What a night!'

Matthew drove cautiously, with the rain drumming on the hood from behind them. This sinister music was added to as soon as they left the farmyard drive and turned down the private lane. Water splashed from the wheels, like rags being torn.

'Gently, old girl, gently,' said Matthew. 'It's like setting off on a night raid over Germany. Remember those days, Anna?'

'I don't want to remember them, Matt. You're sure that child is safe alone?'

'They brought us together, after all. That's worth remembering. And stop fussing. Now, here we go! The flak's rising!'

Two sheets of water rose from the Land-Rover as Matthew accelerated. But he kept on, and, as the headlights flashed round the curve in the lane, the bungalow shone, white and desolate, sheeted by the rain and standing in its own reflection in the flooded garden.

'Look at that! I'm glad Kingdom's paying for the decoration! It's money thrown away. We'll have to do it all over again before we can put a man and wife into it.'

'Shall we be long, Matt?'

'What, finding a couple?'

'No, getting to Sheerness.'

'Why, you feeling signs?'

'I'm not sure. It's so long ago since I started with Madeleine.'

'Well, I think I can step on it now. We're leaving the water.'

They reached the nursing-home in Queensborough, however, to find that it was vacating patients to Minster General Hospital. Matthew was instructed to take Anna there. This meant driving on against the rain. Half-way there, Anna's pains returned, with violence. She had to grip the seat, in the effort not to groan, but Matthew realized what was happening, and put on speed, passing several cars and lorries carrying refugees from the low-lying parts of Sheppey. The rain lashed at the windscreen and over the hood. Every car moved in a nimbus of spray.

'Hold tight, love,' said Matthew, peering ahead, exultant in this return to active service, as it seemed. The triumph of it almost allayed his anxiety over the fantastic situation into which the placid life at 'Doggetts' was suddenly dissolved.

The hospital was nearly full: old folk, children, casualties already from the onset of the floods. But Anna was taken in, and hastily examined. Matthew was told to wait, and given a cup of strong tea.

He did not have to wait long. Half an hour after Anna disappeared, a nurse came to him with the news: both well: a son: and his wife's urgent wish that he should get home without delay. He could come again to-morrow. With that, he turned the Land-Rover for home, speeding before the storm, humming to himself as he had done during wartime forays, alert for the unseen danger and intoxicated by it.

When he and Anna set out, neither of them had looked up at the front of the farmhouse. So they did not see the face at the window of Madeleine's room. As soon as her father left her in the dark, the child knew that she dared not allow herself to fall asleep. This kind of darkness was something new. It filled the whole house and not only her room. It was the darkness of the world outside, full of strange life.

She was not afraid. She was too much used to solitude to be afraid. Since Tom Small left she had been driven to the courage of loneliness. It was a cold, empty kind of courage, but it sustained her now as it had done day after day after Tom's disappearance.

She had to watch her father and mother go, however. It was part of the desperation. She stared out, hard-eyed, at the fluffed shape of the Land-Rover in its dark halo of rain. She saw and heard it move away. Then the solitude added something to itself and came back upon her. Now that the back-glare from the headlights had gone, darkness thickened and solidified. She cut her way through it back to bed, and banged her knee against the side-table, setting the candlestick rocking. But it did not fall to the floor. She groped for it, and was reassured. Yes, there were the matches too.

The wind grew stronger, Madeleine covered her head again with the bedclothes, but the whipping roar of the elms penetrated, and she gave up the effort to shut it out. She turned on her back, and listened. She wondered if she had slept, and how long Father would be. The noise was so regular that she began to doze off. Suddenly, another, sharper sound roused her. She sat up in bed.

It was the clatter of hooves, galloping hooves. Prince Albert had broken loose.

Madeleine groped for the matches, but her hands were trembling. At last she found the wick and persuaded it to light. She struggled into her dressing-gown, took up the candlestick and made for the door. It shut behind her, and caught the cord of her gown. She had to pause to open it and release herself. In doing so, she created a draught that blew out the candle-flame.

By the time she had set down the candlestick and struck a match, the sound of Prince Albert's hooves was lost in the general din of the storm.

She was sobbing: a hard, dry sobbing of utter fear. But she moved more cautiously down the stairs to the hall, and found a storm-lantern which her father had brought in from the barn. She lighted it, and exchanged the candlestick for it. Then she opened the front door. Instantly, the candle-flame vanished. By the feeble light of the lantern she saw for a few yards into the farmyard. The water was creeping up. It reached beyond the gate and was approaching the house. One long arm ran in advance up the drainage gully to the middle of the yard and spread out round the manhole there.

She could see that, the body and the arm, black as an octopus, living, and moving closer. But she could not see Prince Albert.

She called him, assuming that he had gone down the drive.

'Prince! Prince! Come back!'

But her cry was tossed aside. She stepped down to the flagstones, but the rain blinded her and broke up the lamplight into a spongey glare. She knew he would be drowned, destroyed by his own panic.

'Prince Albert!'

She shouted the full name, hoping it might carry better. Then she waited, shouted again, waited, straining to listen.

What she heard was the sound of the Land-Rover. Then the mad darkness of wind and water was turned to flashing steel by the headlights.

Matthew drew up, jumped out and ran to her.

'Go in, Maddy! Go in, you'll catch your death of cold! What are you up to?'

She cried out, holding up the lantern for him to take it and go search for her Prince Albert. She tried to tell him what she had heard, but the sobs interrupted. Nor was Matthew listening.

'Go in, you silly. And what d'you think, Maddy? What d'you think? You've got a brother, a baby brother!'

Her sobs ceased. She stared at him, and her lips ceased to move.

The tragic spectacle brought Matthew to a standstill, but only for a moment. He took the lantern from her and hustled her back into the house.

8

Father and daughter, with the worried Corgi, were alone in the house. Matthew did something unexpected, which would have startled Madeleine had she been in a condition to notice it. He carried her up in his arms and put her, not into her own bed, but into her mother's.

'Bit rough for you to be by yourself tonight, Maddy,' he said. 'Don't you fuss about that pony. He was born in the forest, remember, and knows how to look after himself.'

Madeleine did not hear. She was deaf, blind, frozen with horror. She was not even aware that she was in Anna's bed, with the caress of her mother's perfume around her, the bitter-sweet cedar. All her senses were arrested; she felt nothing, not even the knife-blade of jealousy that pricked her when Matthew announced the arrival of a baby brother.

She lay open-eyed in the darkness, while the house shook under the increased violence of the storm. The disturbance was continuous, a steady roar of the north-easter flinging itself and its tresses of rain against the walls and windows like a mad woman battering herself to death.

Something was happening amongst those

midgets, the human beings on the island, for distant cries, shouts, flashing of lights, crashes of metal and timber, made a miniature punctuation of the rhythm of the weather. It was as though a nest of ants were registering despair and anger, stirred to some frantic effort in the engulfing darkness and chaos.

Madeleine was unconscious of all this. In the dead coldness of her mind she could recognize only that Tom Small was gone out of her world. He had been gone a month: a month as long as 'for ever'. Now Prince Albert was gone too. She had heard him galloping down to the flood, leaving her. To be left: she knew what that meant. There was nobody, nobody for her. Mother and father: they were one. They were always looking another way, or at each other.

She twisted the turned edge of the sheet in her hands until it was hard as rope. No use to call out for Tom. She suddenly saw him rolling one of his cigarettes and looking at her as he licked the paper. He always did that, with a glance that was warmth, safety, happiness. It faded away now into the coldness. There was no Prince Albert for her to mount and follow Tom.

Why had Father put her into Mother's bed? She must have been there a long time, for she was suddenly startled out of her coldness, her indifference, to realize where she was. Matthew stood over her.

'Had a good nap, Maddy? I think you'd better get up and dress. It's two o'clock in the morning and the floods are out all right. We may have to go up into the attic, or even out on the roof, so you must be warm. Put everything on, your overcoat too, and mackintosh on top of that. We'll wait up here. I'll just go down again and have a reccy. We might as well eat something. I've rescued the food from the larder and the fridge. Can't make anything hot, Maddy, for the power's cut off. We haven't many candles left either. Thank God Mother's safe. What a lark!'

His effort to sound cheerful meant nothing to her. She obeyed mechanically, her fingers almost as frozen as her mind. Matthew had ransacked her bedroom and brought in a pile of clothes. She dressed by candlelight, to the accompaniment of Matthew's flounderings on the ground floor.

'It's over six inches down here, Maddy!' he shouted. 'I'm looking for the paraffin-can to fill the lantern. Getting on all right up there?'

She murmured something, but there was no life in it. There was no meaning in what was going on around her. Whatever happened, she was alone; she must do everything by herself. It was like walking in a circle: no beginning, no end.

The Corgi sat trembling at the head of the stairs, whimpering and making little false starts to go down to his master, then sub-siding on his haunches with a yap of despair. He played no part in Madeleine's life, nor she in his, at this time of crisis.

Matthew came up again, his gumboots glittering and clean except for a top rim of mud.

'Ah, good! You're ready for emergency action! I've found some milk! My God, milk! What's happening up at the top there? Too much general din to hear anything of them. But I thought I caught a sound, lowing and – but if they take fright I can't think what will happen. We can do nothing until daylight. Then you and I will *have* to venture out, Maddy, and get some more fodder up to them. If only we can last out a couple of days, people will get to us in boats, or something, and take us off, animals and all.'

He calmed the dog, pulling his ears and patting him, and the terrified animal was happy again, for a while at least. Nothing could last for long in this vast flux of wind and water. Its fury filled the universe.

'Come on, Madeleine, pull yourself together!' Matthew was trying harshness, to make the child return to life and realize what was happening. 'Now, drink this milk, and here's a slice of Mother's seed-cake. We

340

can't waste that, for she won't be cooking again for a while. Never mind, we must face it, Maddy. We're not the only ones. Seems to me the whole estuary is under water. The Government will have to do something about compensation. It's more than the blasted insurance companies can cope with. Act of God my foot!'

He stood over Madeleine while she drank the milk and tried to chew the impossible mouthfuls of cake. But suddenly her stomach revolted. She ran out to the landing and was sick over the balusters, into the flood now flowing through the ground floor of the house.

Even this physical manifest did not wake her mind. Her movements were still those of a sleep-walker. Matthew was now frightened. He tried petting her, rubbing her hands and cheeks. She made no response, offered no resistance.

'Why isn't Tom Small here?' he demanded at last, exasperated beyond reason. At the sound of that name, Madeleine looked up, over her father's shoulder. Then, as she saw nothing, the gleam of intelligence subsided, and she was indifferent again.

Matthew left her to it, and went to the head of the stairs, to flash his torch over the scene below.

'Rising,' he murmured. 'This is the end of "Doggetts". What comes next, Anna?' Then

341

he recalled himself to the reality, and away from the fears.

He heard the faint sound of an engine: something regular in the moody raging of the weather. It grew stronger, chugging steadily. He ran back into the front bedroom, seized Madeleine who was sitting on Anna's bed, and urged her to the window. He flung up the lower pane, and the storm whirled about the room, blowing out the wet curtains and knocking over the pieces of the trinket-set on the dressing-table.

'Hear that, Maddy? Hear that? Somebody's out in a motorboat. It's making this way!'

He began to signal with the torch, summoning up his recollection of the Morse Code. 'SOS,' he flashed into the darkness. 'SOS.'

The sound of the engine grew, and then a beam of light struck across country. The boat was following the submerged lane, navigating by the recognizable pattern of the trees and hedge-tops.

'They must know the way,' cried Matthew. 'It's somebody who knows us.'

The beam of light began to swing round towards the farmyard, passing over the row of bent and naked elms. It found the gate, which suddenly stood out, its top bar above the water, white and clean.

Round came the beam, straight through the yard, followed by its source, the glare of a headlamp at the bow of the boat. Now the beam found the house, revealing Matthew and Madeleine at the open window. The signal of the flashlamp was seen, for the people in the boat answered 'O.K.', and again 'O.K.', using the headlamp.

The engine slowed, coughed, started again, stopped, and the wide, shallow boat glided over the lake of the farm-yard, dark behind its blinding headlight. Nobody spoke from it, but Matthew did not notice this, for he was shouting inarticulate directions which nobody heeded. The boat was drawn up to the pillars of the front door of 'Doggetts', floating over the paving-stones, the threshold of the house. Then someone shouted back to Matthew.

'You all right, guv'nor? We've come to fetch you.'

It was Harry Kingdom. A human whiff from his pipe was sucked into the open window with the storm.

Matthew leaned out, and in the confusion of lights and reflections from wall and water he saw a man step from the boat up to his knees in the water, and wade into the house. As he opened the front door, a swirl of wavelets beat back against the side of the boat.

After more splashing down below, the

343

rescuer found the staircase and left the waterline. A moment later he was in the bedroom.

'Sorry, Boss,' he said. 'No use! I've done no good since I left. And Shirley came after me tonight: said we must see what's happening here in view of the warning.'

Then Tom Small saw Madeleine, who was standing, turned from the window, staring at him as though he were returned from the grave.

'That you, Maddy?' he said. 'Come to fetch you, we have, Shirley and me.'

For a moment she hesitated, still doubting the shadowy reality after the solid substance of the nightmare. Then she was in his arms, being carried downstairs and through the rising waters in the hall. Tom, to reassure her, was whispering to her, his head pressed to hers: 'That's it, Maddy. Don't you fret. We got you safe and sound. Shirley found this boat drifting inland, dozens of them, coming up river. And we got Prince Albert. Shirley rescued him. He was down by the bungalow: had tried to swim out to the open and got his bridle caught in the holly tree where you often tied him up. He'd have been a gonner if she hadn't spotted him with the headlight. She jumped out and waded to him, and we lifted him into the boat. What d'you think o' that, Maddy?'

Madeleine could not speak. She was

sleepy. She snuggled into Tom Small's shoulder, clasping him round the neck and hiding her face there, away from the storm, the cold, the loneliness.

The blast recalled her, and she looked down to the boat. Mr Kingdom sat in the stern, his arm on the tiller. He was laughing up at them, pipe in mouth.

Behind the headlight in the prow two figures, shadowy under the penumbra, slowly took shape. Shirley sat with an arm round Prince Albert's neck, to reassure him after his fright and near-drowning. He stood in the centre of the boat, quite calm, his coat dripping steadily.

'That's us, Maddy,' said Tom. 'So we've all come back.'

Prince Albert turned his head as Madeleine was handed down into the boat. He shook himself and a shower of drops spattered her.

'Oh, you little devil!' cried Shirley. 'That the way to welcome your mistress?' She laughed, and drew Madeleine to her. 'There, kid, we're all together again, as Tom said. Let's forget the rest, eh? And now we've got to rescue that old Mrs Weston – and the doll's house!'

She shook Madeleine, with one arm round her and the other still over Prince Albert's neck.

Matthew appeared, his arms full of household treasures, which he passed to Tom.

'Now for the Missus, Boss,' shouted Harry Kingdom. 'Don't leave her behind.'

He roared with mirth at his own joke.

'She's safe! All over and done with. Had her baby this evening in Minster Hospital. A boy! Yes, a boy!'

'What?' cried Shirley. Then she cuddled Madeleine, drew her close and kissed her warmly.

'Hear that, Madeleine? It's a boy!'

'Yes, I know,' said Madeleine, now fully awake, reaching out and clasping a tuft of Prince Albert's wet mane. 'I've got a brother.'

This Large Print Book for the partially sighted, who cannot read normal print, is published under the auspices of

THE ULVERSCROFT FOUNDATION

Other MAGNA Titles
In Large Print

LYN ANDREWS
Angels Of Mercy

HELEN CANNAM
Spy For Cromwell

EMMA DARCY
The Velvet Tiger

SUE DYSON
Fairfield Rose

J. M. GREGSON
To Kill A Wife

MEG HUTCHINSON
A Promise Given

TIM WILSON
A Singing Grave

RICHARD WOODMAN
The Cruise Of The Commissioner